Praise for the *Witches of East End* series

۶ے

"Move over, zombies, vampires, and werewolves, and make way for witches. Melissa de la Cruz, author of the bestselling *Blue Bloods* series, ably sets the stage for a juicy new franchise with *Witches of East End* . . . De la Cruz balances the supernatural high-jinksery with unpredictable twists and a conclusion that nicely sets up book 2. B+"　　　　　*—Entertainment Weekly*

"Centuries after the practice of magic was forbidden, Freya, Ingrid, and their mom struggle to restrain their witchy ways as chaos builds in their Long Island town. A bubbling cauldron of mystery and romance, the novel shares the fanciful plotting of *Blue Bloods*, the author's teen vampire series. . . . breezy fun."

—People

"A magical and romantic page-turner . . . *Witches of East End* is certain to attract new adult readers . . . The pacing is masterful, and while the witchcraft is entertaining, it's ultimately a love triangle that makes the story compelling. De la Cruz has created a family of empathetic women who are both magically gifted and humanly flawed."　　　　*—Washington Post*

"For anyone who was frustrated watching Samantha suppress her magic on *Bewitched*, Ms. de la Cruz brings some satisfaction. In her first novel for adults, the author . . . lets her repressed sorceresses rip."　　　　　　　　　　*—New York Times*

"What happens when a family of Long Island witches is forbidden to practice magic? This tale of powerful women, from the author of the addictive *Blue Bloods* series, mixes mystery, a battle of good versus evil and a dash of Norse mythology into a page-turning parable of inner strength." —*Self*

"*Witches of East End* has all the ingredients you'd expect from one of Melissa's bestselling YA novels—intrigue, mystery and plenty of romance. But with the novel falling under the 'adult' categorization, Melissa's able to make her love scenes even more . . . magical." —MTV.com

"De la Cruz has, with *Witches*, once again managed to enliven and embellish upon history and mythology with a clever interweaving of past and present, both real and imagined . . . [it] casts a spell." —*Los Angeles Times*

"De la Cruz is a formidable storyteller with a narrative voice strong enough to handle the fruits of her imagination. Even readers who generally avoid witches and whatnot stand to be won over by the time the cliffhanger-with-a-twist-ending hits." —*Publishers Weekly*

"Fantasy for well-read adults." —*Kirkus*

"A sexy, magical romp, sure to bring de la Cruz a legion of new fans." —Kelley Armstong, *New York Times* bestselling author of *The Otherworld* series

serpent's kiss

also by

melissa de la cruz

witches of east end

serpent's kiss

a witches of east end novel

melissa de la cruz

HYPERION
New York

Copyright © 2012 Melissa de la Cruz

Library of Congress Cataloging-in-Publication Data

De la Cruz, Melissa.
   Serpent's kiss: a witches of east end novel/Melissa de la Cruz.—1st ed.
      p.   cm. — (The Beauchamp family; 2)
   ISBN 978-1-4013-2396-7
  1. Witches—Fiction.   2. Long Island (N.Y.—Fiction).   I. Title.
  PS3604.E128S47   2012
  813'.6—dc23

                                       2011052471

ISBN: 978-1-4013-2396-7

Hyperion books are available for special promotions and premiums. For details contact the HarperCollins Special Markets Department in the New York office at 212-207-7528, fax 212-207-7222, or email spsales@ harpercollins.com.

FIRST EDITION

Book Design by Fearn Cutler de Vicq

10   9   8   7   6   5   4   3   2   1

SUSTAINABLE FORESTRY INITIATIVE   Certified Fiber Sourcing   www.sfiprogram.org

THIS LABEL APPLIES TO TEXT STOCK

We try to produce the most beautiful books possible, and we are also extremely concerned about the impact of our manufacturing process on the forests of the world and the environment as a whole. Accordingly, we've made sure that all of the paper we use has been certified as coming from forests that are managed, to ensure the protection of the people and wildlife dependent upon them.

for Mike and Mattie

Surely the serpent will bite
without enchantment.
—Ecclesiastes 10:11

serpent's kiss

Once upon a time in North Hampton . . .

∼✺∼

Three extraordinary women led very ordinary lives. Silver-haired and green-thumbed Joanna Beauchamp lived in a stately colonial on the northern and easternmost tip of Long Island with her two daughters, Ingrid, the local librarian, and Freya, a sexy bartender. For years beyond count, they lived quietly and peacefully among the residents of their small, mist-shrouded town.

Joanna spent her days redecorating her home, gardening, worrying about her girls, and lavishing all the affection she had for her missing son on the housekeeper's six-year-old boy, Tyler. Brazen redhead Freya won the heart of wealthy philanthropist Bran Gardiner, whose family owned Fair Haven manor on eponymous Gardiners Island. She celebrated her engagement by having a torrid affair with Bran's younger brother, Killian, he of the dark, smoldering good looks and devil-may-care attitude.

Ingrid, blond, haughty, and painfully shy, was the library's ranking archivist of historical architectural blueprints. When she wasn't fighting to save her beloved library from extinction from a smarmy local developer, she was turning down a variety of suitors, including voracious reader Matthew Noble, a handsome detective on the North Hampton police force.

But despite their seemingly normal lives, all three women shared a powerful secret. Goddesses from Asgard, they were witches in our world. The residents of North Hampton never suspected that Joanna, Ingrid, and Freya were just three of the many gods and goddesses stranded in Midgard after the legendary Bofrir bridge that connected the two worlds collapsed under mysterious circumstances.

Trapped in our world and unable to return to theirs, they had been restricted from using their powers ever since the White Council enacted the Restriction of Magical Powers after the Salem witch trials, which effectively ended the practice of magic in mid-world. But the three women became restless after suppressing their true natures for so many years, and slowly began to use their otherworldly abilities. Joanna's specialty was recovery and renewal; capable of raising the dead, she brought toy soldiers to life. Ingrid, a healer who could tap into people's lifelines and see the future, began to dole out her spells and charms to any patron with a trying domestic problem. Freya specialized in matters of the heart and served up heady love potions at the North Inn Bar.

With no seeming repercussions to their magical escapades the Beauchamp girls became bolder in their practice: Joanna brought a man back to life, Ingrid gave the mayor's wife a powerful fidelity knot, and every night at the North Inn became a wild, hedonistic romp because of Freya's potent cocktails. It was all a bit of harmless, innocent, enchanted fun until a local girl went missing, several locals began to suffer from a rash of inexplicable illnesses, and a dark menace was found growing in the waters off the Atlantic, poisoning the wildlife.

When the mayor turned up dead, the finger-pointing began, and for a moment it felt like the Salem witch trials all over again.

RUSHING TO UNTANGLE the mystery, Ingrid discovered archaic Norse symbols in a blueprint of Fair Haven manor, the Gardiners' ancestral home. But just as she was close to cracking the code, the document disappeared. Freya discovered she was caught in a centuries-old love triangle with Bran and Killian that harked back to the days of Asgard itself, back when the world was made and she was not yet a witch in Midgard but rather a young goddess pursued by her true love, Balder, the god of joy, and his brother, Loki, the god of mischief. Bran and Killian Gardiner weren't mortals at all, they were the brothers Balder and Loki—but who was who? And had she chosen correctly? Not to mention, it looked as if there was a zombie on the loose. Joanna's resurrection had gone awry.

Soon, Norman Beauchamp, Joanna's long-lost ex-husband, was back in the picture, and everyone was trying to save not just their little town but all the nine known worlds of the universe from *Ragnarok*, the ancient legend that foretold the end of the gods.

They succeeded, and Loki was banished from mid-world, sent back through the hole he'd made in the Tree of Life in the hopes his return journey would heal it. But the mystery of the collapse of the bridge remained, even as two young gods had been punished for its destruction—malevolent Loki and Freya's twin brother, Fryr, whose magical trident had been found in its ruins.

The Beauchamps thought Fryr was lost to them forever, but to Freya's surprise, her twin suddenly reappeared to her in the alley behind the North Inn Bar one evening. He had escaped from Limbo, and revealed that he had been framed for the destruction of the Bofrir, and he knew the identity of the real culprit.

No, it wasn't Loki, who Freya had known as Bran Gardiner.

According to Fryr, or Freddie, as he now wanted to be called, it was Balder who had set him up to take the fall. Balder, or Killian Gardiner, who Freya loved, who was responsible for its destruction.

Now Freddie was out for revenge, and he wanted Freya to help him win it.

halloween

wicked
games

chapter one

Back in Baby's Arms

～੭੮～

Patsy Cline's mournful contralto warbled a love song on the jukebox at the North Inn. It was a departure from the usual rock 'n' roll fare that prompted summertime patrons to leap from their seats to raise pointer-and-pinkie devil signs in the air, music befitting the early October mood—intimate, cozy, sweetness with a tinge of nostalgia. Indian summer was over. When the light tinted golden before sunset, a nip crept into the air, laced with an autumn tang. The Atlantic, visible from the windows of the North Inn, was rough now, huge breakers crashing on the shore. There were no more bikini-clad bodies frolicking on the beach or fireworks erupting in the sky. The high-season crowds had dispersed, leaving the secluded seaside town to the locals, the beaches deserted and the popular meeting spot almost empty.

A lone couple slow danced in the middle of the floor, while a few regulars wandered in after a day's work, scattered in small clusters. The resident bartender, Freya Beauchamp, was taking advantage of the slower pace and had taken a break from slinging drinks for the time being. The pretty redhead was sitting with her elbows on the bar, her face in her palms, eyes aglitter as she watched Killian Gardiner sing along from behind the counter. His low, deep voice, like a caress in the middle of the night, made for a fitting duet. *"I'm back where I belong, back in baby's arms."*

Freya loved this about Killian: he continued to court her un-relentingly. Unapologetically. Even if they were engaged and soon to be married, the game of seduction never ended with him. There was never any fear that they would turn into two bored people flicking through television channels, desperate for enter-tainment, frustrated with a life spent on a couch, their red-hot romance just a faded memory. It was a good thing, too, because Freya thrived on drama, the perpetual titillation of flirtation, the constant chase, the rush from unexpected tender moments like this sultry serenade.

She swooned, watching Killian's hair fall over his dark lashes as he grabbed the cocktail shaker to mix the usual for a cus-tomer who had straggled in. He poured the vodka with a flour-ish, added a dash of vermouth over ice in the silver container.

Freddie couldn't be more wrong about him, she thought. When her twin brother, Freddie, had returned from Limbo a month ago, he was burning with wild accusations, all of them directed at her beloved. Freddie believed Killian had stolen his trident, used it to destroy the bridge, and planted it at the scene so that the gods would blame the golden-haired son of the sea for the bridge's destruction.

Her twin was hell-bent on revenge, but he reluctantly agreed to give Freya a chance to suss out the situation on her own if she promised to help him find the truth and dig up what she could on her boyfriend. Freya had relented with a heavy heart. She could hardly believe that Killian was capable of such treachery. He knew how close she was to her twin brother, so how could he have done something so grave and cruel and—unforgivable? And if so, how could she not see it? Could her feelings, along with the earth-shattering, mind-boggling sex they had, have marred her judgment? No. Freddie had to be wrong about this. He'd been in Limbo too long; he wasn't thinking straight. She *trusted* Killian. They had been separated for so long, but now that they had found each other again, it felt *right*. Perfect, really. Back in baby's arms, just like the song.

Killian caught her staring at him and smiled, his blue-green eyes flashing.

Freya smiled back, looking deep into his eyes, but all the while she was searching for a hint that might give him away. What secrets was he keeping? With her witch sight, she looked for something hidden deep within the recesses of Killian's soul, but all she saw was his simple, pure love reflected straight back at her.

The Patsy Cline song ended. Killian flipped the cocktail shaker up in the air and caught it deftly behind his back, all without breaking eye contact. He slung the shaker onto the counter, winking at Freya, and—just then—for perhaps a fraction of a second, a millisecond maybe, Freya swore she saw something she hadn't seen before or ever wanted to: the tiniest malevolent flicker. It was already gone before she could pinpoint it, although it was enough to give her a shiver.

"Cold, babe?" Killian asked, reaching over the bar to warm her hands in his.

Freya shrugged. "I'm great." But she was asking herself how much she actually knew Killian. They had been apart for centuries. Something could have changed him in the interim. Yet the warmth of his hands seemed to assure her that none of it was true. His fingers slipped away from hers, to pour the mix from the shaker into a martini glass for the regular at the end of the bar.

Since the Restriction had been lifted, Freya, along with the rest of the Beauchamp family, was now allowed to use her powers, so these days the bar was truly enchanted. At the North Inn, prep work consisted of dozens of knives hanging in the air, chopping mint, slicing lemons, limes, and oranges, peeling twirls of rind. The love potions were back, and drinks sometimes mixed themselves, but her magic also extended into other areas, like fixing a bad haircut or giving a dowdy customer a glamorous makeover

9

on the spot. The patrons told themselves it was sleight of hand or smoke and mirrors, or that maybe they'd just had one too many.

Killian went downstairs to fill the ice buckets and while he was gone Freya convinced herself she was becoming paranoid— that she hadn't seen a thing. His eyes had merely caught the light from the setting sun. That was all it was.

Someone put a quarter in the jukebox and the atmosphere shifted as the room filled with the sound of Kings of Leon's jangly guitars. It had been like that all evening ever since Sal had added oldies to the queue—a Roy Orbison ballad followed by Feist, Aretha Franklin before Metallica, the Sex Pistols segueing into the Jackson 5. The music moved back and forth through the history of the charts, much like this odd little pocket of Long Island that existed outside of time itself. As the couple on the dance floor began to shimmy, Freya spied fortysomething Betty Lazar enter the bar.

She looked downright haggard, the poor thing. Freya hadn't seen Betty around town in a while. As the paralegal trundled over, a series of images flashed in Freya's mind: the grueling day, the pesky attorneys, the microwavable dinner, the three cats. No sooner had Betty taken a seat than an oversize martini glass, filled with a pool of electric blue topped with the tiniest bit of ocean froth, appeared before her in a swirl of mist.

Someone yelled, "A pop-up drink, a pop-up drink!" and the dozen or so customers clapped and cheered.

Dazzled, Betty took a sip and let out a sigh. "Wow, Freya, how did you know that was exactly what I wanted? I haven't been here in eons. Talk about *service*! What's happened to this place?"

"Just a few improvements," Freya smiled, thinking a nice lady like Betty shouldn't waste her nights alone with television procedurals.

_____

THEY CLOSED UP SHOP EARLY. It was a Tuesday night and the last customer rolled out at ten. The temperature had plummeted by the evening, and the footbridge to Gardiners Island rattled, swaying precariously as the waves broke against it. Freya held Killian's hand as they wended their way across in the dark, with only the faint glow of Fair Haven and the lighthouse in the distance.

"Nice night," she said, squeezing his fingers. She loved fall. It was her favorite season: the golden leaves, the crisp air, the smell of pumpkins—earthy and full, signifying a good harvest.

"Mmm," Killian agreed, leaning down to give her a kiss.

She kissed him back, pulling him closer so that they were soon locked in a tight embrace. His kisses were strong and forceful, the way she liked it, and they pressed against each other, the heat rising between them. They could never wait to get their hands on each other, and Killian lifted her from the narrow walkway so she could wrap her legs around his hips. He pressed forward and Freya felt herself pushed a little too far against the parapet and she lost her balance, slipping out of his grasp. She fell backward over the railing, strawberry-blond curls and scarf whipping out on the wind. For a few terrifying seconds, she believed she would plummet into the inky waters until Killian managed to grab hold of her knees. But instead of pulling her back up, she heard him laugh.

"Killian! Stop it!" she cried. But he made no move to help as she continued to dangle over the edge.

"I'm serious! Pull me up!" she said. "It's not funny!" She felt as if she couldn't breathe and her heart thudded wildly in her chest.

It was over in a flash as Killian pulled her up and righted her, letting her body slide down the length of his until she was back on solid footing.

She stared at him, frightened to find his face a mask, his eyes muted and dull. *What the hell just happened? What was that all about?*

"Hey, c'mon. I was just teasing," Killian said, looking concerned as Freya moved away and huddled by herself, hiding her face behind her hair.

"I'm sorry," he said, coming over to lean over her shoulder so that he buried his head in the crook of her neck, and she could feel his warm breath on her skin again, making it tingle. "It was a bad joke. I didn't realize you were really scared. Usually you like that sort of stuff."

His voice was so gentle, and she knew he was still Killian, her sweet, her beloved. He would never hurt her, *never*. She knew the truth of that deep in her bones. And he was right: she was an adrenaline junkie; she liked dangerous games. "I'm sorry, too," she said as she turned to face him, running a hand over his stubble, his soft lips. "I don't know why I freaked out."

BACK ABOARD THE *DRAGON*, they tumbled into bed and Freya looked down at him through half-lidded eyes. Killian was gritting his teeth, eyes drowsy and glazed by the pleasurable sensation of their lovemaking. His strong hands guided her by the waist, his thumbs pushed on her hips as she rocked on top of him and the cabin heaved in a rhythm.

Afterward, Killian gave her a sleepy kiss, but Freya lay awake for a long time, as the strange, uncomfortable feeling began to grow. She couldn't lie to herself. She had seen what she had seen, at the bar and on the bridge.

She had looked into Killian's blank eyes and she had seen her own death in them.

chapter two

Stranger in the Night

～

Ingrid Beauchamp walked down an aisle of the North Hampton Public Library, humming as she shelved a handful of books on the way to the children's reading area. Her blond bun was neatly brushed back from her face, and she was wearing a smart tailored blue suit and pretty new spectator pumps. She was taking a break from restoring an Edwardian blueprint that had been found inside an old roll-top secretary desk in a ramshackle manor on the edge of town that was going up for auction.

School had let out about an hour ago, and kids had begun to file in, the teens to check out the latest "trauma porn" (as Hudson called the newest crop of "dark" books for the age group), or study in the carrels, the younger ones huddling up for Tabitha's reading hour. Tabitha had a mellifluous voice, and perhaps she had missed her calling as an actress, Ingrid mused. She kept those kids on tenterhooks. Ingrid wanted to make sure it was comfy in there for Tab. Not quite five months into her pregnancy, the girl already looked as if she were about to pop.

Ingrid let out a happy sigh as she surveyed the busy area with bay windows facing the library's garden, out to the shore and the splashing gray-green waves. A teen lay sprawled on two oversize orange pillows, and Ingrid would need to find a small one for Tabitha's back, so she set herself to the task. The boy had a jet-black faux hawk and was hunkered down over one of the new e-readers she'd bought at Hudson's urging. "We can't get left behind! The future is here, and you should know that more than anyone," he'd said, alluding to her other talents.

The summer's end fund-raiser meant the library was no longer on the verge of extinction and the money had even allowed her to get a half dozen of those devices. She couldn't imagine how anyone would want to forego the intimate experience of a book—pages whispering between the fingers, hurried glances at the colorful cover before immersing oneself again. She didn't understand the allure of reading a flat screen, but if it kept the library alive and well, so be it.

That the previous mayor had died a scandalous death—hanging himself in a roadside fleabag motel after killing an underage girl who had rebuffed him—*was* indeed a sad and tragic fact. However, it had saved Ingrid's beloved library, her home away from home, her domain. There was a lot of silver lining there. The tragedy had ushered in a young, intelligent mayor, Justin Frond, who was all about preservation and keeping big businesses and ugly run-of-the-mill chains out of the quaint and sleepy town; he even wanted to turn the white-columned library building into a historical landmark.

"Large cargo ahead! Coming through!" boomed Hudson, who was guiding Tabitha into the reading room, one hand on her back, the other at her wrist.

"Hudson!" chastised Ingrid, who was arranging pillows in neat half circles facing Tabitha's reading chair.

"Well, it's true," said Tabitha. "But I still have two legs and can walk, *Hudson*!" Her face was rounder and her cheeks flushed; pregnancy had made her look younger, vital, full of life, her long blond hair glossier. She couldn't stop eating, though, and had taken to packing two lunches—just in case. "I know. I'm getting *so* big."

Hudson squared the knot of the violet tie beneath his argyle vest while he studied Tabitha. He placed the tip of an index finger between his lips and bit the nail. *"Mmm . . ."*

"For god's sake, she's *pregnant*," Ingrid cut in.

"Library voice, Ingrid," he reminded. "I was actually going to say *'gorgeous.'*"

The three friends laughed.

"Anyway, Tab, you'll lose the excess superfast once you start . . . What is that *whatsy* thing called again?" He snapped his fingers, searching for the word.

"Nursing . . . ?" asked Ingrid, not quite sure herself.

"Yeah, *that*!" He lifted his brow. "Burn those calories, baby!" Hudson spun on his heels, leaving them with the rest of setup for reading hour.

INGRID FELT WORN OUT as she punched in the code to the alarm, then locked up the library. After-school hours had gotten especially harried, and she had stayed late, working on her magnificent new blueprint. Plus, she had resumed *witching hour*, or "counseling services," weekdays from noon to one. As for payment, there was a list with a full range of suggested donations. SPONSOR YOUR FAVORITE AUTHOR TO COME TO THE NORTH HAMPTON PUBLIC LIBRARY TO DO A READING. SUPPORT LITERATURE, the sign said. THE FRONT COLUMNS AND NINETEENTH-CENTURY GARDEN TRELLISES NEED YOUR HELP! She was back in the magic business and this time she didn't have to look over her shoulder while she practiced it. She found the work fulfilling. Helping people with her magic made her feel refreshed and invigorated. Ingrid was doing her part. Hadn't there been a study that showed that even the smallest acts of kindness made people live longer, happier lives? Well, she would live forever anyway, but she did get a thrill out of being of service. But today, it had been *bang, bang, bang,* one emergency case after the next, and she was ready to go home.

Ingrid crossed the street, making her way toward the adjacent park, tugging the collar of her light wool coat around her neck. There was a chill in the air and the wind had picked up. Autumn had finally kicked in. It was dark, and the park—filled with pines, maples, and evergreen oaks, along with a bench and lamppost here and there along the winding paths—was full of shifting shadows, most likely the tree branches lifting and swelling in the wind.

It was quicker to cut through the park than to circumvent it, walking straight toward the beach and hanging a left on the small sandy alley that led to Joanna's house. Ingrid always took this route, but for a moment she hesitated.

She reprimanded herself for being such a scaredy-cat just because it was darker than usual, or for even considering summoning her familiar, Oscar, to accompany her home. Most likely the griffin was already curled up in a corner of the house, making those little snoring noises. She had done much scarier things than walk through this safe little town's park at night before.

Nevertheless, Ingrid braced herself as she entered the park, taking the little cement path. She picked up her speed as the trees whooshed around her. It was all so dimly lit, and the click of her heels echoed too loudly. She heard a moaning, creaking sound that made her start, but she sighed when she realized it was coming from the children's playground ahead, most likely a swing pushed to and fro by the wind.

As she approached the play area—it was hard to see because of the black rubber mats covering the ground and the sudden glare of a lamppost—Ingrid thought she spied something. It looked like several child-size forms on the monkey bars and the swings. Now that was weird—children playing at this hour. The few parents she knew in North Hampton advocated very strict and early bedtimes. A gust pushed through the trees, and Ingrid heard whispers, a patter of feet, or maybe she was just hearing things, mistaking the sound of rustling pine needles and leaves for something more. Maybe she was seeing and hearing things that weren't there.

Sure enough, as she came around the lamppost, the playground was deserted and the swings were swaying on their own. She heaved a sigh of relief too soon, though. She had been so worried about the creaky noises that she had missed the lumpy, ragged silhouette lumbering toward her on the path about fifteen feet ahead. Her breath caught in her throat, and she immediately recalled a tidbit from the local news warning the residents of North Hampton of a recent rash of burglaries. No wonder she had been tentative about taking this shortcut: the information had slipped her mind, but unconsciously it must have been nagging at her. She could turn around and take off at a clip, but in her pencil skirt and heels, she couldn't exactly sprint. The fearsome figure continued to limp toward her, stopping now and then on the opposite border of the pathway with an awkward, halting gait.

Ingrid kept her head high and her pace steady, and did not change her course. Partly, this was stubbornness on her part. Why should she turn around? She had made it this far and was almost across the park. She didn't have very much on her, about twenty-six dollars and change, and she would happily hand it over if the thief let her go on her merry way. In all likelihood, it was just a poor homeless person searching for a place to sleep.

As she and the stranger neared each other, she could make him out better in the faint light: the strangely small head on that tall body, almost seven feet tall; a grimy face; a stoop or a bit of a hump; shiny, dark beady little eyes; and a long, draping coat that was ripped and frayed.

Just a few feet apart now, she was close enough to attune her senses, quickly sweep through the underlayer to scan for the pulse of a lifeline.

But there was nothing. Ingrid frowned.

As they crossed each other, the stranger unexpectedly swung sideways, lunging at her, grasping her, and cupping her mouth with a hand. Ingrid screamed, or tried to, but there was something in her mouth now—a hanky steeped in chloroform—deep and noxious; she felt immediately drowsy. She sensed a disturbing commotion around her, but she just couldn't open her eyes to see what it was: people moving this way and that, talking in hurried whispers in a language she didn't recognize. She tried to kick her legs, fight back with her arms, but her body wouldn't respond to her brain's commands. She couldn't recall a spell to undo paralysis, not a single word came to mind.

"You're right. It *is* Erda!" a voice said urgently. There was something soothing about hearing her old name. Or had the voice said Ingrid? She didn't know any longer, and she gave in, because now she was too, too tired as she was pulled off the path and dragged over pine needles and stones.

chapter three

Two Princes

૭૮

Joanna Beauchamp stood over the sink, washing dirt off the root vegetables she had dug up in the garden: fat, juicy carrots, beats, parsnips, and rutabaga, encrusted with clumps of dark soil. She had baked two rhubarb pies, which were now cooling on the old Aga stove—one for her family, the other for Gracella's. She wondered if Tyler would like the tangy sweetness of rhubarb and hoped he would. Her girls would probably complain loudly as they ate a piece or two. "Mother! Not another pie!" Freya would say while Ingrid shook her head.

Where were they anyway?

Freya usually came home to take a hot bubble bath or pack a small travel bag every two days or so to spend nights with Killian on the *Dragon*, but Joanna hadn't seen her in—was it four days? The seas had been choppy lately and Joanna couldn't imagine sleeping on a keeling boat, all shook up like that. She should mention to Freya that she and Killian should just shack up in one of the many rooms of Fair Haven if they were going to spend this many nights together. But perhaps the main house held too many bad memories.

Ingrid, on the other hand, was late getting home from work again. Joanna remembered that the other week her oldest had told her about some blueprint she was excited about, and there was no telling how late she might stay at the library once she had immersed herself in a project.

Why was she worrying? Her girls always took care of themselves, had for centuries. And just because this house had become their new pied-à-terre of late, it didn't mean she should start fretting over them as if they were babies. Joanna finished scrubbing the dirt off the vegetables and was about to wash her hands when she noticed yet another anomaly in her kitchen. The little black flowery Chinese soap dish to the right of the sink was gone.

All day long it had been like this. She'd found baking pans upstairs in the bathtub, cups and coffee mugs inside the oven, her hairbrush in the freezer, and now it was going to be a hunt for the Chinese soap dish. There were small items that had gone missing altogether: tweezers by the bathroom sink, along with a pair of small scissors, and, later, her sewing kit. Was Gracella busting out—to use an expression of Freya's—new cleaning techniques? Had she lost it? But that would be very unlike Gracella, who was steady, observant, and almost too thoughtful (in the bathroom, she aligned Joanna's lipsticks with the color labels facing upward from dark to light).

Was one of her girls playing tricks with her? But why? Logic dictated it couldn't have been Freya, who *had* seemed distracted lately and had been a no-show for several days. Freya always made a point of letting Joanna know she was home, singing audibly as soon as she walked through the door, then greeting her mother with a hug and a kiss. Ingrid wasn't exactly the prankster type. If Ingrid had been peeved with Joanna for whatever reason, she wouldn't take it out on her by hiding Joanna's things.

"Aha!" uttered Joanna as she scooted a chair out from the table after trying the breadbox and every other unlikely nook and cranny in the kitchen she could think of. The antique soap dish, which she had bought eons ago at a market in Hong Kong and had managed not to break all these years, sat smack in the middle of the chair's seat. It was clean and contained a brand-new bar of soap. Puzzling. Perhaps Gracella had been forgetful, had had an off day. Everyone did from time to time, even the best of housekeepers.

Joanna washed her hands, content that everything (or so it seemed for now) had been put back in its rightful place. She pulled the ancient wand out of her loose bun so that her long silver hair fell down her shoulders. She needed a shower.

As she strode through the living room on her way upstairs, the blinking answering machine caught her eye, and she stopped in her tracks. The red button winked twice at her, then paused and blinked twice again. *Ah,* she thought, *they aren't as inconsiderate as I thought and are finally learning that a mother does worry even when her girls are immortal.*

She walked over to the machine and flicked her wand at it. She could, of course, press the button, both acts requiring a single gesture, but somehow this felt easier, plus Gracella had taken care to clean the vintage machine: she had seen her doing so with Q-tips and rubbing alcohol.

"*Uh* . . . this is Norman. *Uh* . . . your husband?" the machine said.

"Oh!" She was caught off guard. She crossed her arms over her chest and waited for Norman to continue. Why did he have to announce himself like that? They had known each other for millennia, and she certainly hadn't forgotten his voice. What was with the upbeat word *husband* with the question mark at the end? Well, she had to admit that she herself didn't know what their status was. Being apart this long, would they actually be considered divorced?

"I've been thinking . . . *How to put this?* . . . Maybe this is not the right place to say it, Jo . . . I probably should speak with you directly instead . . ."

Joanna waved a hand at the machine as if to urge it to speed up.

"Yes, I know, you're getting impatient with me right now, so I'll get on with it . . ."

Joanna snorted. She couldn't help but feel a slight thrill at hearing Norman's soft gruff voice, which suggested a nose-in-the-books-all-day kind of weariness. There was also the pleasure of the deep familiarity of his voice, like hearing from an old friend who anticipated her thoughts.

Norman continued. "Ever since that little shindig of Ingrid's— the library fund-raiser—well, even before that, I thought . . . Well, maybe we can just talk a little?" The latter came out rushed. "I would really like that, Jo. Call me! I was thinking it would be truly terrific if—" Just as Norman had been gathering some momentum, the machine sounded a long beep, cutting him off. It reminded her of that *Gong Show* from the 1970s and she laughed out loud.

"Hi, this is Harold Atkins calling Joanna Beauchamp," piped in yet another male voice, this one more self-assured and to the point. "I wanted to follow up on that little conversation we had about letting me take you out to dinner. I heard about some new place down by the waterfront. Would you like to try it out? By the way, how's that raven of yours? Hope to see you soon. Tomorrow at the preschool? Are you picking up Tyler?"

Harold Atkins, a dashing gentleman widower, had recently moved to North Hampton. His daughter and son-in-law, both doctors at the local hospital, worked long rotation hours. Harold had proposed that rather than raise little Clay with a series of nannies who came and went, better to have the child's own grandfather for the job. He was retired from his veterinarian practice in New York City and had nothing keeping him there any longer. His wife had died of ovarian cancer three years earlier, and the city was filled with painful reminders of the woman he had dearly loved. So Harold had sold his Manhattan brownstone for a handsome sum to buy a house on the beach in North Hampton and be a grandpa.

Joanna didn't find Harold's message intrusive; it was flattering that he had taken such an interest in her instead of that bunch of sexy grannies at the preschool. What did Freya call them? Not cougars—*snow leopards*—slim, glossy silver–haired ladies with their *light work* (expressionless foreheads), weekly manicures, and monthly visits to the salon, who eagerly sidled up to him or threw him salacious sidelong glances. Harold was a very young, very urbane-looking seventy-year-old, and it didn't hurt that he was also rich.

23

She and Harold had become friendly since early September when school had started, and he always appeared especially pleased to see Joanna. She *had* noticed that her jeans fit more loosely lately; maybe it was that she had lost a few of her extra pounds and didn't look so bad herself. She and Harold had exchanged numbers to set up playdates for Tyler and Clay, who were buddies.

It's raining men, she thought with a sudden bout of angst. How funny to find herself the object of two suitors. Norman wanted to talk. *What was it that would be "truly terrific,"* she wondered. It was hard to imagine stodgy old Norm excited about anything. He was so ensconced in academia, very much fulfilled by life in the ivory tower—although his small, monastic cell had elicited a twinge of sadness in her. Now here was Harold Atkins asking her out on a date. The truth was that Joanna had grown comfortable in her singlehood; she enjoyed being alone. Plus she had Tyler now, who took up much of her thoughts, although perhaps it was a way to assuage the longing she felt in her son's absence. Joanna deleted both messages and replied to neither.

It was all so overwhelming. But finally she had to admit hearing from the two men wasn't what was troubling her. Something was not sitting right, and it had to do with the girls, Freya in particular. Freya was hiding something. Joanna could not exactly pinpoint how she knew, but she trusted her mother's instinct that something was wrong.

chapter four

Girls, Girls, Girls

⌐⌐

There was someone skulking around the *Dragon*, and even asleep Freya heard it: creaking in the crew cabin starboard, then in the salon and kitchen galley. It wasn't Killian. He was lying next to her with his arm looped around her waist. She needed to wake up but couldn't quite push past the layers of sleep to the surface. There was the noise again. This time it was footsteps on the companionway. She forced her eyes open, her ears finely attuned, but now there was nothing. The night was still, and the only noise was Killian's soft breathing.

The glow from the lights on the dock shone through the portholes of the cabin. There was nobody in the room except the two of them. Freya slowly extricated herself from the blanket and sheets, dressing quickly and quietly, careful not to wake Killian. She was soon stepping onto the footbridge, where only the *Dragon* was moored. There was no one around, but she figured whoever it was had taken care not to get caught.

Deciding to give up on going back to sleep, she walked against a strong gust along the path that traversed the darkened beach until she reached her car. Instead of taking the right toward Joanna's, she swung the Mini Cooper in the opposite direction, driving west, taking the narrow sandy road, flanked by cattails, that ran along the shore. Not fifteen minutes later, Freya reached a dilapidated two-story beachside motel on the outskirts of town, half of which appeared sunk in the sand, perilously tilting sideways. The neon sign read UCKY STAR, the *L* permanently extinguished. The puke-pink and mint-green facade, as well as the rusty white railings along the upper story, had eroded in the briny air. Despite the motel's appearance, about a dozen cars were parked out front, so Freya backed up, preferring to pull up in the shadows, lest her Mini be spotted by someone she knew.

She got out and walked toward the motel's front lot. It was so quiet this time of year without the constant thrum of cicadas and insects screeching in the grasses; only the sound of the wind as it whispered through the reeds and the waves crashing before slithering away.

Just as Freya entered the lot, she heard heels clicking on the upper walkway of the motel. The stranger, a tall woman, tottered forward unsteadily, then seemed to sense Freya's presence because she leaned against the railing and peered out to the lot. Her clothes were rumpled, and wayward strands of light blond hair had come loose from her bun. Freya hid, hunkering down behind a car, but one glimpse was all it took to know that Freya had just seen Ingrid, looking uncharacteristically disheveled. *What the hell is she doing here?*

Perhaps Ingrid and that detective of hers had finally gotten around to getting it on? Freya smiled to herself. Being an expert in all matters love, especially when it came to other people's romantic quests, Freya had not been unaware of the torch Ingrid carried for a certain Matt Noble. In this case, it hadn't been images in her head but that sweet little kiss she had witnessed them exchange at the last annual library fund-raiser that confirmed it. However, when she had asked Ingrid about it, her sister shrugged it off, saying, "Oh, Matt, but he's just a friend!" Yet Freya had seen the blush spread in Ingrid's cheeks and decided that for now she would leave it alone and respect her sister's privacy. Strange to think Ingrid and Matt would rendezvous at such a run-down hotel. Maybe it was a kink of theirs. Oh well, everyone had their little secrets.

She heard one of the doors open then close, and when Freya rose from behind the car, Ingrid was gone. Freya sprinted across the lot to a door on the lower level, on the sinking side of the motel—the cheaper rooms. She tapped out the secret knock.

"Will you get that, babe?" she heard from behind the paperthin wall among sword-clanking sounds, muffled grunts, and blows coming from the TV.

A young woman with a ponytail, the golden-brown mane swept onto a shoulder, cracked open the door. She wore a snug T-shirt that blared WRONG ISLAND UNIVERSITY, a skirt as big as a handkerchief, tights, and calf-hugging high-heeled boots. "What do you want?" she said, giving Freya the once-over.

Freya stared back at her with equal disdain. *"Uh . . .* I'm here to see my *brother*?"

"Let her in," said Freddie from inside.

The coed swung open the door, and Freya strode in. She stopped abruptly, taking in the sight: everything in the room— the floor, the beds, the desk strewn with leftover fast-food wrappers, the TV, the armchair where Freddie sat wielding a Wii remote at a video game on the TV screen—pitched slightly to the right. There was a pile of neatly folded clothes on one twin bed, while the other was unmade, covers and sheets spilling onto the floor. Freddie, in a tank and boxers, sat with one very long, muscular leg swung over the armchair's side and the other foot, like that of an ancient Roman sculpture, resting on the floor among other discarded food wrappers. His lips broke into a huge grin as he turned to Freya. A dwarf boar, Freddie's familiar, burst out from beneath the blankets on the floor, waddling over to root around in the wrappers as if he were taken with a sudden urge to hunt truffles.

"Buster!" said Freya to the piglet.

"So *cute!*" said Wrong Island University.

"Buster or Freddie?" asked Freya, curious.

The girl cocked her head to one side so that her ponytail flipped over. "Well, both, really."

"Ugh!" harrumphed Freya, annoyed that her twin continued to play his video game even when he knew she hated it—all that cartoon violence. After she had refused to play along with his revenge fantasies against Killian, Freddie devolved into a slug. Funny that: he lived with a pig and had become a slug. But at least he had done his laundry; that was a start.

"Babe," said the girl, "I did all your laundry, so now all you've got to do is put it away. I really should be getting back to the dorms. It's late. Do you think you'll be needing anything else?"

Freya was amused at her twin's resources. He had somehow managed to procure his very own personal assistant despite being holed up in self-imposed exile.

"I'm great," said Freddie, swinging his leg over onto the seat, getting up to rub his flat belly.

While Freya watched, appalled, the coed pecked him on the lips, then stared at him a moment. "You're such a god, Freddie!"

"If you *only* knew," he said, raising an eyebrow as he walked her to the door.

"Okay, bye . . . um, Freddie's sister, whatever your name is!" After the coed was gone, Freddie locked the door behind her.

He swiveled around toward Freya, his arms open wide for a hug. She begrudgingly returned his affection even as she felt a twinge of guilt. She patted him on the back before she went over to one of the twin beds to sit. He returned to the armchair across from her.

"Talk to me!" he said, clapping his hands together. "What's up?"

Freya couldn't help but smile at her sleepy-eyed twin, recalling the little boy he had been, her best friend, who now made a valiant effort to sit at attention. She longed for that kind of closeness with him again, the intimacy of twins who shared their own secret language, as they once had. But she held herself in check. There wasn't going to be a truce, not yet, not until Freddie got these stupid ideas about Killian out of his head.

"Gotta hand it to you, bro," she said. "Little college girls doing your chores, getting you food? What is this, a harem?"

"Whatevs," said Freddie with a shrug. "They like doing stuff for me."

"I'm sure they do." She smirked.

"So, why are you here so late? Did you find it?"

Freya shook her head and didn't answer. "This is very unhealthy, you know, the video games, the laziness, this fixation on Killian, which has gotten *way* out of control. Why don't you just let me take you home? This can all end right here, right now, but you've got to stop with these crazy, unfounded accusations."

"They're not unfounded!" Freddie insisted. "How many times do I have to go over it with you? I remember it *very* clearly."

Freya put a hand up. "Please don't! I remember what you said."

"Well, did you look for it even?" he asked.

Freya stared wordlessly at him. Buster nosed his calf, and Freddie gave the pig a gentle squeeze, which made the little fatty roll onto his back. Freddie flicked his hair out of his eyes and glared at Freya. He was stubborn, sure, but he was also beautiful: dear Freddie, who'd always been a love. Freya understood exactly why a girl might do his laundry, then place it like an offering at his feet. Freddie's features were a striking contrast of delicate and bold: creamy gold skin, large green eyes like hers, the sweet dimple in his strong chin. With that head of flaxen

29

hair, he did exude a celestial kind of radiance. He was a ray of pure sunshine, beaming at her from the squalor of this run-down motel.

"So?" he asked, the question still hanging between them.

She sighed impatiently. "Freddie, I looked everywhere! Every freaking nook and cranny on that boat! Then I looked again. I found nothing. *Nothing*, Freddie!" She was annoyed to have given in. She was reluctant to let Freddie know that she had conceded to his request, because that meant she didn't fully trust Killian; it was an acknowledgment that he could possibly be guilty. "You've been here all night?" she asked, thinking of the noises she heard on the boat earlier.

"Right here," he said.

The toilet in the bathroom flushed, and Freya did a double take at the closed door. "Who else is here?"

Freddie winced. "Uh . . . I forgot her name," he mumbled as a long-legged, towel-wrapped maiden, another college girl most likely, they were obviously Freddie's new weakness, emerged from the bathroom.

"Oh, hi!" she said to Freya.

Freddie smiled at her. "Hey . . ." he said.

"Hey yourself," the girl retorted. She'd obviously heard his confession about having forgotten who she was.

"Well, you're obviously busy," Freya said. "I should be going." She rolled her eyes at her incorrigible twin. Apparently, even cooped up in this motel, he had managed to meet plenty of young ladies—and she'd been worried that he was lonely.

"Freya, if you don't act, I will," Freddie warned, following her to the doorway. "There are all kinds of hiding places you know, doors within doors. It's got to be there. He's keeping it nearby. You haven't looked hard enough."

Freya turned to him, her arms crossed. "He didn't take it. I *know* he didn't."

"What did you lose?" the girl asked, confused. She was now wearing a lacy bra and Freddie's boxers.

"One of his video games. He thinks my boyfriend took it," Freya said, rolling her eyes. "Bye, Freddie," she said, then slipped out into the night.

chapter five

Here Comes Your Man

~≈~

Ingrid repaired to a back booth at the North Inn to wait for Matt Noble, safely hidden in one of the high-backed banquettes for now. While she wanted to go somewhere she was comfortable, she didn't want to see Freya just yet. Her sister would tease her mercilessly about the detective and Ingrid wanted to avoid it as long as she could.

It was hard to imagine that someone who had lived so long had so little experience with romance, but Ingrid had always preferred reading about love to getting involved in messy dramas herself. Love stories never ended well. Look at Tess of the d'Urbervilles, Anna Karenina, Lily Bart, Lady Chatterley, Emma Bovary; the list of tragic heroines went on and on. Love was frightening territory, and Ingrid had always steered clear. Now, of all things, she'd gone and fallen for a mortal, and she suddenly understood how one could be inexorably drawn to a person, no matter how wrong or ill-fated the circumstances.

She sipped her water and looked up to see Freya standing in front of her, with a hand on her hip and a smug smile on her face.

"Oh . . . hi," she said.

"You're meeting *him* here, aren't you?" her sister asked. "Nice of you to come by and say hello."

"I was going to, but . . ."

Freya grinned. "I'm just busting your chops, Ingrid. I like the guy even if he did lock us up for a day."

"I'm nervous. It's our first date," confided Ingrid.

"There's nothing to be nervous about—wait—what do you mean this is your *first* date?" Freya demanded.

But Ingrid didn't have time to explain because Freya was called away to the other end of the bar. Ingrid sighed. Of course her sister wouldn't understand. Freya always called Ingrid a tortoise, especially when it came to men.

It had been a little over a month since Ingrid's first spine-tingling kiss with Matt on Labor Day. Since then an investigation had taken him out of town for a couple of weeks, and every time they had tried to get together, something came up, like the library conference Ingrid had needed to attend in the city, or some other work commitment for Matt. They'd finally agreed on a couple of drinks at the North Inn, then dinner at that new French restaurant by the beach. She wondered if he still felt the same about her—and she alternately dreaded and longed for the moment she would glimpse his handsome freckled face when he walked into the bar. Every time a customer came in, she flinched, looking to the door, her spirit lifting and then falling with disappointment when it was someone else. Matt was usually prompt—at least when he'd been dating her ex-coworker, Caitlin. Ingrid tried not to be too miffed.

She twirled the straw in her drink. The ice had nearly melted, and her nerves were too raw to take even one sip. It was eight minutes past the appointed time. She tugged at the scoop neck of the little black dress she'd bought in the city during the library conference.

"Don't worry. You don't look like a floozy, Sis. That's my department," Freya said, coming back with a glass of champagne and setting it on the table.

Ingrid glanced dubiously at the champagne flute, strings of pearly bubbles floating on the surface. "This isn't one of your potions, is it?"

"Um, you've got plenty of your own magic. You certainly don't need mine. It's champagne with a touch of cassis, a Kir Royal. I can sense your anxiety from all the way over at the bar, and it's making *me* anxious. Relax, you look great!"

It was true. With her hair down, in a tight black dress that showed a hint of cleavage, a thin red ribbon around her small waist, Ingrid looked ravishing, her arms and face shimmery, a flush in her cheeks. She followed orders and bravely downed most of the Kir Royal. "I'm not overdressed, am I?"

"God, no! You look elegant, but not overstated," said Freya, giving her sister a reassuring smile. "I'm sorry about before. It's just that I thought—"

But Matt was standing by Freya's side, which made her instantly change the subject. "Ah, there he is, the Beauchamp family savior!" she teased fondly, for it had been Matt who had pressed his colleagues to drop the investigation. Even if he had hauled all three of them in for questioning originally, he was also the detective who had solved the murder cases that cleared the sisters and their mother of any wrongdoing. "What can I get you guys? On the house!"

Matt wagged his finger at Freya and craned his neck to catch a glimpse of Ingrid. Freya leaned over and took away Ingrid's empty champagne glass. In a flash, the table was set with a bottle of the bubbly in an ice bucket and two full champagne glasses.

Ingrid came out of the booth to greet Matt. They stood slightly apart, looking so shyly at each other with excited smiles that they didn't even notice how quickly the drinks had arrived.

"Hi," Matt said.

"Hi," Ingrid returned. She gathered he had gone home, showered, and changed. His hair was still a tad wet, and he looked clean shaven, dapper in a dark suit with a crisp green shirt and blue tie. She liked him in his dress up civilian clothes, and admired his solid shoulders inside the suit.

Matt moved toward her, putting a hand at her waist. It was all so natural, no fumbling for each other's cheeks, just that same ease she felt when they had last stood face-to-face—and then the jolt that went straight to her heart as he touched her.

"You look amazing," he said. "I couldn't wait to finally see you again."

"You, too. I mean me, too. I mean you look amazing as well and I was looking forward to seeing you, Matt." Ingrid blushed, embarrassed for being so voluble.

For a moment, Matt didn't look sure whether to sit beside her or across from her, and finally decided on the latter. They sat. Ingrid stared into his clear blue eyes. "So, uh, that author of *The Cobbler's Daughter's Elephants* has a new one. Should I place it on hold for you?" she asked. He looked stricken for a moment, and then saw that she was teasing him and they laughed together.

She took a sip of her drink, and when she placed a hand on the table, Matt stared at it as if he was contemplating whether to touch it or not. She sort of wished he would. "I really am sorry for making you read all those boring books. I'll make it up to you. I have a bunch I think you'd really like," she said.

"Ah, I would have gone on reading them just because you recommended them."

"Really?"

"Truly." He smiled. "I'm glad we finally got together. It's pretty obvious that um . . . I mean at this point, I'd say it's a pretty incontestable fact that . . ." He shook his head. "I mean I want to apologize. Clear the air. It was lousy of me to date Caitlin when I wasn't interested in her . . . and I don't want you to think that

melissa de la cruz

that's the kind of guy I am . . . because I'm not." He looked down, shaking his head.

"You don't have to explain. I understand. I was sort of awful to you, and I'm sorry."

"No, no you weren't." He looked up at her.

"What?" she said when he didn't say anything after a long time.

He grinned. "You're just so adorable, Ingrid. Can I ask you something?"

"Sure, anything," she said, feeling a bit flushed. How many glasses of champagne had she had? Two?

"I'd really like to kiss you right now. Can I?"

How formal of him. She liked it. There were tiny beads of perspiration on his forehead. He was nervous, probably as nervous as she was. This brave man was nervous about kissing her. Ingrid felt even warmer toward him.

"Here?" she asked, looking around.

But either he'd decided to stop being shy or not to wait for an answer, because Matt was already leaning over the table toward her. She leaned forward to meet him, and he cupped her chin with his hands, gently pulling her face toward his, and Ingrid closed her eyes, feeling that same trembling sensation as the first time, even with the table between them. It was even sweeter than she remembered, the warm, melting softness of it all. When they parted Ingrid sat back down, a little dazed after the experience. She'd always thought kissing came at the end of the date, not the beginning.

Matt exhaled. "I just needed to get that out of the way. I couldn't get that first one out of my head." This time when he saw that Ingrid's hand was on the table, Matt reached for it and clasped it in his.

Ingrid wanted to say, *Neither could I.* But she was breathless, and she also thought she might need to—what? Slow things down maybe? She had no clue how to go about any of this. "You know, I was attacked the other day," she blurted out, not sure why she was mentioning it now.

It caught Matt off guard. "Excuse me?" His expression changed, and Ingrid saw a sudden spark of anger in his eyes, but when he saw her distress his face softened. "Did I hear that right? You were attacked? When? Are you okay?"

Ingrid pulled her hand away from his and took a nervous sip of her drink. "Sorry, it occurred to me just then. It was nothing, just a harmless homeless person," she lied.

"What happened?"

"I was walking through the park at night, taking my shortcut home from work—"

"You were walking through the park alone at night? What time was it?"

"I don't know. After midnight?"

"Ingrid!" Here Matt did the strangest thing: he took out a small, rectangular leather-bound pad and began scribbling notes in it. "Continue," he said, looking up at her.

She launched into the story, deciding to stick as close to the facts as she could. "It was actually a band of homeless kids, and I did think at first that they meant some harm, since I couldn't speak their language, but it all turned out fine. I'm fine!" she stressed. It had been scary at first when she woke up in that room at that dingy motel, but she didn't want to tell him that.

"Hold on a sec. Besides the fact that you shouldn't be walking alone in the park at that hour, first you tell me it was 'a harmless homeless person,' and now you say it was a roving band of foreign kids. Kids can be dangerous in groups, you know."

"They're not dangerous. I swear. Forget I mentioned it," she said.

"Ingrid, look at me."

She looked at him.

"This is serious. There have been a bunch of burglaries in town, and we're convinced it's a group that's not from around here, which sounds very much like these kids you're describing."

"You sound like a cop," Ingrid said.

"I *am* a cop."

There was really no way of explaining this properly, so she backpedaled. "They're just a bunch of desperate kids who're new to the area. They're not from here, Matt, and they don't know this culture—how things work." This was all *kind of* true.

She was being honest. Her attacker had not been a homeless person at all but rather a group of pixies. The reason the stranger in the park had appeared tall and lumbering was because the five pixies had climbed one on top of the other's shoulders and covered themselves in a long, draping coat—thus the bizarre gait. But the pixies *were* homeless, since they certainly were not from this world. So in a sense they were foreigners, refugees really. They were not allowed to use money, only barter, and in a pinch they resorted to theft. The pixies had kidnapped her—*stolen* her from the park— since that was the way they operated. But it was all very harmless. Pixie magic, while powerful, could be contained, and they had contacted her because they needed help. Still, she couldn't exactly tell Matt that they were magical creatures somehow trapped in mid-world and had sought her help to find their way back home. Ingrid wasn't sure exactly how much Matt believed in her magic; he still seemed a bit skeptical, unlike most of the towns- folk who had easily acclimated to the small enchantments that now pervaded daily life in North Hampton. She hoped it was just his careful nature and not a sign of closed-mindedness.

"They don't mean anyone any harm. Please, let's just forget about the whole thing," she said. She found she didn't much care for Matt's tone, and he was making her feel as if she were in an interrogation room.

"Well, you'll have to tell me where they are, so we can bring them in for questioning," Matt said, looking piqued.

"Oh no, I sent them away. And they promised not to return or ever trouble anyone in North Hampton again."

"Great!"

Ingrid did not like the sarcasm, and she saw that Matt had picked up on her displeasure.

"I'm just worried about you . . . for your safety," he said. "I know you do some amazing—some people even say *miraculous*—things for people in this town, but you need to leave police matters to the police."

"What do you mean 'some people say miraculous'?" Ingrid asked, her nerves on edge.

"Come on now, you don't really expect me to believe . . ."

"In magic?" she prompted.

"Well, yeah. I mean . . . there's no such thing."

"No such thing?" Ingrid snapped. "You're sure about that?"

"Ingrid—did I say something wrong?"

Ingrid shook her head. Patronizing she could stand, but complete disbelief? She was shocked. If Matt didn't believe in magic—if he couldn't accept that she was a witch—what kind of future did they have together? If he couldn't see her for what she was, truly, then there was no hope for a romance, or any relationship at all. Ingrid couldn't change or hide who or what she was for him. If she could accept that she could love a mortal, then he would have to accept that he was in love with a witch.

"Detective Noble, while I'm grateful for your concern, I've taken care of myself for years, and it just so happens that I've done a fine job all on my own." She heard how cold she sounded and instantly regretted it. Was it just moments ago that they were kissing across the table?

Now they were glaring at each other, and when Ingrid finally broke eye contact, she took her purse and rummaged through it for her wallet.

"I've got it," he said.

She couldn't find her wallet anyway. She nodded curtly. "Thanks for the drink. I'll see you around." She'd been looking forward to this date for weeks. How horrid that it had to end this way, with not even a friendly kiss on the cheek or a final hand-shake or plans to see each other again.

Matt stood up. "Ingrid—hey, come on. We're supposed to have dinner."

"You know what? I'm not hungry."

He looked hurt. "At least let me drive you home . . ."

"No. I prefer to walk. It's way before midnight," she said. She stormed out of the bar, glad that Freya hadn't seen her so she wouldn't have to answer any questions.

Ingrid stormed away, furious with herself. She didn't know what had happened back there, but she sensed that she had ru-ined any chance with Matt. And it filled her with an acute and unbearable sense of loss.

How many centuries would she have to wait for the kind of love that could wake her sleeping heart? Even though he had acted like a condescending *policeman*, Matt had mostly just showed how much he cared for her. But that didn't matter now, because she was sure that after tonight he wouldn't anymore. That was the thing that cut her through the heart: she'd lived a long time and met many different men, but she knew there would only ever be one Matthew Noble.

chapter six

All in My Mind

~∾~

Joanna couldn't believe it. Either Gracella had gone mad, or she had. Gilly watched, perched on a chair, as her mistress moved frantically around the room, setting things right again. Joanna had walked in to find the furniture in her study had been rearranged: her desk was no longer facing the view of the Atlantic the way she liked it, but rather it was placed below a tableau of a countryside landscape against the hunter-green wall, like some kind of practical joke. The love seat now occupied the spot where the desk had been, as if two lovers had sat there, staring out at the sea after performing the switcheroo.

It had been a long day and she had been looking forward to some nighttime pleasures—a bit of reading, some light sewing before bed. She only enjoyed rearranging furniture if it was her idea, and she liked the room the way it had been. This would not do.

It was not just that, but the books on her shelves had been rearranged as well, conspicuously out of alphabetical order with *Wizardry and Its Very Essence* placed at the front and *The Abracadabra of Real Magic* all the way in the back. Joanna had been hunting for a particular ancient and rare book of spells, which she'd always been able to spot very quickly because it was in a Ziploc bag to preserve its worn leather cover with the fading gold-leaf letters, delicate spine, and yellowing pages.

But now it was nowhere to be found. She'd have to use, well, magic to find it. She kept her wand inside a secret compartment of her bureau drawer when she wasn't using it, but when she opened the lock, she found it was gone. This final coup was the most alarming. She turned the entire office upside down in an effort to locate it.

"Where is it, Gilly?" she asked her familiar, but the raven only cocked her head, pecked at her chest, and gave no response, which was also troubling.

"Well, I give up," Joanna announced. She needed a break, and went off to find some comfort after the confluence of frustrating events in the kitchen. She'd baked several miniature pies for Tyler that morning, and she was looking forward to eating one, especially since she had skipped dessert.

Upon setting foot in the kitchen, Joanna gasped. The sight was more than she could bear. Just moments ago she had left the kitchen pristine, but now it was in disarray. Several of her pretty little pies lay half-eaten among crumbs on the kitchen counter and another on the table beside a half-consumed glass of milk. She took a huge breath to calm herself and, as she was doing so, Freya came out of the pantry.

Her younger daughter wore a lumpy leather jacket that she was attempting to zip up, but a telltale Lindt chocolate bar slipped out and fell onto the floor, followed by a bag of nuts. What on earth? Joanna stared at that lumpy jacket. What else was in there? A box of pasta? A bag of cookies?

The two women stared at the items on the floor, then looked at each other.

"Oh, hello, Mother," Freya said, as if there was nothing out of the ordinary in her actions.

"So *you* are the one behind all of this," Joanna said.

"Behind what?"

"Well, for one, the messy kitchen and my poor half-eaten pies."

Freya came over to the table and let the items inside her jacket slide out, then began setting them upright. "Mother, I just got here, and I myself was wondering about the mess. I thought you and Tyler had a little party or something. It's not like you to leave the kitchen like this."

"So if it wasn't you who made the mess or ate my pies, why, may I ask, are you stealing food? "

"Oh, these are just snacks to bring to the *Dragon*. You know, it's late, and I couldn't find an open market, and there wasn't anything in the pantry to put this stuff in," Freya said, jabbering.

Joanna retrieved a shopping bag from beneath the sink and began placing the foodstuff in it. She could tell her daughter was lying to her—probably not about the pies, though. Freya didn't like coconut and key lime. No, she was lying about the snacks from the pantry. Freya talked fast when she was hiding something, ever since she'd been a little girl, like the time she'd told Joanna that her classmate's hair was purple because she was a Goth and not because Freya had hexed her for stealing her purple crayon.

She knew enough not to point out Freya's tell—it was a mother's secret ammunition—but extracting the truth would be a delicate operation. "By the way, how are you and Killian doing? I miss that sweet boy. You should bring him around here more often," she said.

"Everything's great!" Freya replied too cheerfully, so that it sounded conspicuously false. "You really shouldn't worry so much, Mother. And you look . . . I don't know . . . as if *I* need to worry about *you*." Freya walked behind Joanna and began to massage her mother's shoulders.

The massage felt soothing, and Joanna realized how tense she had been. She was about to confide in Freya about the very odd,

43

frustrating goings-on around the house that were making her think she'd gone crazy when the front door opened and Ingrid trundled in, shrugging off her coat and looking extremely upset.

She looked so pretty in her black dress with just a hint of red, her blond hair loose on her shoulders. *What possibly could be wrong?* Joanna wondered.

Ingrid placed her coat over her arm. "Hey, you two," she said, forcing a smile.

Freya came and grabbed her by the shoulders, looking into her eyes. "Hey! Why are you here so early?"

"It's nothing," Ingrid said, but she looked on the verge of tears.

Joanna clucked her tongue. Something was obviously not great or fine, but if she asked, then she would never know. Now she had two tight-lipped daughters, which was nothing new, and the front door buzzer was ringing.

They all stood silently for a moment, until Joanna said, "I guess I better get that." As soon as she walked into the hallway, she could hear her girls hurriedly whispering back and forth. It really pained her that they were so reticent to include her sometimes. What was it about herself that elicited such mistrust, or was it just the nature of all mother-and-daughter relationships?

Joanna opened the door to find Harold Atkins, her gentleman caller, beaming at her and closing a long black umbrella. A light rain had just begun to fall. It was nice to see his calm, amiable face after such a taxing evening.

Freya pushed past her mother to get through the door, holding the bag of groceries.

"This is—" Joanna began, but Freya was already rushing down the path, yelling good-bye over her shoulder. "I mean that *was* my daughter Freya."

She and Harold shared a complicit smile. *Kids.*

"I was just driving by on my way home and thought I'd drop by to see if you got my message about taking you out to dinner. And since I was here anyway, I thought I'd check on Gilly. You said she was losing feathers and . . . 'gloomy' was it?" He twirled the umbrella, its tip planted on the step.

Joanna swung the door open. "Yes, yes, of course! Please come in! It's raining. The house is in shambles, because . . . long story, which I'll tell you over some pie, and we can talk about dinner and Gilly."

45

chapter seven

Almost Paradise

ص‍

"What is it called again when someone goes to a party they haven't been invited to?" a brunette asked her equally pretty blond friend as they each took a stool at the bar.

"Uh, going to a party you haven't been invited to maybe?" said the blond as two cocktails materialized before the two young women.

"Ooh," they said in unison, staring down at the drinks.

"Pop-up drinks!" a customer yelled from the other end of the bar, and the man next to him reluctantly handed over a dollar.

"This place is cool!" the brunette said, taking a sip.

"*Crashing,*" Freya said, placing coasters beneath their drinks. "These are on the house. We're doing a promotion on the new cocktails." Freya handed them the love potions list. "They're called Smarty-Pants in case you like them and want more."

"Huh?" they both replied.

"You *crash* a party," Freya said with a smirk.

"*Oh, right!*" they said.

Friday night at the North Inn, the east end of Long Island was the place to be. It had only been two weeks since Freya had slipped Betty Lazar one of her potions, and now the former wallflower was wilting no more. Betty had sauntered in wearing a red silk sheath, strappy heels, and a killer smile, headed straight to the bar and asked Freya for another one of those "addictive blue drinks." Soon Betty was standing by the jukebox singing Meat Loaf and Ellen Foley's duet, "Paradise by the Dashboard Light," with Seth Holding, a young, handsome junior detective Freya recognized from the precinct, one of the more affable ones who was always more than happy to hear Freya's take on a case.

A small crowd had already gathered around Betty and Seth. They were great singers, both closet thespians who had forsaken Broadway aspirations for more reliable paychecks.

Seth was singing the refrain, *"Baby, baby, let me sleep on it!"* an elbow lifted, his unbuttoned shirt revealing a wicked set of abs. Freya knew he didn't need to sleep on it. As she watched them, she saw snippets of their first night together: Seth walking Betty home from work under a light drizzle, Seth breaking out in song with "Singin' in the Rain" as they ambled down Main Street. She caught a glimpse of him shyly standing by Betty's door, waiting for her to ask him in. Then came a series of snapshots—singing, kissing, laughing—and she heard Seth's tender admission in the morning: "I have a thing for older women, you know, but really I think I just have a thing for you, Betty."

It was all supersweet, as it should be for Betty, who had been waiting for so long for the right guy to arrive. Seth Holding wasn't just some young buck or blockhead who wanted to get into an experienced woman's pants or avoid the "drama" women his age had a reputation for. He was a good egg. And, boy, could they both sing! Sometimes magic acted only as a catalyst, and the rest was serendipity. Still, Freya was proud of her handiwork. She looked around and saw her magic everywhere.

That couple with the now-seven-month-old—Becky and Ross Bauman, whose marriage had frighteningly and violently derailed—were in couples counseling. Freya had gleaned this from a vision of them talking in a therapist's office (the framed print of Monet's water lilies on the wall a dead giveaway), sharing feelings they hadn't even known they possessed. They were currently sitting in a booth, making out like teens. Apparently all those Serenities she had served them over the last month had worked: a touch of star-of-Bethlehem, valerian root, and the tiniest bit of the night-blooming belladonna.

Then there was some brand-new witchery at the pinball machine: a girl Freya's age leaning into the machine, a hunk behind her doing some upright spooning as they both pressed the flipper buttons and he slammed into her jeans. He had ordered the Playful, she the One-Night Stand.

Now two college boys were flanking the blond and brunette at the bar, and the girls had started a contest to show them who could remove her bra the fastest without taking off any clothes.

It dawned on Freya, who was tending bar alone tonight, that nearly everyone around her was either doing it or about to, all of them happy, sated, smug, or excited. She granted love, fertility, sexual desire. She offered Eros on a silver platter, Venus on the half shell. Cupid and his arrows were at her command. Every fiber of her being was made up of sensuality, passion, and raw emotion, yet lately she had been experiencing none of that fervor; lately, it was like she was dead down there. Or was the word *deadened*? That sounded a tad better.

Sex had never been an issue, certainly not for her, not even the times she had lost her virginity (in her many lives), during which she had taken to lovemaking as if she were an old hand at it, the passion and excitement of those first unions erasing any pain with a soft, shivery caress. There *had* been that one weird time with Bran Gardiner, but that was because she had already sensed something was off. Plus, she had been thinking of Killian.

Killian . . .

He was her love. Or was he? She didn't know what to believe

anymore. Ever since that night when she'd almost fallen off the bridge, things had cooled. When they'd made love that night, she had pretended to feel the same way and had gone through the usual motions and noises but her heart and her head weren't in it. Freya had experienced enough relationships to know that power shifts were intrinsic—the roles of Lover and Beloved flip-flopping with every little change. But it had never been so with Killian; they had always each played both parts: Lover and Beloved or Beloved-Lover or Lover-Beloved.

Since that night, however, Killian had slowly pulled away as if he sensed Freya's mistrust and resented her for it, which had thrown everything off. In a sense, Killian was pouting; he was the longing Lover wanting to be the Beloved. She felt the same. Perhaps once you got into the nitty-gritty of a relationship, this was to be expected, but Freya hated it to happen with Killian. It had all been so perfect and idyllic until Freddie came along and sowed doubt in their little garden.

Killian was not just her lover; he was her best friend, and she realized with a start that she was terribly lonely. *God, no,* she said to herself. *Not lonely, never lonely. If ever there were a sin, it is loneliness.* She panicked.

Thankfully, the solution to her funk came traipsing through the door.

Hudson Rafferty, Ingrid's good friend from the library, walked in with an extremely good-looking man in tow. It was his boyfriend, Scott, Freya thought, suddenly cheering up. Hudson and Scott always had the best gossip.

Hadn't Joanna always said that Freya should focus on helping others whenever she was feeling down? It wasn't good to get too self-involved.

Freya set down two coasters and hoped she could be of help to these handsome boys.

chapter eight

Haunted while the
Minutes Drag

❧

T he Edwardian blueprint from the old manor was a diazo
print, a paper used beginning in the early twentieth century.
It was oily to the touch, the edges crumbled and the fine lines of
blue ink degraded and blurred in spots. The problem with such
old blueprints was that back then they were considered dispens-
able, with no other use than their practical function as a guide to
build a house. No effort had been made to preserve this one other
than rolling it up and plopping it into the cedar escritoire, where it
had fortuitously been saved from light and dust and other sources
of decay. However, the quality of the paper itself was poor. Steaming had made it less brittle, but Ingrid was still careful as she now
applied another treatment.

She felt brittle herself, as if exposure to the light could turn
her into dust. A weekend had come and gone, and she hadn't
heard from Matt; their affair appeared to have ended without
ever really beginning.

After a few sprightly knocks at her office door, Hudson burst
in. "Hey, I just had a second and didn't get a chance to tell you
yet. Guess who I saw this weekend? Ew, it stinks in here. Witchy
stuff?"

Ingrid laughed. "No, solvents for the blueprint."

Hudson studied her, chewing on the nail of his index finger, then placing it along with two others in the upper pocket of his tailored jacket to give a tuck to his turquoise pocket square. "Something's wrong. You don't look happy, Ingrid."

She glanced up from her glasses, pulled at the wrists of her gloves, and continued applying the chemical. She felt like a failure after her date with Matt and was too ashamed to admit to her friend that she had botched the whole thing. She hadn't told Hudson about the date at all, neither before nor after. She felt like a traitor as a friend but her lack of experience had kept her mum, just in case something like this happened. Well, at least she'd been smart about that. "It's just the chemicals. They make my eyes water."

"Yeah, right, it's just the chemicals. Uh-uh, you are no good at hiding it, my dear. But I'll leave you in peace for now. Just know my shoulder's here any time, okay? I'm wearing cotton so there's no harm in crying on it."

"Okay," said Ingrid, smiling. So who'd you see this weekend? Did you and Scott go out on a date?"

"I saw Freya! It is really, truly remarkable, the whole *vibe*—to use that reappropriated hippie word—she is giving to the North Inn. Talk about bacchanalia! You two with your magic!" He gave her a wink as she peered up at him from behind her glasses. "Anyhoo, we got to discussing my little problem."

"That Scott is angry with you because he can't meet your parents when you've met his?"

"Yeah, that one."

"*Big* problem!" Ingrid emphasized. *As if she were one to talk.*

"Well, Freya made us some of those . . . love potions? Phew! Let's just say Scott and I had the most incredible, romantic, earth-shattering night! I'm still reeling from it." He spun around.

Ingrid began putting the caps back on the bottles of the solvents. "So does this mean you're ready to introduce Scott to your mother? Although that would mean you'd first have to come out to her."

"No, not ready for that yet."

"Oh, Hudson!" she said.

SHE LEFT THE LIBRARY EARLIER than usual; Tabitha and Hudson would do the closing up. Caitlin no longer worked there, because she had started—of all the unexpected twists—law school in New York City. Perhaps heartbreak had changed her, made her want to prove herself in some way. Ingrid only felt empathy for the girl now and, she had to admit, a lot of admiration.

Clipping along in her work heels, Ingrid took the roundabout way, skirting the park, even though she knew it was a ridiculous waste of time. But part of her hoped that somehow, if she followed Matt's instructions and stopped using the dark-alley shortcut, it would bring him back. *What am I thinking? That's ridiculous!* Ingrid was annoyed with herself; it was a longer walk and it was so unlike her to let others tell her what to do.

Not even one of her magic knots could fix this problem. She would never use magic on him anyway. She wanted him to be drawn to her on his own volition, without any external aid, like spells or charms or incantations. Besides, true love was the very essence of magic.

Even though she had been appalled by his behavior, she understood him better now that she had probed every detail of that evening with a fine-tooth comb. His anger had come out of feeling protective of her as well as out of a sense of duty. He saw the situation as a police matter, even though she knew it was beyond anything the police would understand. As for the matter of not believing in magic, well, he was a logical, practical guy, but she was certain he wasn't closed minded. All he needed was a little time to expand his worldview.

But if he felt protective of her, why hadn't he called her by now? She couldn't get around that one. Enough thinking about Matt Noble, she told herself, but for the rest of the walk, she couldn't help herself and her thoughts were consumed by him despite her attempts to chase them away.

WHEN INGRID ARRIVED HOME, she stopped before climbing the steps to the door and made an effort to wipe the disappointment off her face. She tried a smile, and though it didn't feel right, she kept it there, placing a foot on the first step.

The door swung open and out came a squealing Gracella, Tyler following on her heels, imitating his mother, arms flailing and little hands flapping in the air. On the pathway, Gracella turned toward Ingrid, a hand on her bosom as if to steady her heart. "Miss Ingrid, this house is haunted. This is a haunted house!" she said, appearing terrified. "I am not coming back until these ghosts go away."

Ingrid walked over, concern on her face. "What happened?"

"I don't know! Things are moving around in that house. I put one thing in one place, then *boom*, gone, then *boom*, in another place, or I cannot find it." Gracella spoke hurriedly, as Tyler clung to her leg. "Then strange noises upstairs. But no way am I going up there in the attic, Miss Ingrid!"

It was getting dark outside, and the lights hanging from the eaves of the house automatically lit on their own, which made Gracella jolt and start to hyperventilate.

"It's okay, Gracella. Those lights are on a timer," Ingrid said, attempting to reassure her. She put a hand on the woman's shoulder, reciting a calming, protective spell in her head, and Gracella's breath quieted.

"It's the strange ones," said Tyler.

Ingrid crouched to be at Tyler's level. "What did you say?"

"The strange ones. I talk to them; they talk to me. They're nice but very clever," the boy said, screwing his face at her.

Ingrid laughed at the word *clever* coming from a child's mouth. "You mean, like, imaginary friends, Tyler?"

He shook his head no.

"I must be going, Miss Ingrid. I must get home. Will you tell Miss Joanna what is happening in this house, that I could not finish all my work today because of these crazy ghosts. Please make them go away, so I can come back and do my work. I don't like this. I am not coming back until you tell me they are gone."

Ingrid promised Gracella she would tell her mother and that she would take care of the house and make it a safe place for everyone. "I'll get to the bottom of it. You have my word, Gracella."

She watched as Tyler and his mother peeled out of the driveway in their Subaru, the little boy looking sad as he waved to her from the back window.

GHOSTS? WHAT WAS GOING ON? Joanna hadn't mentioned anything to her, and she hadn't noticed anything out of the ordinary herself. Ingrid let herself inside and checked all the bottom-floor rooms of the rambling house. Everything looked clean, neatly tucked away and properly set to rights by Gracella's careful hand, but upon entering the living room, Ingrid heard a noise, a scraping sound followed by thumping. Those burglars, maybe? Unlike Matt, she didn't think the burglars and pixie refugees were one and the same. Well, he didn't know they were pixies, just a band of homeless kids, and she had definitely sent them on their away. *Ugh, Matt again!* He occupied her every thought. Even when she thought she had found a respite, there he was again. If this was what being in love was like, she wanted none of it.

She climbed the stairs and checked the bedrooms. All four looked fine, including the one that sat empty, sadly waiting for her brother's return, although Ingrid knew poor Joanna might have to wait an eternity, until this house had long turned to ruin.

Now the attic. It looked as it usually did, books on a shelf, boxes piled on top of boxes, dusty discarded furniture, old day-beds, couches, lamps, desks, Joanna's large steamer trunk, but nothing egregiously amiss, and she couldn't imagine where the noises had come from. There was one box lying sideways on the floor, clothes spilling from it: their childhood costumes, wings, tutus, and taffeta dresses. Perhaps that box had made the noise. Maybe it had fallen from the other and squished the one beside it, gravity doing its work until it succumbed and tipped.

There was one final place to check. She returned down the flight of stairs, heading toward Freya's bedroom. Once inside, she opened her sister's closet, which smelled like Freya's perfume: sweet and sultry. Ingrid waved her hands in front of her face. Did Freya spray her clothes with the stuff? Her feathers and furs and microdresses and décolleté blouses and the collection of heels dating back to a weathered pink leather pair of 1920s flapper-girl shoes? Oh, how she had worn those out!

There was a "silky corner" where Freya's slinky lingerie hung from pink satin hangers: baby blues with beige lace, red satin, taupe silk. Ingrid felt envious of all this femininity dangling on the hangers. She was not jealous of Freya, but she felt so ignorant when it came to these sorts of things. Hudson always told Ingrid she had great style. But perhaps she needed to work on being a little more—sexy? Then maybe Matt would . . . ugh, thinking of Matt again. It had to stop.

Ingrid drew her wand from her shoulder bag, then pushed past Freya's garments and the sign with the quip about Narnia and made her way down the long ebony-floored corridor until

55

she arrived at Freya's Manhattan apartment. Magical passage-ways were so much more useful than commuting, Ingrid thought.

There was the smell of charred wood in the air, as if someone had recently lit a fire. A lone pillow and crumpled blanket lay on the plush velvet couch facing the fireplace, and in the kitchen Ingrid found an unfinished cup of coffee by the sink (the milk hadn't turned yet). She saw her sister's telltale red lipstick on it.

Well, at least it was Freya who had been here and not someone else. Or something else. Whatever had scared off their housekeeper.

Now why had Freya been sleeping here, Ingrid wondered. She was under the assumption that Freya spent most of her nights on the *Dragon*. Freya hadn't mentioned anything amiss, not even when Ingrid had told her all about the awful date with Matt. Freya thought Ingrid had overreacted and that it was far from over; she was sure Matt would call Ingrid soon.

Ingrid hoped her sister would come to her for advice if she were having relationship problems. On second thought, how could she solve Freya's problems when she didn't even know how to solve her own?

chapter nine

Don't Look Back

J oanna walked outside with a basket and garden shears to gather some fresh bouquets for the house. From early spring through fall, her garden blossomed with different flower varieties, bursting in a multitude of colors along the perimeter, climbing the fence, in the beds, a fragrant onslaught to the senses. This time of year the burnt-orange roses had bloomed, as well as her coral gerberas and rich purple dahlias, pink and white winter daphnes, marigolds from vivid yellow to orange to a deep, rich red. She began cutting the tall-stalked sturdy ones before moving on to the more delicate flowers, placing them on top so they wouldn't get crushed. She wound through foliage and plants in her clogs, snipping here and there.

She stopped at the bed of Japanese anemones, where ferns poked through along the chocked fence—pink, violet, and snowy white flowers, dainty bright yellow pistils resembling little suns at their centers. *My son inside each one of them,* she thought wistfully. She reached to cut the stem of a set of white ones, when suddenly its leaves withered, petals falling to the ground.

"Huh!" Perhaps there had been a morning frost.

She reached for another, chose a perfectly healthy-looking one, and just as before when her fingers grazed it, it withered instantly, bending and falling to its death. She tried again, and this time a slew of them died, petals spilling like tears into the undergrowth.

No, it wasn't a frost but something entirely different. She finally had to admit that she knew what was happening inside the house—with all the objects being moved and misplaced, especially now with the flowers dying in the garden. It wasn't the first time it had happened, but the last had been such a traumatic ordeal that Joanna had pushed it out of her mind, denying that something similar could recur.

IT HAPPENED IN 1839, when she was visiting England for several months. Events had unfolded in the same way: the belongings in her flat moving around, roses wilting in the garden, and then the mischief had escalated with the frightened horses on the landau she rode around town. The carriage had tipped and been dragged at a gallop along the cobblestone streets of London, killing the coachman. After that, Joanna could not ignore it anymore and had been prompted into action.

The story began with the death of a young English aristocrat from a long illness at the very same time that a farm girl in the countryside of Dorchester plummeted to her death inside a well. Neither had known the other in life due to their geographic distance and entirely different social spheres.

It was in death that they fell in love. When they arrived in the first layer of the glom toward the Kingdom of the Dead, they immediately recognized each other as soul mates. Somehow they learned about the Eurydice clause under the Orpheus Amendment, which stated that if two iterant souls met in the Dead's Kingdom before the first gate and fell in love, they could be granted a second chance at life as long as they remained true to each other. If they did not, then their punishment entailed dying anew, but this time they would never encounter each other again in the glom or beyond.

Philip and Virginia could not imagine ever forsaking each other, and so they campaigned for the chance to live and love each other in mid-world. Joanna's sister, Helda, the Queen of the Dead, was not pleased about their request but, unable to refute the existence of the Eurydice clause, directed the couple to appeal to Joanna instead. "You must make your plea to her, not me. She is the only one charged with the delicate business of resurrection, the only one among us who can bring you back to life. That is not my territory."

The two hapless romantics roamed the glom, striving to contact Joanna however they could, using their abilities to push objects without touching them, or choking the life out of small plants. They became increasingly desperate as Joanna—either deliberately or obtusely—failed to hear them and they eventually resorted to frightening the horses that pulled the landau.

That finally got Joanna's attention. Since Joanna had no desire for others to be harmed by such recalcitrant spirits, such folly, she acceded to their request and brought the lovers out of the spirit world and back to the land of the living. Philip was still on his deathbed, while Virginia's body was just rescued from the well when the "miracle" happened. Upon revival, they found each other and immediately wed.

Philip's family cut him off and disinherited him for marrying a commoner, but for a while they lived happily in the Dorchester countryside. Then the bills came, and the fights. Philip took to gambling, and his losses piled up. He blamed Virginia for his misery, and she in turn blamed him for failing to provide for them. Virginia was pregnant and became ill during the final months of pregnancy. Destitute and penniless, Philip begged his family for money and help with medicine and food. By the time he returned to his beloved's side, she was dead, the child a stillbirth. He shot himself and that was that, a tragic story.

Joanna sighed, thinking of how beautiful those two had been, how rosy and happy when she had visited them in their little Dorchester cottage.

There was always a catch. Philip and Virginia had tried to cheat death, and more recently Joanna had tried to bring back Lionel Horning. Lionel was only in a coma; he hadn't gotten past the seventh circle where his soul would have been forever bound to Helda. Still, on his return, he was, as her girls called it, "zombified." Helda always won her souls in the end.

Joanna shook her head, thinking of her stubborn and proud sister. But at least now she knew what was going on. A spirit, or spirits, sought to contact her. She couldn't ignore the signs anymore.

Joanna closed her eyes in her garden, letting the perfume of the flowers wash over her and feeling the sunshine on her face before moving fearlessly into the glom. She stepped into the twilight world. It was dusky, and above her were tiny, dim pinpricks of light that illuminated the sandy path just well enough for her to make it out.

She heard an owl's call, and she hooted back at it. The scent of something rotten filled the air, something heavy and viscous, the smell of death. Joanna moved off the path, toward the sound of the owl. A spirit who sought contact would be on the first level, the one closest to the seam. She didn't need to continue any farther.

"Is anyone there?" she whispered as her words echoed back toward her. She kept her voice as quiet as she could, not wanting to bump into Helda. Her sister could be vindictive.

She heard the flapping of wings, the owl lifting from a branch. She wished she had her wand, so she could see better, but instead she extended her hands to feel around in the darkness. She ran smack into a tree, the bark dead, dry, papery to the touch. She picked at it with a fingernail, and it began to ooze a shiny, dark liquid.

"Anyone?" she asked again, and again only her voice came back to her: *Anyone? Anyone? Anyone?*

She did not feel the presence of a soul seeking her here, so she found the path, returned to mid-world, opened her eyes, and was happy to be standing once again in her lush garden.

chapter ten

Love Shack

～✦～

Freddie Beauchamp sat at his desk in the Ucky Star, playing hunt-and-peck on his laptop. Now how could a god recently returned from Limbo, new to the modern era, come about such technology?

Girls was the obvious answer. He didn't need any magic to hook up other than his lovely smile. When Freddie Beauchamp smiled, all a girl wanted to do was kiss him. After that, they tended to leave presents, like the Wii console, the video games, and the laptop.

It all started with Gigi McIntyre, a college girl he met by the motel's ice machine, when he first returned. That first night Gigi was there, too, for a friend's weekend-long bachelorette party in early September. She stood with the empty bucket, wearing a midriff-baring T-shirt and the smallest denim shorts. Gigi was a lot of fun, a glorious revelation after the years of dull nothingness in Limbo.

One might imagine a night with the god of the sun would involve cinematic flourish—the immediate tearing off of clothing as soon as the motel door clicked closed, doing it in every imaginable position, on every surface. No.

Freddie understood that each woman possessed her own distinctive set of rules when it came to sex. Every girl had a different key and Freddie's gift was knowing how to find it—its particular shape, and how it might turn in the lock. Freddie had unlocked Gigi—*did he ever*—had given the college girl her very first full-body, writhing, shaking, screaming orgasm. But it had taken hours of talking, teasing, conversation. At the ice machine, he'd asked her if she knew how to work the television remote and they'd watched some old movie before he even made a move. It had taken almost all night to get her in bed, but then Freddie had all the time in the world.

Gigi had returned the next day to the Ucky Star in a Porsche convertible filled with boxes and clothes. It all belonged to her brother, she'd explained, who had recently left for his freshman year at NYU. "What does he care? We're rich. Consider these a welcome gift, Freddie," she'd said with a toss of her dark mane. "When he gets set up at his apartment in the Village, my mom will just buy him all new stuff. All this is from last year. Nearly vintage." He thanked her, and she had smiled sweetly. She was still grateful to him for that orgasm.

Gigi zoomed off to New York City, and there were no more college cuties partying at the motel. Things died down. The motel filled with traveling salesmen, couples having illicit affairs, which Freddie found tawdry and sad. He puttered around the boxes Gigi had left, quickly discovering the Wii console and the laptop. The video games were a fun distraction, but the laptop opened a whole new world, one even bigger than the nine worlds of the known universe. He'd missed so much while he was in Limbo, and he caught up on his favorite subjects: sailing ships and oceans. He discovered a deep and instant love for sports cars.

But these were not as cool as the dating sites, where one could choose a girl as easily as picking from a menu. Freddie put up his profile, using the laptop's Photo Booth application to take snapshots of himself. His pictures were nothing like the ubiquitous male profile pictures one saw on these sites: bare-chested guy in the bathroom mirror, the reflection of his cell phone's flash covering most of his face.

No, Freddie used his magic to create more appealing scenarios: Freddie in a tuxedo, laughing it up at a cocktail party; Freddie in a cowboy hat on a bull (he'd morphed Buster for that one); Freddie in a gray suit and slightly loosened gray polka-dot tie, looking serious. The kicker was the casual one: Freddie on the beach in a plain T-shirt, jeans, and black Converse (the caption read "This one's the real me").

The girls arrived in droves, so many of them Freddie did not know what to do, and so there were threesomes and moresomes and somemoresomes. He indulged every whim, courted every girl, made each and every one of them feel special. There were no unsatisfied customers.

His latest obsession was one Hilly Liman. They had been chatting online for a while now, and it was becoming more intense, messaging each other back and forth in the evenings until it was almost morning. For the last few days, the communiqués had become so frequent and impassioned that Freddie had been forced to call off the cavalry of coeds. He had no interest in any of them since meeting Hilly.

Something formidable had happened: Freddie had fallen in love. There was no other way to explain it. Hilly was different. She made him wait. Unlike the other girls who appeared at his doorstep after one posting, she had only told him her real name after they'd been e-mailing for a few weeks. She was reserved and cautious, and he didn't think she was playing hard to get. The strangest thing was she didn't even have a picture of herself on her profile, only a shadowy illustration of a silhouette. He didn't even know what she looked like, but he was certain she was gorgeous. He could just feel it. He couldn't explain it, but he was drawn to her from the beginning.

<<so in two weeks, after your exam?>> he typed.

<<yes, can't get away till then. all I can do is think of you, tho. just to be able to touch you. even just a little hug.>>

<<a little hug?>> he wrote.

<<you know what i mean.>> Hilly responded. After a few minutes, she typed again. <<i really like you.>>

Freddie paused, staring at Hilly's words on the screen, putting his hands behind his head as he stretched his back, which was sore from sitting. He exhaled, then typed <<ditto.>>

Three knocks sounded at the door. Freya's signal.

<<brb. my sister's here. i might have to go.>> Freddie wrote.

<<ok. i'll let you go. even tho it's hard.>>

<<u have no idea. <3>> he typed and on-screen, in the chat box, Freddie's heart icon turned red, then swiveled upright, and Hilly typed one out for Freddie on her end, and he watched it do the same thing, smiling to himself. You had to love technology.

Buster nudged his calf as Freya continued to knock.

"Freddie, you there?" she whispered from outside.

"Coming!" He closed the laptop and opened the door a crack.

Freya stood at the doorway, looking wind tossed and holding two shopping bags full of groceries. She stared at him. "Are those . . . pajamas? Have you been wearing them all day?" Behind her, the sky was gray, and it was almost evening.

"So?" Freddie asked, annoyed with the sisterly nagging. "It's not like I go anywhere."

"But that's your fault. I've told you so many times to come home." She shook her head. "Well, aren't you going to let me in? I brought you healthy stuff from Mom's garden, some nuts and dried fruit, instead of all that junk food you've been eating."

Freddie took the bags from her, poked his head outside, looked each way, and then fully opened the door. Freya walked in past him. "You seem distracted," she said.

"A little," he said. He put the bags down as she crossed the room and sat at the end of one of the beds. "Some of those girls won't leave me alone. I wanted to make sure none of them was out there."

Buster scuffled over to Freya, and she kneeled down and pet him, then tickled his snout. "I thought you liked all the attention. Don't tell me you're here alone. What happened to the harem?" She observed him with genuine concern and wondered if her twin had truly lost it. He looked a real mess: tousled hair, dirty pajamas, unshaven. He shouldn't be living this way. She looked around and noticed the computer on his desk.

"Ooh, you have a Mac!" she said, sauntering over to inspect it.

"Don't touch it!"

"It's not a bomb!"

"It kind of is," he retorted. He moved the grocery bags on the desk, put a hand on the laptop protectively.

"You're acting so weird," she said, squinting her eyes at him. "Are you going to tell me what's going on?"

"All right." He sighed. He realized he was dying to tell Freya, so it all gushed out: the social media sites and how he'd met someone special—a girl named Hilly Liman. After that he couldn't say her name enough times.

As Freya listened, she finally understood how Freddie had kept his loneliness at bay. He'd obviously gone delusional. She was reluctant to burst his bubble about this Hilly girl, who was probably just some slutty college chick, not that there was any other kind, and not that there was anything wrong with that. Freya, of all people, understood the need to experiment, the desire to see just exactly how much fun one could have when one was beautiful and young.

However, this whole Freddie-in-love thing was too much. She'd grown weary of his whole situation—the motel, the accusations, the sloth.

Freddie sat on the armchair, legs extended. "She's the one, Freya. I'm telling you. It's for real this time." He smiled.

"Yeah, right. Every week you fall for someone new, and you haven't even met this . . ."

"Hilly Liman."

"Yeah. I should really know her name by now. You say it enough." Freya pushed a hand through her hair. "Look, I'm tired, and I can't do this. I can't find that thing you're convinced Killian stole from you, that will prove he did it, and we really need to move on. I'm going to let the family know you're back. Mother will be so happy!"

Freddie jumped from his seat, his face flushed. "You can't do that, Freya. No one can know! If the Valkyries know where I am . . . they'll . . . they'll drag me back. I can't go back to Limbo! You don't know what it's like there! I need to prove I wasn't the one who destroyed the bridge!" Freddie made a frustrated gesture, then fell back into the armchair, deflated. His head fell. When he looked back up at her, tears welled in his eyes. "I can't go back. You have to help me, Freya. Please." His voice broke.

Freya shook her head, staring ruefully at her twin. "Oh, Freddie, stop," she said. But her voice was cracking, too.

chapter eleven

The Gang's All Here

～&～

A shaft of light poured through the attic gable, illuminating particles of dust. On the floor, leading through the sundry pieces of furniture, was a Hansel and Gretel–like trail of candy wrappers, paper clips, glitter, DayGlo-colored mini Post-its, and childhood costumes.

Ingrid had come up to search for a book she couldn't find in Joanna's study. She glared at the odd trail. When she had last set foot here after returning from Freya's Manhattan apartment, she had placed those costumes back in the box and set it upright. Tyler couldn't have done it because Gracella had yet to return after the other day. Was it Freya maybe? Her sister was certainly the messiest of them, but what would she be doing digging through old costumes? Ingrid set about straightening up, picking up a pink tutu here, a plastic glass slipper there, a black leather mask—hmm, that didn't look like a child's costume but like something from Freya's closet—and when she arrived at the end of the trail, she was standing before Joanna's large steamer trunk. Was that really cigarette smoke? She sniffed at the air.

She hovered over the trunk and noticed the latches were undone. When she lifted the top, she stared down at five small heads tucked between five pairs of grungy knees. The heads looked up, and she immediately recognized the pixies. They had glitter all over their dirty faces: three boys and two girls.

Well, it wouldn't be accurate to say they were children, although Ingrid thought of them as such. They were adult in years but had childlike bodies and childlike minds, as well as mischievous spirits. With their blackened faces, they reminded her of the chimney sweeps of Victorian England, although they were quite the opposite of those poor abused children who had the maturity and jaded attitudes of adults, drinking ale, smoking pipes, and shooting the breeze at the inn after work. The pixies *had* taken to cheap booze and smoking in mid-world—that much Ingrid had observed at the motel where she'd first met them—but there was something rather naïve about these creatures.

"Well, look what we have here," she said, thinking she sounded a bit like Hudson right then.

"Don't hate on us, Erda!" said Kelda with her tiny rosebud lips. She lifted a hand in a ragged fingerless glove to protect her face as if Ingrid might smack her.

"I see you've picked up the local slang. Isn't that just fantastic!" returned Ingrid as all five of the pixies sheepishly rose and stepped out of the trunk. *The clever ones*, Tyler had called them. Clever boy.

Their clothes were an array of grimy hues, from dark army olive to black: skinny jeans, ripped T-shirts, frayed sweaters, safety pins, wool caps, and heavy black boots. Ingrid could not have determined what kind of look they were aiming for—punk, grunge, grebo, or crusty. All those rebellious styles looked the same to her no matter the decade; only the year and the label changed. The pixies looked as if they had just returned from war, and they had grown quite odiferous since the last time she'd seen them.

There was Kelda and Nyph, the two female pixies, petite and small boned like teenage ballerina rebels with their tough clothes and heavy dark eyeliner. While Kelda was fair, with white-blond hair and pale-blue eyes, her skin as nacreous and white as pearl, offset by arresting crimson lips, a tiny bloom, and her ruddy cheeks, Nyph was her opposite with a darker complexion—sleek black hair, olive skin, huge liquid-brown eyes tilting up at the corners, puffy lips. The boys huddled behind the girls of course. There was scruffy, dark-haired Sven with green eyes, whom Ingrid thought of as a grumpy old man, always with the five o'clock shadow and apathetic manner; Val, who had a spiky fire-engine-red Mohawk, who was a perpetual nervous wreck; and finally Irdick, with his tousled head of flaxen hair and round boyish, rosy-cheeked face. He was wearing a T-shirt that read HUGS NOT DRUGS.

The thing about pixies, both male and female, was they were rather comely creatures, their features refined, delicate, as if carefully carved out of ivory. But at this particular moment, it was difficult for Ingrid to tell exactly what any of them truly looked like because they were so damned filthy.

"Will you tell me what is going on here before I cast a spell on you and turn you all into frogs?" she said. Although it was more a reproof than an actual threat.

"Please don't do that!" Irdick yelped. There was something so vulnerable and sweet about Irdick that he made Ingrid feel guilty for scolding them. Also, the T-shirt was hilarious.

Val moved forward from the huddle, speaking so fast that Ingrid could barely make out the jumbled words of his endless run-on sentence, which turned staccato whenever he ran into a word that began with an *J*. She did, however, catch a phrase here and there, getting the overall gist.

From what she could tell, they had tried to fulfill the promise they'd made to her to return home following her instructions to follow the yellow brick road—a real path that led between the worlds. At the motel where they had been staying, Ingrid had showed them where the path was in the seam, but when they had set out on it, the path faded, and besides, they could no longer remember where home was, or even what it was. So after they'd failed, they'd caught Ingrid's scent and followed her home, where they had taken shelter in Joanna's attic.

"It's nice here!"

"There are pies!"

"Yummy!"

"Don't make us leave! Erda, please!" Kelda donned the black leather mask and began doing fast cartwheels across the room, which made Ingrid dizzy.

"Did we mention there are pies?" said Val.

"We promise to stay out of the way!" said Kelda, landing on her feet.

"Hush!" yelled Ingrid. "I can't think with all of you shouting and moving around like that!"

The pixies instantly quieted and stood still.

"Okay," said Ingrid, crossing her arms. "I'm going to let you stay, for now, but you have to promise to be *quiet* and stay hidden and not make such horrible messes. Also, you guys stink and you need to bathe. Do it when Joanna is out of the house, of course, and leave the bathroom as you found it. We'll do this until I can figure out where home is and what's wrong with the yellow brick road. But if you don't behave yourselves, I'll put a curse on you!"

The pixies were delighted and thanked Ingrid, who tried not to breathe so she wouldn't smell them. Sven, however, stood off by himself, his arms crossed over his chest, a sour look on his face.

Ingrid gently shrugged the pixies off and rearranged her clothes.

"Thank you, Erda, thank you," they kept saying.

"It's all right. You're welcome," she said.

Kelda spun around on the heel of her combat boot. "We stole something for you." Her clear blue eyes, white eyelashes batting, peered up at Ingrid through the mask while she reached into the pocket of her pants. "A little thank-you gift."

"That's another thing," Ingrid said. "No more stealing! You

can't use money, which I think says something about where you guys are from. But absolutely no more stealing. I'll bring you food."

"What about cigarettes?" asked Sven in his gruff voice. He sounded as if he had had been smoking and hitting the hooch for years, although when Ingrid stared at him long enough, she could tell that he didn't look that old. It was all in the jaded attitude and cooler-than-thou posture. "I've been jonesing for a cig. Could you buy me a carton of those wicked Kool Smooths that taste like thin mints, Miss Erda?" He smirked.

Ingrid was flustered again. The pixies had completely lost their funny accents and were speaking like the local teen derelicts now, some of whom, she had noted at the library, were quite erudite despite all their street jargon. "No, no smoking in here!" she said. "You could start a fire! Sven, I'm serious. Besides, I don't know about pixie physiology but I'm sure it's bad for you."

He lifted an eyebrow at her while Kelda shoved something in her hand.

"What's this?" asked Ingrid, holding the crumpled piece of paper.

"Our gift!" said Kelda.

Ingrid set about flattening it. Nyph came and stood at Ingrid's other side to watch.

On the scrap, torn from a small, rectangular spiral notebook, was the name "Maggie" followed by a phone number. Ingrid stared at it, perplexed.

Her work with blueprints had endowed her with an adept eye for analyzing idiosyncratic longhand styles. She often had to match the unsigned notes on sketchpads and working drawings to the handwriting on blueprints. In this case, the writing on the scrap of paper tilted ever so slightly to the left (backhand, it was called), indicating a left-handed person, and then there was the distinctive *M* with its two pointy peaks and the *a* that resembled the numeral *2* with a loop. She had seen this *M* and *a* before.

Ma . . .

Matt Noble. These were exactly the same letters she had seen him use to sign his name on the credit card slip at the bar. Not only that but there was also the fact that Ingrid had immediately noticed that Matt was a lefty when he had begun to scribble in his notepad, a small spiral notebook inside a leather cover. The paper was the same light green–lined one she was now holding. There was no doubt in her mind that Matt had written this woman's name, this Maggie's number on this scrap of paper. Ingrid's heart fell, and her stomach twisted. Maybe this was the reason their date had ended so badly, because Matt had his mind set on someone else.

She immediately crumpled it back up and threw it away, to the consternation of her pixie friends.

73

chapter twelve

I Get a Kick out of You

༄

"Two daughters?" asked Harold.

"Two daughters and one son," said Joanna, then immediately regretted complicating things. She couldn't explain that her son was in Limbo for an eternity or why; it was just that of course he was never far from her thoughts, and it had slipped out. "Do you have other children, Harold?"

"What you see is what you got!" said Harold, smiling. "Just my daughter."

"She's darling, really. I know her from the hospital. She was great with Tyler when he was ill."

They were sitting in a private alcove facing the ocean at the swanky new French restaurant in town, and so far everything was going smoothly. They were halfway through their entrees—grilled salmon in a triple-citrus glaze for her and a duck confit with blackberry drizzle for him—and the evening had been very pleasant. They made a striking couple: Joanna elegant in a gray cashmere sweater and dark skirt, her silver hair in a loose updo, showing off her pearl earrings; Harold, impeccably groomed, in one of his signature three-piece suits, black with pin-stripes, a crisp white shirt, and red tie. He had entrancing navy-blue eyes, raven hair with thick white streaks (Joanna had noted the ironic *widow's* peak). His face was what one might call strong but at the same time refined—emphatic cheekbones, nose, and jaw. He was courtly but didn't fuss or act slavishly attentive. He exuded just the right amount of care, so as not to make her feel claustrophobic. He was well-read but not pretentious, eloquent but not glib, and cultured but not in an Olympian way. Harold and his late wife had traveled abroad nearly every summer of their professional lives, going as far as Southeast Asia. Traveling and sailing had been one of their passions, he reminisced, before Joanna delicately steered him away from further talk of his wife.

"So, Freya works at the North Inn and Ingrid's a librarian. What about your boy?" Harold continued.

"Oh, him? He's perfect. Handsome, thoughtful, loving, a sweetie, really." There. She was done.

"And he lives here?"

Joanna coughed, covering her mouth with a fist. She was going to have to tell an untruth. "Abroad!" she said matter-of-factly but squirming a little.

Harold was an intuitive man, and she saw that he had observed her discomfort. "Allow me, my dear," he said, taking the bottle of white from the ice bucket to refill her glass. He wasn't going to pry any further. "You look splendid this evening, and I'm so glad to be here with you tonight."

She went ahead and poured Harold's red wine as he poured her white, their arms parallel as they reached over. It was a nice restaurant, and nice of Lucien to leave them alone and not disturb them, she thought. He was an excellent waiter, knowing just the moment to stop by and check on his diners. "Well, enough of me, tell me more about you," said Joanna. "Any new interests, hobbies, postretirement?"

Harold cleared his throat, hesitating. Was he embarrassed? But why? "I'm starting a little business with a friend. Don't want

75

to say too much. Don't want to jinx it. But you'll eventually find out, Joanna dear."

"Oh, how nice, I'm sure it will be lovely."

"I hope so," he said, then winked. Was he flirting? Was she?

THE NEXT MORNING Joanna had a slight hangover, a pinch at the temples and nape, but it had been worth it to spend a lovely evening with a new friend. To her great relief, the objects and furniture in the house had been staying put lately. Although now it appeared as if the pantry and refrigerator were being raided nightly. Just yesterday she'd baked a whole batch of cookies, but when she returned from errands only a tray of crumbs remained. There was also the vexing issue of Gracella refusing to come back to the house because it was haunted, no matter how much Joanna tried to explain that there was no such thing as ghosts. Even if his mother had effectively stopped working for them, Tyler was still very much a part of her life. Joanna still picked him up from preschool and they spent many an afternoon together.

Last night, she and Harold had laughed like kids, but they had also crossed a new frontier. After acknowledging Harold as a friend from the start, Joanna was beginning to think she might actually like him *that way*. She hadn't anticipated something like this ever happening to her again and had been resigned to being single without a complaint. Not that she was truly single of course, since there was Norman to think about—but could they even consider themselves still married? It's not as if one of them had ever filed for divorce, but who ever heard of a thing like divorce among immortals. She supposed she would have to ask her daughters what they thought.

The thing was, she didn't think she would ever have this problem. Harold had caught her by surprise, and now she was walking around the house with a smile on her face, which she had noticed when she crossed the antique cheval glass mirror in the living room. *Who's that?* She started before realizing it was herself. Then she examined her reflection, pushing a strand of hair behind an ear, noting the glow in her face. She appeared years younger, which made her smile even more, but then she grimaced.

"What am I doing?" she asked her image.

Then Joanna saw Gilly above her, pointing her onyx beak, the same black-blue shade as her feathers. She turned around to face her familiar, who was perched on the grandfather clock. Whatever Harold had done with Gilly the other day had worked. The raven looked so much healthier, glossier. Joanna was thrilled to see her up and about, not just listlessly whiling away her time in her cage.

Gilly cawed. She was telling Joanna she wanted to take her somewhere, and she appeared anxious, moving from one foot to the other. The raven fluttered down from the clock, landing on Joanna's raised forearm. "What is it? Where are we going? Out? Okay."

JOANNA DONNED A COAT and her Wellingtons, tied her handy red bandanna around her flyaway hair, and stepped outside, following Gilly. The raven flew from branch to branch, perched on the fence in the garden, guiding Joanna past the gate to a path that cut through an overgrown field. They wound past a few neighboring properties, a barn and corral, and then headed toward the woods.

They moved quickly and Joanna soon grew winded, but the brisk walk in the cool breeze felt hardy and good. The air smelled of earth and wild thyme. Having nearly reached the forest, her familiar alighted in the weeds. The raven waddled along, bringing

77

Joanna's attention to ground level. Gilly stopped, pointing her beak, and Joanna saw the path of wilted, shriveled weeds and wildflowers, violet asters and goldenrod, surrounded by other flowers that were still thriving. It was as if someone trampled on the overgrowth, leaving death in his or her wake.

Joanna kneeled and touched the desiccated flowers and weeds. They crumbled at the slightest contact. She rose to her feet and followed the dried path that led into the forest. Gilly flew up onto her shoulder as Joanna ambled along, and they arrived in a clearing, where the grass was still green. Here the path wove desultorily through the grass, as if searching where to go next, then further veered uphill through more weeds and wildflowers.

Gilly began to caw as if she were eager for Joanna to keep moving, let her know she was getting closer, but then Joanna heard her name being called. The voice was immediately familiar and welcome that she turned around, abandoning the path.

"Joanna, what a pleasant surprise," Harold Atkins said. "I was over at the barn back there"—he motioned with his head—"and saw you two passing, but I was in the midst of administering a shot to a mare." He smiled as he took wide strides through the open field toward her.

"Nice to see you so soon, Harold," she returned. Even on one of his veterinarian calls, Harold wore a suit and polished tan leather shoes. It made her feel underdressed—her country clothes, red foulard around her unwashed hair, jeans, wool coat, big rubber boots.

"I couldn't just let you wander by and not say hello." His smile was contagious. "I see Gilly is doing well."

"Oh, yes, she's suddenly very spirited. I'm so relieved. We were taking a walk."

They kissed on either cheek, European style, and Joanna noticed that she liked the way Harold smelled—like soap and the woods, but also the ocean mist. Perhaps it was just the fresh scent of the North Hampton outdoors.

"Well, I'd love to walk you home if you don't mind. It's such a glorious day," said Harold.

She accepted his offer, and the two chatted all the way back to her house, making plans for dinner again sometime soon, and she forgot all about the strange trail of dead flowers.

chapter thirteen

Hide and Seeking

~~

The *Dragon*, a sixty-foot-long sleek white sport-fishing yacht
with a seventeen-foot-high beam, could cruise at up to 44
knots at 2,330 rpm, but for now ropes held it tautly moored to the
dock of Gardiners Island. The boat comprised three levels. At
the top was the exterior gallery with a mezzanine-style cockpit
replete with a freezer, two tackle drawers, a drink box, coolers,
various storage bins, a transom fish box, and a live well—in other
words, plenty of places to hide something. Below that was the
second tier, the flybridge with a peninsula-style console, a teak
deck containing a trapdoor leading to more storage, and starboard and forward bench seating, beneath which were yet more
compartments for ropes and rigs.

Moving farther down from the deck through the solid teak
door to the companionway, the steps led to the interior gallery:
teak flooring and cherrywood walls, cabinetry and bulkheads
with bas-relief carvings, and fawn leather seating. Aft was the
master stateroom with a biometric safe, which could only be
opened with the fingerprint of Killian's index (but it was too
small for what Freya had been searching for), and multitudinous
cabinets and closets; starboard, the crew cabin with three berths
that lifted to reveal more storage units; then forward, the salon
attached to the galley with black granite counters and cabinets

everywhere. There were also the three heads and the engine and pump room, which Freya had already inspected several times.

Every inch of the *Dragon* contained some kind of stowaway space. Freya had searched the boat from stem to stern, but one compartment could possibly be concealing another, like a series of Chinese boxes, so she started all over again.

Now she was downstairs in the crew cabin that doubled as a guest room. She had lifted the top of a berth and, from the container inside it, removed all the bedding, which was piled high on the third larger berth. Just as she thought, she discovered a hidden door in the bottom planks. She tried to lift it, but there was no handle, and her nails wouldn't do. She needed something to slip into the groove to jimmy it.

She turned around to retrieve a knife from one of the galley drawers and found herself standing face-to-face with Killian, who had apparently snuck up on her and been observing her—for how long, she didn't know. She hadn't heard him board or come down the companionway; it was as if he had floated down here.

He looked bewildered, but there was also something else in his piercing eyes, and she couldn't tell whether it was anger or disappointment. "What's up? What are you looking for?"

Freya tried to look sheepish. "An extra pillow. I think I pulled my back at the bar carrying those stupid ice buckets. I don't know why I didn't use magic to get them upstairs. Now I'm going to need something to prop myself up just right when I sleep, so it doesn't hurt so much." She squeezed her right arm. God, that was lame. Plus, why did she have to always talk so fast when she lied? Joanna always could tell when she did that, and probably everyone else.

Killian stared at her for a long moment, behind his thick dark bangs, and then his face broke into a slow smile. "Cut the crap. You and I both know that is bullshit." He laughed.

She laughed, too, but she couldn't come up with any other excuse. She could act jealous, say she suspected him of having an affair. But why would she be searching under the floorboards? Accusing him of hiding a woman inside the berth would seem a bit psycho.

Killian leaned inside the door. He was so unflappable, his voice and movements always so relaxed, reminding Freya of their nights of languorous sex. Not that they'd been having any lately, but she couldn't help but feel the pull.

"You've been avoiding me lately," he said. "You haven't been sleeping here. *At all.* Every time I call you to ask if you need help at the bar, you say it's too slow, whereas that never, ever mattered before, and what's going on with you and the boat? How many times do you have to turn it upside down? What's going on? Why won't you tell me?"

So much for thinking she had left the boat intact. "I lost something," she said. There. That wasn't that much of a lie. Freddie *had* lost something.

"Are you going to tell me what it is?"

She stared at him, pinching her lips, then adamantly nodded a no.

"Maybe I could . . . *help*?" Killian said. "Ever think of that?"

She was quiet for a moment and took a breath. "You can't. I'm sorry. And I can't tell you. Not yet. I hate it, keeping anything from you, but I just can't."

"Okay if that's how it's going to be . . ." He let his head fall and his shoulders went up and down. When he looked back up at her, she saw the sadness in his eyes. It was very genuine and clear, and she felt terrible for it.

She loved him so much, but she loved Freddie, too. There was no way her twin could be right, but she needed to find this proof, or at least be sure there wasn't any truth in his accusations. She was in an awful position caught between two people who were very dear to her.

The Valkyries did not let go of their prisoners, and somebody had to pay for the collapse of the Bofrir. Somebody had to go to Limbo—there was no way around it—and if it wasn't Freddie, then who? After all, Loki had served his time. Freddie was so sure it was Killian, and Freddie had never lied to her.

Killian suddenly punched the wall and Freya jumped back. She knew he was frustrated with what was going on, that he thought he was losing her. "Killian, don't, please," she said, feeling a wave of love and pity for him. But pity was death to a relationship, that much she knew, and she didn't want to feel pity for Killian.

He didn't say anything. Instead he abruptly turned around and left her alone, making her feel horrible, abandoned, and suddenly the one who needed to be pitied. She ran up the deck, calling his name, and even climbed up to the cockpit, but he had vanished. She came back down and stood at the gunwale, calling his name in the darkness. "Killian! Come on! Come back!" But there was no answer. No Killian.

She knew what he was trying to say. *Go ahead, Freya. Go ahead and search my boat all you want. I won't stop you. If you think you can't trust me, if you think I'm hiding something from you, then go ahead and look. I dare you to find something.*

She felt like a fool.

83

chapter fourteen

Night and Day

I t was a little after two, and Ingrid had already returned the COUNSELING SERVICES placard to her drawer and begun typing a report on the new blueprint. The recent funding to the library had allowed them to replace all the PC dinosaurs with iMacs as well as acquire archiving software to keep track of the many blueprints the library owned. There was much to do: she had to go through every print and its accompanying materials to enter the data, but since this Edwardian one was still fresh in her mind, she started there.

She looked up from the computer screen, hearing Hudson rapping at her office door.

"Entrez," she called.

He swung the door open just wide enough to slip through, then quietly closed it behind him. *"Bonjour, Mademoiselle Ingrid,"* Hudson said with a huge grin. "A very handsome officer of the law is here to see you." He raised his eyebrows at her.

"You can't mean . . ." she huffed, then panicked, glancing at Hudson for a second. "Is it really him?" she asked as she began nervously squaring things away on her desk, arranging pens, pencils, erasers, stapler, and Scotch Tape dispenser just so.

"Uh-huh, well, should I bring him back here?"

"Well, yes, I suppose. Go ahead." Her voice got a little high-pitched, and she didn't want to make eye contact, lest he see her absolute terror.

While Hudson went to get Matthew Noble, Ingrid worried her hair and bun with a hand, corrected her posture, then tried to decide which hand should rest on the desk. She tried one, then the other, but decided on fake typing instead, which would make her appear just the right amount of insouciant.

Matt strode in. He was wearing his NHP uniform for a change—detectives wore plainclothes, and Ingrid thought he looked rather dashing in it—the fitted navy shirt, snug pants, gleaming heavy black holster at his hips, and shiny black shoes. He wore no hat, which Ingrid found to be an intelligent style choice.

She rose, coming out from behind her desk, extending a hand in a formal manner. "Hello, Detective!" she said with a little nod.

He smiled at her crookedly. "Always so formal, Ingrid," he said.

"Have a seat," she said, swinging an arm in the general direction of the chair and small couch along the wall as she returned behind her desk.

Matt chose the chair facing Ingrid's desk and sat with his elbows on his knees, a hand on his forehead, staring down at the floor, shaking his head with what seemed like disapproval. He righted himself and looked Ingrid in the eye. He actually seemed downtrodden.

"I thought I'd come by and talk to you directly, since you won't answer any of my calls," he said. "I'd rather just know in person if you have chosen to end . . . um . . . our . . . this . . . *thing* we've got going . . ."

"Your calls?" she asked.

"Yes, my calls," Matt said sharply. "I've left you several messages with my sincerest apologies for the other night. I'm sorry about what happened. The cop in me kicked in. I was worried about you. I was out of line. I'm *so, so* sorry, Ingrid."

She was staring at him, eyes wide. This was the last thing she had expected to hear, and she'd been bracing herself to be the one to make an apology. She was confused, but another part of her just wanted to smile. She made an effort to keep her face neutral. "Well," she attempted, "there must be something terribly wrong with my phone, because I never got your messages."

"Really?"

She shook her head.

Matt laughed. "Wow, we really suck at this, don't we?" He stood, kicked at the floor, putting his hands in his pockets. He looked timidly up at her.

"Indeed," said Ingrid.

They stared at each other shyly again, a hint of a smile on both of their faces.

"Listen, you don't have to apologize, Matt. I'm the one who acted rudely, and I've been feeling awful ever since," she said earnestly. "Except I'm worse because I didn't even try to call you. Crikey, what was I thinking?"

"No, it's my fault," he said, picking up on the thirties lingo she'd suddenly adopted. "I had to go and act like a copper."

"Why are we talking like this?" she asked, thinking that any minute now scratchy music might start swelling in the background.

"Well, you started it," said Matt. "I was just picking up my cue."

They laughed. So they had that in common, too, not just classic American novels but sprightly golden age of Hollywood movies starring Humphrey Bogart and Lauren Bacall, a yen for sweet but gritty black-and-white romance.

"Can we try it again, again?" he asked. "You and I? We really ought to. You're so swell and peachy, Ingrid."

"Stop it," she said, giggling.

"I can't," he said. "You're aces."

"I'd like to give it another shot. I really would, Matt," she said huskily, just like a heroine in a film noir.

INGRID WAS CERTAIN the pixies were behind all those missed calls. They had probably messed with her phone. She wouldn't put it past them. And that piece of paper with that girl's number on it? Most likely another of their mischievous pranks. After work, she was going to give those mooching pixies a piece of her mind. She had to find out where they were from, pronto, so she could send them back there as soon as possible.

chapter fifteen

Jigsaw

～

It was a few days before Halloween. Joanna had been so distressed about the spirit trail that she had barely noticed anything else, not least of which that the house was slowly sinking
into its former squalor since Gracella had stopped working for
several weeks now. She had also forbidden Tyler to visit the house
for fear that he would be possessed by evil spirits. Joanna had
mentioned it to Ingrid the other day, and her older daughter had
muttered something about "refugees" and "I'm taking care of it."
Joanna had been looking forward to celebrating the holiday with
her "adopted" grandson, carving pumpkins, buying candy for the
trick-or-treaters, creating a real haunted house. But there was no
time for that now.

She set out, a backpack on her shoulders, Gilly leading the
way to the trail of wilted flowers. They arrived at the clearing in
the exact spot where Harold had called her name. It was a cloudless day, around two in the afternoon, when the sun reached its
zenith, shining through the pines and lighting up the glade. In the
middle was the path left by the spirit that was trying to make
contact with her. The grass along it slanted in different direc-
tions, crunching into powder underfoot as Joanna followed it. Of
course, it would be quicker to go straight across the glade, but she
wanted to keep an eye on the path itself in case she came upon any
new clues.

When she reached the end of the clearing, she saw that the trail continued among the evergreens, but there it turned black; the pine needles blanketing the forest floor were scorched. She crouched down and studied them, picking up a handful, inspecting, sniffing; they were indeed charred and turned to soot in her hand. She clapped her palms to rid them of the black dust, then continued to climb the hill. Gilly flew ahead.

She stumbled on a bed of stones, then got back to her feet, ascending to the top, where the ground leveled off. Here the path came to an abrupt halt, but straight ahead in this small upper clearing stood a large gnarly oak, and beneath, in the shadows of its sprawling branches, rose a singular mound with a grave marker. Gilly flew and alighted on top of it.

Something like glass caught the light on the mound. Joanna strode ahead until she was standing before it. The stone marker had no name or epithet inscribed on it—just a blank weathered and pockmarked tombstone. But there on the mound, arranged neatly on the dirt, the pine needles and leaves pushed aside, was a message.

The spirit had used six rune stones, two Scrabble tiles, and two dice that were missing from a fancy backgammon set that had been a gift from Ingrid. The wooden Scrabble tiles could have belonged to anyone, but the runes, made from the same matter as her dragon-bone wand, which she noticed was there, too—the spirit had used it to underscore the message—were unmistakably hers.

She had not noticed that the runes were missing. She usually kept them in a red velvet pouch on the desk in her study. Once in a while she would consult the runes to sort out a conflict or look into the future. Unlike Ingrid, Joanna couldn't directly tap into a person's lifeline but instead needed the aid of these ancient Norse stones to act as an oracle.

Joanna took care not to touch anything at first. She removed

89

her rucksack from her back, found a pen and notebook to begin copying down the message so she wouldn't forget it and could study it further at home. Obviously the spirit was using the runes to tell her something.

Gilly cawed excitedly, and the sound echoed through the woods.

"Yes, Gilly, *X* marks the spot," she said. "Well, more like an *E*? Hmm . . . kind of. Thank you for bringing me here. You did well."

Runes were an alphabetic script, and each letter etched onto the small tablet possessed a special meaning, like tarot cards. The order in which each rune was laid out also held significance. At first glance, she saw that none of the runes was reversed, which heartened her because this meant this was most likely a propitious portent. Usually when a rune was upside down, it took on a negative meaning.

The runes had been placed in a straight horizontal line that included the Scrabble letter tile *A*. There was a gap after the first three runes, then another three followed, the *A* among them. In the practice of ancient oracles, such as runes, tarot, or I Ching, the number *3* was commonly used for divination purposes, denoting past, present, and future, a triangle that was complete, the trinity within—blood, water, spirit. A three-rune spread was known as the Norn spread, representing the Norn sister triad, goddesses of past, present, and future, who presided over the fates of gods and men. But why the roman letter *A* in there, too?

Beneath this first line was another composed with the two dice, *1* then *5*, followed by an upside-down *L* Scrabble tile. Was the reversed *L* meant to be a *7*? This would then indicate the number 157. What could that be? Could it be a year—BC or AD? So long ago! Because objects other than runes had been introduced, she knew this message would require more than a reading of runes to decode it; this was a puzzle to be solved.

She sketched it out on her pad:

ᚻᚠᛈ ᚣᛗAᛖ

⚀ ⚄ 7

_____

When she was done with the sketch, Joanna searched around the gravesite for other clues—a stray rune or letter, maybe even another object—but she didn't find anything, so she folded the runes, tiles, and dice up in the kerchief she kept in her bag, then knotted the pieces of the puzzle together inside it, so she could pore over the reproduced message at her desk.

The temperature had dropped and the wind had begun to lash at the pines and maples.

"We are done here for now, Gilly," she said, shouldering her pack.

"Caw, caw!" responded the raven, lifting off to lead the way back to the house.

chapter sixteen

Sexual Healing

~S~

There were fewer kids than last year, Freya thought as she put away the candy bowl. Halloween had come and gone, and it wasn't the same, not without Tyler, whom they had been looking forward to spoiling. Joanna hadn't decorated—their mother was not herself lately—and Ingrid didn't approve of the "commercialization" of one of their high holy days, although it had been a long time since they'd celebrated a proper All Hallow's Eve. It was a shame. Since the Restriction had been lifted there was nothing to stop them from really getting down and dirty and—*pagan*. Ah, well, maybe next year.

Freya's phone vibrated. It was a text from Killian. <<come to the dock asap. i want to show you something.>>

They hadn't seen each other since that last stupid fight on the *Dragon*. It was as if Killian had disappeared, and Freya had kept an eye on the *Dragon* in the evenings to see if the lights went on, but it had remained dark since she had last set foot there. This was the first she was hearing from him.

That day after Killian had left, Freya had gone back to searching every corner of the boat, which had felt like a deplorable act of betrayal. She believed she had found all the secret hiding places, opened every last Chinese box, but the search, which lasted till dawn, had once again yielded absolutely nothing.

Ever since Freddie had introduced doubt in her mind, Freya had been rattled. She'd been seeing things in Killian: malevolent flickers, evil intent when she had almost slipped off the footbridge. But what if it was just her imagination? She was very impressionable after all. Her emotions clouded everything. What if she was seeing things that weren't there?

She had holed up in her New York apartment every night, not wanting to bump into her mother or sister. They would fret and pry, and she was too vulnerable, on the verge of confiding everything. She had made a promise to Freddie that she wouldn't reveal his secret—that he was back, that he had escaped from Limbo. If it were anyone other than Freddie, she would have told by now, but she always kept her twin's secrets. They were sacred, no matter what, no matter that it was killing her. Already, Joanna and Ingrid were getting suspicious about her actions.

The worse of it was that she missed Killian. She felt as if she were missing a limb, as if some part of her had been severed, and she lay there bleeding out. It felt as if she'd lost him just as she'd found him again, but now, with this message, she felt a glimmer of hope.

Besides, there was nothing on that godforsaken boat. Freddie was welcome to search it himself if he didn't believe her.

<<i'll be right there.>> she texted.

When freya arrived at the footbridge, Killian was waiting for her on the other side, casually leaning against the railing. His face was unreadable. She hurried across, but no sooner had she reached him than he hushed her and gently slipped a white scarf over her eyes. The feeling of his fingers putting the blindfold in place, making sure not a sliver of light crept through, calmed her. He placed his hands softly on her shoulders and whispered, "Can you see?"

She shook her head no. She knew this was his way of asking her to trust him, give him her blind faith, and at the moment she was so relieved and thrilled to be in his presence, to feel his touch again, that she would have gladly let him lead her straight to the edge of a precipice to push her off.

He made her spin around, doing five revolutions, then spun her the other way. He took her hand. "Come on," he said.

He guided her along, but after all that spinning, she wasn't sure whether they were moving toward the dock or in the opposite direction. Either way, she could still smell the brine on the air. But eventually the ocean scent thinned, so she deduced they were moving away from the water. Now he was behind her, his hands at her waist, pushing her slowly ahead, and she sensed she was on a path among trees; she heard birds chirping overhead. She guessed they were moving away from Fair Haven.

"Where are you taking me?" she asked.

"Shh," said Killian. They walked silently for a while but soon he was making her stand in place. "Okay," he said. His hands undid the blindfold, slipped off the knot at the back of her head.

The scarf fell and she opened her eyes. They were on the southeast side of Fair Haven, where a greenhouse abutted a wall of the manor.

Through years of disuse, it had gone to disrepair. Its domed roof and walls had grown bleary with age and many of the panes between the 1800s smith ironwork had broken. The inside had turned into a pandemonium of weeds, brambles, and ivy, so that it had become impossible even to step inside.

Freya stared in awe. The greenhouse had been completely revamped, and the glass shone in the light. The scene inside reminded her of the tropical conservatory greenhouse at Kew

Gardens in England: slim, twisting palm trees, agave ferox, african violets, swiss cheese plants with bright green lacy fronds, a reflection pond with pink water lilies. Resurrected, the greenhouse was a reminder of what Killian had always been for Freya: Balder, the god of tranquillity, joy, and beauty. This was an extension of him but also a manifestation of his love.

"You did this?" she asked.

"Well, it's really just to showcase your new herb garden," Killian said. "I got a little carried away, and it took a while to get it all growing the way I wanted. You always mentioned wanting to cultivate your own herbs for your magic."

Freya felt her eyes blur and Killian took her by the hand as they entered the thick, wet, sun-warmed air filled with the perfume of flowers and the song of cicadas. He gave her a tour, pointing out the herbs he had planted throughout as he called out their names: damiana, hyssop, burdock, feverfew, valerian, catnip, angelica root.

"Moss," he said, stopping at a large, round green rock.

"I see!" she retorted. She put her hand on the moss and pressed, admiring its springy texture.

He grinned with an irresistible glint in his eye. "It's nice." He pressed her against the mossy stone.

It was really the perfect place to rest her back as Killian moved his lips to her neck, then face, kissing away her tears. Soon they were naked, rolling around among african violets; then her face and hands were pressing against the glass as he entered her again, and she saw her breath form a patch of vapor on the pane.

They were drenched in sweat, their bodies slick, slipping against each other; then she was pressed against the moss again, as he moved tenderly inside her. He was so strong, and she loved that he held his strength in check as she ran her hands over his muscled torso, and he lifted her knees above his shoulders,

pushing them to her chest. They were in sync now, making love—
that was what it was—and it was all she could ever remember doing with him. She was screaming as he shuddered in her arms,
grasping her tightly, and she peered above at the sky and clouds
moving beyond their glass haven.

They let go of each other, arms at their sides, their foreheads
still together, as they gasped.

"I fucking missed you!" said Killian.

"Me too!" said Freya. *And I missed fucking you.*

He cupped her face in his hands and pulled her mouth to his.
He was wonderful. He was all Freya wanted. Only Killian could
rock her body and soul that way, and he was the only one who
ever had. All she had to do was let go, trust him.

Freddie was wrong about him. She should never have doubted.
Killian would never deceive her. She stopped kissing him, and
before she knew what she was saying, she was saying it. "I've been
hiding something from you. My brother's back from Limbo.
Fryr—I mean Freddie. He's called Freddie now."

Killian stared at her, joy written all over his face. "That's incredible news! Freddie! You're not the only one who's missed him,
you know? Where is he? Let's get him. Right now!" He tugged
her hand and with the other began gathering the clothes they had
scattered throughout the greenhouse. He handed her the blouse
and pants she had worn.

Freya leaned against the moss-covered rock, holding her
clothes to her chest. "It's not that simple, Killian." She looked
down at the brown mulch covering the ground, then watched
him as he dressed. She was going to have to explain.

Now that she had revealed Freddie was here, she couldn't
hold anything back. She had taken the leap of faith and trust.
"Freddie *escaped* from Limbo. The Valkyries didn't exactly let
him go—and there's more . . ." She told him what Freddie be-

lieved had happened, that Killian was his nemesis, that Killian was the one responsible for the collapse of the Bofrir bridge and stealing the gods' powers as his own, leaving him and Loki to take the blame. "I can't talk him out of it. He really believes you did it. I've tried, but he's insisted on hiding out, on plotting his revenge against you."

Killian stood barefoot in his jeans, his shirt unbuttoned. He stared at her the same way he had looked at her last on the *Dragon*—jilted, hurt, confused.

She still hadn't put her clothes back on, and now they fell to her feet. Her brow was creased as she stared back at him. "But he's wrong about you, right, Killian? Tell me he's wrong!"

Killian didn't answer, only set about buttoning his shirt, without looking her in the eye, without answering her question.

chapter seventeen

Teenage Dream

ھ

It was windy on the beach, but none of it mattered: sand hitting their faces and getting in the food, the blanket lifting from their shoes, placed as ballasts at the corners to hold it down, their hair mussed by the sudden gusts. All of it only made them laugh.

Matt had picked up Ingrid after work and driven her to the tip of Long Island, near the Montauk Point Lighthouse, to watch the sunset. The spot, a deserted sandy alcove surrounded by rocks that cut jaggedly into the sky, was right on the outside of the disoriented pocket, and so the two of them, in a sense, had stepped out of another dimension into real time, or perhaps they were still tottering between the two. They were inside the border of ordinary and extraordinary, but there seemed nothing ordinary about either side at the moment. Perhaps it was a dream zone, because that was how Ingrid thought of it—this second first date. They were starting all over again.

Matt had brought a blanket and further surprised Ingrid with a picnic basket containing an elegant spread: a white tablecloth and napkins, champagne flutes, a chilled bottle of Veuve Clicquot, duck mousse pâté, cornichons, a soft brie, olives, and a baguette, deliciously crunchy on the outside, soft and nutty on the inside.

"Since we didn't make it to that restaurant, I thought I'd bring the restaurant to you," Matt said as he bit into a piece of bread and pâté. "I hope you like it. The waiter there said it was *très délicieux.*"

Ingrid was touched and laughed at Matt's effort at a proper French accent. He had a good ear. He was always surprising her like that. No man had ever been so thoughtful toward her before. Well, unless her father, Norman, counted, but of course dads didn't count when it came to this sort of thing.

The sun fell behind a silver-blue cluster of clouds, outlining them in luminous white. Above that horizontal strip, the sky tinged turquoise, below ochre, then tangerine along the water, whose soft ripples reflected back a sunspot and the sky. Waves broke, hissing along the sand. They finished eating, and soon the sun would disappear into the waves.

"This is magic," Ingrid said.

Matt smiled and didn't respond, but he didn't disagree, either. She thought she would leave it for now. There was no point in arguing. She also had no desire to glimpse into his lifeline, although it would be easy to do it right now; he sat beside her, pants hitched up to his knees, barefoot, open, receptive, present—the perfect candidate, really.

He hadn't once mentioned the "band of homeless kids," and she was grateful for that. She felt at peace with him, as if she had finally come home. She watched his animated freckled face changing expressions, peered into the blue pools of his eyes, his hair moving this way and that in the wind.

Matt cocked his head at her. "May I?" he asked. Ingrid blinked nervously, but he turned her away from him by her shoulders and carefully began taking the pins out of her bun. He placed them in her hand, and she faced him again, shaking her hair out.

"Better," he said. He put a finger beneath her chin, lifting it up, so she could look in his eyes. He bent his face down to hers, and Ingrid could barely catch her breath.

"We really should get back to the car before it gets dark, put all this stuff away, don't you think?" she rattled.

"Hmm," said Matt with a dreamy smile. "Oh, well." He laughed.

She stood up and brushed the crumbs off her skirt and began packing away the picnic. She felt stupid and foolish for ruining the moment; she should have just let him kiss her. It wasn't as if it were the first time. Things were going too well, and she wasn't sure where it would lead—where she wanted it to lead.

They hurried to the car as the wind picked up, carrying the blanket and basket over the path through the rocks, putting on their shoes when they reached the parking lot. After they stored everything in the trunk, Matt opened the passenger door for Ingrid and got in the driver's seat.

He slammed the door and turned toward her. She looked questioningly back at him, or maybe her face was blank. She couldn't tell how she was looking at him.

"I'm sorry . . ." she said. "I'm new at this . . ." Her hands twisted in her lap and she felt as if she would die of shame.

"Hey . . ." Matt said. "We don't have to do anything at all. Listen, we can just be friends, okay?"

Ingrid sniffed and nodded, swallowing her disappointment.

Matt put his key in the ignition. It was over. He was going to drive her home, and then they would be friends. She couldn't do this, she thought, have a real relationship with someone she liked. She was a failure and a coward.

But the car remained parked. Ingrid turned to him. He was smiling at her. It was the smile that did it, the one that said, *It's okay. We'll be friends. I'll wait for you.* She didn't have to read minds to know what he was trying to tell her.

Ingrid reached over and shut off the car, then placed her hand on his and guided it to her lips. She kissed his fingers, each one, a penance. An invitation. She didn't have to wait very long. He was kissing her again, longer this time, and as she opened her mouth to his she knew it was unlike anything she had ever experienced before, a longing that ached, a hunger they each sought to satisfy, but at the same time sweet, assuaging. Matt was leaning over her, the back of her head pressing against the headrest, her arms awkwardly at her sides.

She pushed her mouth harder against his, placing her hands, hesitantly at first, on his broad shoulders, then running them more confidently along his arms. She felt his muscles straining beneath the soft sweater. His hands caressed her waist, pushing up her skirt. He kissed her face and her neck, and she heard him sigh audibly, felt the heat rise between them, the windows of the car beginning to fog.

Wind and sand lashed at the car. It had gotten dark. The lampposts around the lot had lit up at some point. She put her hands underneath his sweater, underneath his shirt, on his hard, flat stomach, and all the while they were kissing, pressing closer and closer, so that Matt was on top of her, his knees between her legs, and her head bumping against the window.

She hadn't noticed that while they were kissing she had removed his sweater, that her hands were under his shirt, that while she had been undressing him, he had unbuttoned her shirt, and now his hand was behind her back, fiddling with the clasp of her bra.

She pulled away, and her blush spread from her cheeks to her chest.

"Do you want me to stop?" he asked, his breath ragged, hovering on top of her, his eyes glazed.

She sat there with her knees pointing toward him, her skirt hiked up to her black tights, the lights softly illuminating her pale breastbone, her little everyday white bra showing, which embarrassed her. She always wore a bra, unlike Freya, who liked to "set the twins free." Her bra was so very unsexy, just practical, not lacy or pushup or cleavage enhancing. Just a plain white bra.

A plain white bra that she wasn't even wearing but pressing to her chest, because Matt had succeeded in unhooking it.

She was thirty-two years old. No. She was older than that. So much older. But Ingrid realized no one had ever seen her naked before. No man, at least.

She was trembling.

"We can stop," Matt said, and began to wrench his way off of her.

"No . . . don't," Ingrid said.

His eyes on hers, he peeled off her blouse until it fell on the ground, then slowly, ever so slowly did the same to the wisp of cotton that she was holding so tightly. Ingrid closed her eyes and let him see her.

"You're so beautiful," he murmured, kissing her neck. And then his hands were on her bare skin, on her breasts, and her pulse thrummed in her ear, and their kisses became tremulous. They were both shaking now, skin to skin. *So this is what it's like,* Ingrid thought, although she was past thought. She had surrendered to pure sensation, liking the feel of his warm body on hers, pressing against each other.

Freya would be so proud of me, she thought. Second base! But it was as far as she would go, and she knew she could trust Matt. She wouldn't have to say anything. Instead they kept kissing, like two tentative and frightened but eager adolescents, having their own private awakening, inside the only parked car in the lot.

thanksgiving

we are family

chapter eighteen

Message in a Bottle

ᘒᘚ

Joanna laid out the spirit's message on her desk, just the way it had been displayed on the grave:

ᚺᚠᛈ ᚤᛗAᚱ

⚀⚄🁛

_____

Now that she could read the runes at her leisure, she decided to go by the Norn spread, reading the six of them in groups of threes from left to right, because they had been placed in two distinct clusters. The first one, called Odin's rune, represented the factors leading up to this point (past) and was the overview of the situation, the second summed up the situation (present) and identified the current challenge, and the third was intended to suggest a course of action (future) and its possible outcome.

In the first position she had *hagalaz*, which meant "hail," whose deeper prescient significance was crisis, upheaval, catastrophe, stagnation, loss of power, a disruptive force awakening from a deep sleep. Here the spirit was telling her that something had gone amiss. This wasn't too surprising. If the spirit was seeking

Joanna's attention and had gone through the pains of leaving this message in mid-world, it meant it was in full unrest, desperate enough to breach the thick membrane of the seam separating the dead from the living. The rune had no ambiguous meaning; even upside down it meant the same thing.

The rune in the second position, the current challenge, *ansuz*, stood for an ancestral god, and its underlying esoteric translation was the revealing of a message, a communiqué, advice. "Whoever you are, you want me to read them. That is clear," Joanna said. "Or are you saying that the challenge is that I must find you, so that you can tell me something pressing? You have advice for me? You want to tell me what this catastrophe is about, what perturbs you? Okay." She was speaking to the spirit as if it were in the room.

The final rune, the action she had to take, was *wunjo*. "Aw, that is nice of you," said Joanna. "You want us to become friends, allies, or you are saying that we will be friends in the future?" *Wunjo* was the symbol for "joy" and meant friendship.

She had resolved that the overall message of this first set of runes was simple: some kind of great calamity had taken place and the spirit needed to inform her of its specifics, while offering friendship and meaning no harm. She would need to travel farther into the glom to find it. If the spirit were as powerful as it appeared, it didn't necessarily have to be in the layer closest to the seam.

In the case of Philip and Virginia, their attempts to contact her had become so out of control that they'd killed the landau driver. Had Joanna intervened sooner, she might have prevented that poor man from being impaled on the spikes of a wrought-iron fence as the carriage tipped and hurled him off. The two lovers had intended no harm. It was only that their love had driven them to desperation. They hadn't wanted a man to die. *No one was going to die this time,* Joanna thought. She had to figure out what this spirit wanted her to know before it took similar desperate action. This would require research, the correct spell, and she needed to know where to look for this soul. She was about to read the next set of runes when she felt a presence in the room. She peered over her shoulder and saw Ingrid.

"Oh, you startled me!" she said.

"You're very jumpy, Mother!" Ingrid chided, but Joanna could see her oldest was in a good mood. She was glowing, her light blond hair sleekly draping down past her shoulders, the prettiest hue of pink in her cheeks, her skin pale and dewy. She reminded Joanna of a delicate but robust flower, like a white moth orchid or a slim, graceful calla lily. She smiled, happy to see her daughter so relaxed and well. It must be that new cop boyfriend of hers. Matt Virtuous or something, was it? Joanna was amused and secretly pleased. It was about time Ingrid found somebody.

Ingrid strode to Joanna, and her blond hair fell on the desk as she leaned over her mother's shoulder, studying the runes. "Hmm, interesting," she said. "Why are those Scrabble tiles and the dice I gave you included in your reading?"

"Never mind that, darling, just tell me what you see," said Joanna. She wanted to get a quick first impression from her daughter without conveying all the backstory quite yet, a reading unaffected by any other knowledge, one that was pure and objective. Ingrid, her gift being foresight, was adept at reading the oracle of the runes. Since the Restriction had been lifted, Ingrid had begun to regain her memories and abilities, including the formerly lost talent to read and understand their ancient language.

Her daughter also assigned the Norn spread and came to a similar conclusion about the first three runes. She moved on to the second set, and Joanna requested that she ignore the *A*.

"*Algiz, manaz, laguz,*" Ingrid said, listing the names of the runes. "This means that something or someone has been protecting you until now. Shielding you from evil. However that protection, that connection, this divine structure, if you will, has been disrupted, disconnected, and you need to repair it. You're in danger. That's your challenge. You need to fix that connection to be safe. As for the course of action you must take to do this . . . *laguz* . . . water— you must travel. But it's a good thing. The ultimate outcome leads to healing and renewal."

Oscar came traipsing in, then rubbed his large eagle's head against Ingrid's leg. She patted her familiar.

Joanna continued to stare at the tiles. "You're absolutely right. That would have taken me forever. Thank goodness I have smart children." She explained everything that had been happening lately, how a spirit had made contact.

"Things were moving around the house? Hmm, that's not good! *Darn it!*" Ingrid huffed the latter beneath her breath. "You *thought* it was a spirit?" Ingrid sounded skeptical and appeared distracted, glancing at the doorway worriedly. "Are you sure?" she asked.

"I think I would know, dear." She told Ingrid about her experience in the garden, the flowers wilting at her touch, how Gilly had taken her into the woods where they had followed the path to the grave and found these objects laid out on the mound in this formation.

"You're right," said Ingrid, studying the message. "It is a spirit who needs your help. But this is also a code—the Scrabble tiles, the dice . . . It's an encryption, a cipher, an anagram, of some sort. The fact that there are Scrabble letters indicates that. Maybe it says something else entirely different from what the runes tell us, something horrible, something ominous, a threat. We need to decode this, and I think you should enlist Dad ASAP. He's a great help with enigmas."

Joanna cleared her throat, feeling a bit peeved that her daughter would think she wasn't capable of figuring this out on her own. "Well, I'd like to sort it out by myself for now. The message is obviously for me and me alone. I can decode it without Norman's help. But first and foremost, I think I need to get in touch with this spirit, 'travel,' as you say. It wants to speak to me. I think it wants me to raise it from the dead."

"I *think* you are getting ahead of yourself, Mother. You don't know what this says yet. This isn't just about the runes. There's something else here." She pointed at the line with the dice and upside-down *L*. "Look, that's a number. One fifty-seven."

"I know it's a number," said Joanna a bit too defensively. She realized her daughter was only trying to help. Of course Ingrid was right to caution, but she sensed it was urgent and said so.

Ingrid shook her head. "You can't raise a dead spirit before finding out what it wants! Remember the Covenant you made with Helda. You can't just go around resurrecting everyone! Your sister doesn't take that sort of thing lightly. Plus, it's never gone well in the past."

"I know. I know. You don't have to remind me."

Ingrid attempted another tact. "I know you feel this spirit needs you, but I don't think that's the best way—"

"This spirit is trying to tell me something important, but the only way I can truly find out is to speak directly to it. Cut to the chase, rather than spending hours decoding this."

"But what if it's evil?" Ingrid said.

"Well, we won't know that until I raise it from the dead, will we? I've already gone into the first layer, and it wasn't there."

Ingrid sat down in the chair beside Joanna's desk, resigning herself to the situation. "I guess I'm not going to be able to persuade you to take your time with this, but will you promise to come to me for help if you plan on doing anything drastic?"

"I promise," said Joanna.

"And the Covenant?"

"I'll think about it," Joanna said.

"Good," said Ingrid, appearing only somewhat satisfied.

Now that mother and daughter had reached a resolution of sorts, Joanna thought it might be the right time to ask about the cop boyfriend. "So, how's that young man of yours?"

"What young man?"

"Ingrid—I'm your mother. I *know*."

"What do you know?" Ingrid asked, trying to look innocent.

"You're dating that cop—Matthew Good-Guy or something."

"Matt Noble!" Ingrid corrected, aggrieved.

Joanna smiled wryly. "See."

"All right. I suppose I am . . . seeing him, Mother, but you don't have to look at me like that. I already have to deal with Freya teasing me day and night."

"We're just happy for you, dear," Joanna said, coming to embrace her girl. "We want you to be happy, you know."

"I know," Ingrid murmured. "Thank you, Mother. I am happy." She squeezed her mother in a tight hug. "I've memorized the code. I'll think it over, see if I can come up with anything." Then she released her hold and left Joanna's office before her mother could ask her any more embarrassing questions or call Matt by some other silly name. Oscar followed on her heels, his nails clicking on the floorboards.

Joanna was left to herself once again staring at the message. *Yes, a cipher or anagram, something of that sort,* thought Joanna. *That is exactly what I thought.* She grabbed a pen and paper and began to scribble.

chapter nineteen

When Doves Cry

ഛൟ

B etty Lazar and detective-in-the-making Seth Holding, still going strong, had proposed hosting Friday Night Karaoke at North Inn. Sal had jumped at the idea. That was the thing about Sal. Even at seventy, he was always willing to try something new, as long as it got the joint going.

"We can call it Fri-a-oke!" he said excitedly, to which Freya had responded, *"Eh!"* The other bartender, Kristy, put it more bluntly. "Lame! How about just Friday Night Karaoke?" The two bartenders were game and helped Sal purchase the equipment and disks on eBay from a recently shut down bar in New York City.

Once they set everything up, they saw that most of the songs and accompanying videos appeared to date back to the eighties. The visuals that provided the lyrics featured women with huge hair, dozens of rosary necklaces, pale skin, glossy scarlet lips, and oversize dresses sloping off a shoulder. The men were no better with tight pants and mullets, either business in the front and party in the back or the other way around.

But this was all very much in keeping with the bar's shifts in the time-space continuum, so now on a Friday eve at North Inn, one might hear anything from a drunken off-key version of Prince's "Little Red Corvette" to a superbly belted out rendition of Billy Joel's "Piano Man" to Night Ranger's "Sister Christian" (a drunken group sing-along), AC/DC's "Back in Black," songs by Tears for Fears, Billy Idol, the Fine Young Cannibals, 10,000 Maniacs, Duran Duran, Pat Benatar, and Michael Jackson, of course, as well as a slew of other artists who had either died, evaporated into the pop ether, been recently arrested for a DUI in LA, or become healthy, sober vegans.

The young people of North Hampton and its surrounding environs did not appear to be missing either the tragic Amy Winehouses or the bubbly Miley Cyruses of their generation, and came in droves dressed in Mom and Dad's old duds to pile into the booths and pore over the song lists.

There were also the fortysomethings who had come of age during the era of too much cash flow and cocaine, such as smarmy developer Blake Aland, making good with the townsfolk, discussing a bit of real estate he wanted to get his claws into, and recalling the adage of not being able to sing one's way out of a paper bag. Conversely, Justin Frond, the hip new mayor, had surprised everyone with his perfect pitch and lovely, smooth voice tonight.

Gay men are the best, thought Freya, spying some visual teasers of the mayor's private evenings. She saw Frond with his handsome partner, walking along a moonlit beach, pants rolled up, making out in the tall grasses of a sand dune. The mayor had excellent abs, Freya noted. As for Blake Aland's midnight trysts, Freya had to blink her eyes to ward off the unsavory images: spiky heels digging into a spine, something involving a tongue, a black patent leather shoe, a glass table, and a panting, frothing Mr. Aland.

Seth was singing Queen's epic "Bohemian Rhapsody," which was a strange choice for a police officer, being that it was about a boy who had shot someone, but he was off duty, and Betty was doing backup vocals, neither of them taking their eyes off the other as the crowd began to cheer. *"Mama, life had just begun, but now I've gone and thrown it all away . . ."*

"They really are good, those two," Sal said to Freya. He was working the bar with her. Killian hadn't come in to help—Freya missed him, but he'd become obsessed with getting the greenhouse just so—and Kristy served drinks at the booths while collecting the slips with song choices and manning the karaoke machine.

"You don't know the half of it, Sal," retorted Freya. Betty and Seth had sex at least three times a day when they could: lunch break in a restaurant restroom, Seth's police car, an interview room at the precinct (*of all the places—they really should be more careful*). As she watched them sing, Freya decided to entertain herself beyond casual voyeurism.

She closed her eyes and focused, and when she opened them again, dry ice smoke enveloped Betty and Seth. When it dissipated, they had undergone a costume change and were now in tight white satin one-pieces à la Freddie Mercury. The expert performers and hams they were, they didn't blink, and the crowd only cheered and whooped louder.

Freya joined the hooting but stopped when her cell phone vibrated in her pocket. It was Killian, and she asked Sal if she could take the call in the back room. Killian sounded distressed, but she couldn't hear him over the din. She stepped into Sal's cramped office, with its heavy mahogany desk, card table for poker nights with the local geezers, dart board, and old, scratched black file cabinets.

"You need to come to the *Dragon* right away," Killian said. "We need to talk."

The *need to talk* phrase never went over well with Freya. She was almost like a *dude* in this sense. The words filled her with dread and unease. Had she done something wrong? Was Killian mad at her for some reason she couldn't remember? Everything had been going so well lately. Their sex life was back to normal (giving Betty and Seth a run for their money) and they'd succeeded in avoiding the topic of Freddie altogether.

"It's really busy. You know, that new karaoke night thing," Freya said. "Well, it's more like eighties night."

"Try to get off. I really need to talk to you. Please."

SAL HAD ALWAYS BEEN GOOD at wrangling impromptu help, and one of his buddies soon joined him behind the bar. Freya was already at the wheel of the Mini Cooper, speeding toward the parking lot by the beach that led to Gardiners Island. When she got to the *Dragon*, Killian was outside on the deck. He helped her jump on board. Inside the boat, she saw that he had ordered some takeout—there was pasta in foil containers—and had opened up a bottle of red wine, but his plate of food looked untouched and the wine hadn't been poured.

Freya crossed her arms, not quite knowing what to expect. The sense of dread had sunk to the pit of her stomach, and she felt queasy and faint. What did he want to talk about so badly?

"Have a seat," said Killian. "You want a glass of wine?" Invariably, Killian followed his words to Freya with a term of endearment—*my love* or *babe* or *darling*—but there was none of that, which frightened her even more.

"I've had enough to drink for tonight," she said.

"I'll get right down to it," he said earnestly. "I know we've been ignoring the subject lately, but that doesn't mean I haven't done a lot of thinking about it—what you said Freddie told you about me." His back against the granite galley counter, with his face tilted at an angle and his dark lashes batting, he looked even more handsome than was allowed.

God, my man is gorgeous, Freya thought, and she hoped that whatever he had to say to her wouldn't stop them from rocking the boat tonight.

Killian exhaled. "Here's the thing: I don't remember what happened that day."

Freya stared blankly back at him. "What day?"

"The day the Bofrir bridge collapsed. Freddie might be telling the truth," he continued. "I don't understand. There are holes in my memory. I try to remember, but then I hit a wall, and I just can't recall how it all went down. All I know is that there were three of us on the bridge that day. Fryr and Loki were punished, but I got away scot-free. The gods have always looked upon me favorably, but what if, what if . . ." His words trailed off.

Freya didn't know what to say or think. What if Freddie were right? What if her brother were telling the truth all along? What Killian said was true: the gods loved Balder; he could do no harm in their eyes. He was Frigg's favorite son. Nothing in all the universe was allowed to touch him, to harm him. He was Balder the Blessed. Balder the Beloved.

"I don't know what happened, but I want to come clean, Freya. I was there. I saw the bridge destroyed, and I remember holding something that didn't belong to me when it was over. But that's all I remember."

chapter twenty

Sharp-Dressed Man

ᒐᡐ

She was a vision as she walked along the beach: a tall, voluptuous goddess, long golden-brown hair lifting in the wind, silhouetted by the sun. She tugged her coat around her curves, and even from far away Freddie could see the smile forming on her lips as she spotted him. He had sensed her the moment she stepped onto the sand, before he saw her from atop his dune, where he had been waiting for her to come to him, trusting she would as he surveyed the beach, squinting at the sky, watching the waves.

Freddie stood and waved, then quickly scaled down in his bare feet, moving toward her. Hilly Liman. It wasn't quite love at first sight, for Freddie Beauchamp had already toppled during their fervent epistolary courtship. Hilly had materialized for him through his laptop—her vibrancy, her warmth, her little quirks (how she sucked the water out of her toothbrush or made little dolphin-like sounds at the back of her throat when it itched)—and he could recognize her anywhere. His goddess.

They stopped a few feet apart, his eyes tracing the lines of her face, her square jaw, strong cheekbones, a beauty mark beneath an eye, the long, dark lashes of her almond-shaped hazel eyes that stared unwaveringly at him.

Freddie took a deep breath. "You're just as I thought," he said.

"Really? How did you know?" she said with a laugh.

"What about that little hug?" he said.

She nodded. He took a tentative step toward her and she took a more assured one. He hugged her, exhaling a lungful, a release of everything that had been pent up inside him until that moment. Hilly was real, and all he knew was that he loved and wanted her.

She looked up in his face. "I'm glad I'm here," she said. "I'm glad I'm finally hugging you."

They let go of each other and stood apart. "Me, too," he said.

"I can't stay long. It was a long drive from school, and now my parents are expecting me at the house in the city for the weekend."

He was devastated, feeling as if something would be ripped from his skin as soon as Hilly left him. But instead he smiled, and she smiled back.

"I wanted to meet you in person to make sure it was real. You never know with these things," she said. "There could be a lot of projection."

A seagull squawked overhead.

"And . . . ?" he asked.

"It's real," she said.

"I know." He looked toward the Ucky Star, lifting an arm to encompass the slanting beachside motel with its broken neon light, partly obscured by dunes and reeds. "My palace," he declared.

Hilly turned in that direction, looked back at him, and they both laughed.

"Listen, if we're going to be together, you need to meet my family," Hilly said nervously. Her forehead creased and her countenance darkened. "My dad's sort of strict. He's old-fashioned. I guess I am, too."

"Anything," replied Freddie. He understood from the beginning that Hilly wouldn't be going back to the motel room with him for some sexual gymnastics. Not that he had expected it anyway. Where Hilly was concerned, he wanted to take his time. Freya had warned him about this girl, that he wasn't acting like himself. But Freddie didn't care. So she wanted him to meet her dad. He could do that. Dating. What an odd concept! Did that mean just kissing? Anything for Hilly, though, even if it meant coming out of hiding to meet her father just to be able to gaze longer at her.

"Can you come to dinner tomorrow night?" she asked.

"Sure!" said Freddie, thrilled that he would be seeing her so soon again.

"I'll e-mail you the details," she said. "I really like you, Freddie."

He wanted to reply, *I love you, Hilly*, but instead he nodded. "Ditto."

For the trip to New York City to meet the Limans, Buster morphed into a black Porsche convertible, the same exact model Freddie had been admiring online. The taglines described it as "driving magic." Freddie thought he would see about that. So far, it was divine, as if the car were an extension of his body, responding to the lightest tap of the gas or the brake, then defying gravity altogether by taking off to the skies. They arrived over Manhattan, where lights twinkled like so many jewels in the dusk, and landed in Central Park by the Turtle Pond, kicking up turf as they alighted and swerved to a halt. Buster turned back into his regular form and now was snuffling about fallen leaves, keeping out of sight until Freddie returned.

Freddie didn't like the city. Buses and taxis spewed toxic fumes, nearly running him over as he made his way to the doorman building on Central Park West, wearing appropriate attire— the gray suit and tie from his "serious" profile picture. The problem with such magical clothes was that they came with a short shelf life, an expiration hour, so to speak, and now he was very much in the same predicament as Cinderella. He hoped he would be out of there before the suit and polka-dot tie faded and he was back in his T-shirt, ripped jeans, and black Converse.

IT WAS NOT THAT he wanted to leave Hilly, who was looking resplendent for the occasion—her hair up, a few locks coiling down her cheeks and a delicate strand of silver South Sea pearls around her neck. But since he'd arrived in the Upper West Side apartment, the whole occasion had been a bit bizarre, even for Freddie, who had seen many strange things and many strange worlds over many thousands of years.

For one, the expression *shit faced*, which he had learned on a television show in his motel room, came to mind. In fact, many of the rules of decorum and social mores of the twenty-first century he'd learned came from cable television. Hilly's mother, Hollis, sitting at one end of the table, was shit faced, though dinner had barely begun. Henry Liman, Hilly's stern father, at the other head of the table—graying hair, a thin black mustache, sharp vulpine features—had let Freddie know several times that he was president and chief executive officer of an extremely successful boating company. He also hadn't stopped grilling Freddie since they sat down to dinner, asking him about his portfolio and throwing words at him like *stocks, hedge funds,* and *derivatives,* which Freddie knew nothing about. Besides, what did that have to do with boating?

Meanwhile, Hilly's two older sisters gawked at Freddie. The middle child, Cassandra, a pale, dark-eyed, droopy girl with a slim curving neck and long bony hands, had played a dramatic assonant piece on the piano before dinner. Even Henry had remarked, "Can you play something a bit more melodious next time, my swan?"

Gert, the oldest, looked like a Gert: a bosomy, horsy blond with a toothy, brilliantly white smile. She had managed to monopolize the bread, while still glaring expectantly at Freddie.

It was dark outside, and one could see the tops of Central Park's trees beyond the terrace and, across the park, the glow of the city above the roofs and penthouse gardens. The table, covered in a white cloth, was set with flower centerpieces, birds of paradise, green cymbidium orchids, white lilies, and verdant fronds; silver candelabra with flickering candles; white bone china plates, a small red flag with a star at the center and light blue scalloped trim (from the *Titanic*, Gert had let Freddie know, though he couldn't tell whether it was with a note of sarcasm or if she was showing off); and gleaming silverware that weighed a ton. There was too much space between the six of them at the extremely long table in the vast room with one red wall and a gleaming black wood floor; the color scheme was not unlike that of boardrooms during a certain chilling German era. A private chef brought the appetizer: crispy duck served medium rare on a bed of wild baby greens with pineapple, mandarin, and lychee.

But before they sat down to eat, Freddie had gone to use the downstairs bathroom and heard strange noises coming from inside. Was it retching? Vomiting? The toilet flushed, and Hilly's mother, Hollis, a tall, slim reed of a woman, came out straightening her skirt, smiling at Freddie and handing him her iPhone. He tried to hand it back, but she would have none of it, flipping it back in his hand so that they awkwardly tossed it back and forth like this for a while. When Freddie finally relented and entered the bathroom, he stared at the device in his hand. There was a note to him on the screen:

<<Freddie, you are adorable. Don't let the man bully you! He'll

crush you if he can. I'm on your side. As far as I'm concerned, Hilly is yours. I don't want her making the mistakes I made. Please delete this message when you have finished reading, then give the phone back. XXXX, Hollis>>

Freddie opted for discreetly setting the iPhone down on the credenza in the living room, while Hilly's parents drank their predinner cocktails, Hollis swigging hers enthusiastically, faster than Henry in any case, and he and Hilly sipped Shirley Temples, like ten-year-olds, sitting at opposite ends of the long sectional couch, while Cassandra banged out that earsplitting piece of music and Gert attempted to conceal her laughter, snorting now and then.

BACK AT THE DINING-ROOM TABLE, Freddie was being badgered by *the man*, and the strangest thing of all was that Hollis, swaying hither and thither, watched her husband with an approving smile that seemed perfectly natural albeit—yes—*shit faced*.

"So what college are you attending, Freddie? Hilly's a Yale girl herself, just pledged the most selective sorority there," he said proudly. "What about you?"

"I don't think they'd take me in any sorority," Freddie replied with a smile, but he only received a frown in return.

Gert yawned loudly. Cassandra, whom they referred to as Swan, broke into high-pitched hyena-like laughter, then turned silent and morose. The chef came to remove the appetizer plates, taking Freddie's even though he had only nibbled a few baby greens, then returned with the entrees.

"Well, Mr. Liman, I mean, Henry"—Hilly's father had insisted on being called Henry, his only bit of graciousness thus far—"I decided to take a little time off before college." It wasn't really a lie. Perhaps Freddie would go to college if that meant getting the man's approval to be with Hilly. He would look into it. How hard could it be?

Henry harrumphed, but Freddie understood it was less to clear his throat than to make his disapprobation known. "So, you are taking time off to live in a motel, to find yourself, some soul seeking before the academic plunge? And your family? They are fine with this?"

Freddie nodded.

Hilly's father frowned more deeply, obviously disappointed that Freddie's family didn't seem to care he was a slacker. Freddie tried to win some points. "Actually my dad's a professor, and he always said we should explore a lot of avenues before committing. He's a big advocate of taking a year off. And Mom's . . . a . . . a . . . free spirit." Freddie had no idea whether his father felt that way, but at least he was honest about his mother. Whatever she was, Joanna was certainly a free spirit.

Henry continued the interrogation. "Well, what about an internship somewhere in the interim? Have you considered that? Internships are marvelous, aren't they, Hilly?"

"Yes, Daddy. I enjoyed the one I did at *Vogue* this past—"

"Well?" cut in Henry, glaring inquisitively at Freddie.

"No, I haven't looked into an internship . . . but . . ." he replied sheepishly, searching for the right words.

"A complete layabout in other words," Mr. Liman muttered under his breath as he began knifing the enormous lamb shank on the plate before him.

"Hmm," said Hollis, nodding, as if she were giving careful consideration to what her husband was saying. It appeared as if she were merely going through the motions of sociability and was somewhere else entirely.

Gert laughed again, which no one paid attention to, and Cassandra appeared to be nodding out, like a heroin addict, her fork hovering over the edge of her plate.

Freddie's pride was rattled. He looked to Hilly for help, but she only stared back at him with panic in her eyes. Though Freddie did not have human wealth, he *was* a god, the god of the sea and the sun, able to make crops grow, flowers blossom, arid land turn fertile, oases rise out of the desert. He created beauty all over the world. Conducting his own legal defense in his mind, Freddie began to notice that the suit he was wearing had begun to fade and this added to his anxiety. He needed to wrap things up. He knew about love and emotion and passion, and he wasn't about to let Hilly's father tell him otherwise.

"Mr. Liman, Henry, I know I don't have a job or any prospects. I may look poor to you since I currently live in a run-down motel. But the truth of the matter is that I have fallen in love with your daughter, and all I know is that . . . well, I love her."

Here Hilly smiled at him and nodded encouragingly.

"Yes, I love Hilly." Freddie stood. "And I'm willing to do whatever it takes—whatever it is you want me to do—to have your daughter's hand!"

Everyone at the table had suddenly come to attention, staring at Freddie, mouths open wide. Even the drowsy Swan had awoken, and Mrs. Liman appeared quite sober suddenly.

"My dear boy," said Henry. "Did you go and change your clothes while we weren't looking? Weren't you wearing a suit just before? A gray . . . ?"

Freddie stared down at himself, and to his horror saw that the serious outfit had expired, and now he stood in his black T-shirt, torn Levi's, and humble Converse that were terribly scuffed.

Mr. Liman let out a bellowing laugh, so loud and terrifying it appeared to make the table and walls shake. When he finally collected himself, he said, "I do love a good magic trick. Excellent indeed, Freddie! A very original way to request my daughter's hand in marriage. But you will have to prove yourself further—a real job with real prospects, although you did very much catch

123

me off guard. I have always had a fondness for magic, I must say."
He tittered to himself, shaking his head as he observed Freddie
with a puzzled look.

At that everyone around the table clapped delightedly, although Freddie did not take a bow. Instead, he sat back down in
his seat and sulked.

chapter twenty-one

Like a Virgin

ℯℯ

"A re you sure there's no one out there?" Ingrid stared anxiously at Hudson, whom she had asked to stay late and meet her in the office once the library was closed and the last patrons had left.

"Well, I'd say the library is as empty as a fourteenth-century European village ravaged by the bubonic plague. It's tantamount to the black death out there."

"Oh, good," said Ingrid.

"But no infectious dead bodies in the aisles, which is also good."

Ingrid tittered, then her face turned serious. "We shouldn't joke about such things."

"No, we shouldn't," agreed Hudson with an exaggerated serious face.

"Have a seat and sorry to keep you late." Ingrid sat down in her swivel chair.

"For you, not a problem, my dear." Hudson took the seat across from her desk, one he was quite comfortable in. It was clear he loved their private little tête-à-têtes. He crossed his legs and leaned forward, an elbow on one knee, face cupped in his palm. "What's up, Miss Ingrid?"

Ingrid looked around, steeled herself, and looked him

directly in the eye. "Well, remember how you said you were my old reliable friend, and you would be here when I needed you?"

"Yes, of course," said Hudson. "I'm your Old Faithful. Here to spout wisdom and truth."

"I need you, but I don't know how to put it, and you have to promise not to laugh once I tell you."

He laughed. "Okay, I just got it out of the way. Have out with it, Ingrid."

"I guess there is only one way of putting it, really," Ingrid hedged.

"Yes?" Hudson smiled to help bring his friend out of her shell. He knew she had a tendency to get nervous, shifty, and was prone to making a mountain out of a molehill.

"Well, I'm a virgin, Hudson, to put it bluntly," she said, bravely forging ahead.

"Oh!" He was staring at her, wide-eyed, and he did not laugh at all. "I see . . ."

"God, this is awkward," remarked Ingrid. "This is worse than talking to my mother."

"No, no. Sorry, you just caught me off guard." He looked down and squared his tie, flicked at a bit of lint on his suit. He looked up. "This was just the last thing I expected to hear. You mean to say that you *never*?"

"Never," said Ingrid quickly. She bit her lip.

"But you're, like . . ." Hudson began, then let the incomplete sentence dangle there. He stared curiously at her.

She stared back. "You're starting to make me uncomfortable, Hudson."

"I'm sorry. It's fine, really, really. It's just that in this day and age, I am a bit . . . How to say? Shocked? I didn't think there were any virgins left!"

"I understand," said Ingrid with finality, fixing the papers on her desk.

"I'm sorry. You're a virgin. Okay. So?" He put out a hand, and it rested there in the air between them, then he quickly drew it back to his lap. "What do you want to know? There's not much to it, really, especially with your . . . um . . . kind." He continued to watch her pound the stack of paper upright then sideways on the desk.

"What kind is that?"

"The breeder kind. With my people, it's not quite as simple, although it can be. It's just a matter of . . ." He giggled and did not finish his sentence.

Ingrid looked up at him from behind her glasses. "I mean, I understand the mechanics of the thing. I'm not totally clueless, nor totally naïve, Hudson; it's just, I haven't really done anything except a little heavy petting."

"Petting? As in a zoo? What is this, the fifties? You want me to . . . what?"

"I don't know, Hudson. Would you stop looking at me like that! I don't know, explain things a little. The ins and outs . . ."

They both stared at each other, and then burst out laughing. "The ins and outs," he echoed.

"It's not like I'm asking you to sleep with me or anything like that," Ingrid said dryly.

"Of course not. You're perfectly lovely but far from my type. I'm sorry, Ingrid. It's just you're so discreet otherwise. I never imagined you'd ever talk about your"—he coughed—"*sex life*."

"Well, that's because I don't have one," she said. She hadn't seen Matt since that heady make out session in his car on their second first date because he'd had to go out of town for several days.

"We could look at a *Cosmo*. I can explain the articles ... Is there a reason this is coming up now?" he ventured, with a raise of his eyebrow. "Things with Officer Noble are coming to a head, so to speak?"

"Stop making bad jokes!" Ingrid laughed. "And I've read a lot of *Cosmo*s already."

"I think I need a Cosmo. You know, a cocktail, for this conversation. So, how far have you two crazy kids gotten?"

"I don't know ... Second base I guess?"

"Right, the petting zoo. Well great, that's great. It's a start. Baby steps," said Hudson as he clapped his hands. "This is truly great news, my dear. First off, that's much, much further than Caitlin ever got with him, you know? Okay!"

Hudson stood up and paced the office frantically. "We need to prepare for this, Ingrid. Maybe one of Freya's potions? You know, just to loosen you up." He made a wavy gesture with his hands. "Do you have any sexy lingerie? A girl needs those." He snapped his fingers. "We could order some stuff online! Or maybe Freya can help you with that. Take you shopping in Manhattan? That girl certainly knows how to doll herself up." He had turned into a dervish, whirling this way and that in the office, pointing a finger at Ingrid every time a new idea occurred to him.

"That all sounds great"—Ingrid nodded—"but I was wondering if ... I don't know ... I mean, is there other stuff we could do ... that he and I could do ... without doing ... you know, *it*. I don't think I'm quite ready yet ... but surely we could sort of ... you know ... try other stuff?"

"Other stuff?" The eyebrow shot up again.

Ingrid thought she would die in a puddle of embarrassment.

"I've got it!" he said, pointing at the computer.

"What?"

"Porn!"

"Pornography? We're going to look at pornography? Hudson— no." She shook her head. "Just . . . no!"

"Aw, come on, there's nothing like the Internet to give you ideas on 'other stuff.'" He smirked.

Ingrid sighed and let him click away on the computer. She had come to him in her hour of need, and like it or not, Hudson was finding a way to come through. She had to trust him since this was all, well, virgin territory to her.

chapter twenty-two

That Loving Feeling

ञ

N orman finally explained what he had been trying to get across in his last phone message to Joanna. He wanted things to be peaceful between them. He admitted he had been at fault, had acted the coward during the Salem trials, and added that if she would let him, he would like to make it up to her. He knew this was a mild way of putting it, of course, but there was no other way of saying it. In the meantime, however, he asked for leniency and wanted permission to begin reestablishing a relationship with his daughters. Joanna had settled it over the phone when she had returned his call, agreeing that he could come for a visit. That was where they would start for now: give things a test drive.

Now Norman, Freya, and Ingrid sat on the couch before a crackling fire in Joanna's living room, having their first intimate family powwow since the library fund-raiser that summer, while Joanna hid out in her study poring over various ancient books on *seid*. She had been searching under the topic "rituals of necromancy." She still hadn't decoded the message the spirit left and was on to the next order of business while she took a break from all the letters of the runes pieces swirling around in her brain.

She had arrived at an impasse. From the runes, she knew the spirit wished to communicate with her, but she hadn't found anyone in the glom, so she needed to seek a new approach. She could travel to the Kingdom of the Dead and try to garner gossip or hearsay on this particular spirit's whereabouts, but doing so might bring many a false lead. Resentful of their deaths, new spirits often acted out and could be spiteful and deceptive. She didn't want to waste time on a fool's errand, following leads to dead ends. If this were an older spirit, she might have to appeal to Helda to release it, and Joanna wished to bypass the Queen of the Dead altogether if she could.

The books recommended performing a ritual on the gravesite of the deceased in question. She would have to return to the mound in the woods to do so. Drawing the standard circle around the site would be required, which could be done with salt or stones. All four elements—earth, air, fire, and water—would have to be represented in the ritual to achieve balance in the magic and prevent it from going amiss. Some of the rites included recipes listing sacrificial blood as an ingredient, but Joanna found such a practice outmoded. Wearing garments belonging to the dead person was yet another suggestion, albeit morbid and, in this case, impossible.

For the rite, she would bake unleavened black bread and uncork the homemade grape juice she had made from the concord grapes picked in September from her garden. Consuming such foods symbolized embracing decay and lifelessness, a gesture of compassion toward the spirit itself, becoming one with it, so to speak.

She reread the section in the *Hrólf Kraki's Saga*, involving one Skuld, a half-elfin, half-Valkyrie princess skilled in the art of witchcraft, an unconquerable warrior but a rather merciless one, as she wouldn't let any of her soldiers rest, bringing them immediately back from the dead as soon as they'd fallen in battle so they would continue fighting. She glanced at "The Spell of Gróa" in *The Poetic Edda* to see how Svipdag raised his mother, Groa, whose advice he needed on how to handle the wild-goose chase his stepmother had sent him on—the hand of the fair Mengloth. There wasn't much there but the following: "Awake, Groa, awake! From the door of the dead, I wake you." She would need to come up with a better incantation than that, so she continued searching.

The phone in the living room rang. It was the only landline in the house. Annoyed by the interruption, she walked into the living room, but by the time she had gotten there, Freya had answered the call.

Her daughter covered the mouthpiece with a hand and crinkled her nose at Joanna. "It's that man. The one who was here the other day? He says his name is *Harold*." She grimaced.

This is awkward, thought Joanna, taking the phone from Freya, who went and sat back on the couch with Norman. Ingrid flanked him on his other side. They looked cozy those three, complicit, and Joanna caught herself envying them, feeling left out.

They watched her as she took the call. She turned away from them, facing the window that looked out to the sea. It was pitch-dark out there and they could see her reflection in the glass and she theirs, observing her.

"Hi, Harold," she said. "Good to hear from you. How are you?"

Harold talked enthusiastically and loudly, and most likely they could hear his voice booming from the phone. "I'm great, great, but really I would love to see you again." Joanna tried to muffle him by pressing the phone harder against her ear, which made it hurt.

"Yes, that would be fantastic," she said, then tried to cut the conversation short. "Listen, I have a guest, and my girls are both here tonight. Could I call you back, say, tomorrow?"

"Not a problem, dear. Just checking in, really. I thought we could set another date."

"Yes, yes. I'll be talking to you soon, then, Harold."

The girls and Norman continued to glare wordlessly at her reflection. She and Harold said quick good-byes, and Joanna felt awful for nearly hanging up on the poor man. She turned toward the three on the couch and forced a smile.

Norman's turquoise eyes squinted at her from behind his black-rimmed glasses. He had shaved for the journey to North Hampton, looked polished and well-groomed, which was something she had always appreciated about him. When they'd been together, she had never needed to tell him to shower, trim his nails, or observe any of the obvious rules of hygiene, which some men annoyingly appeared to require. He had taken to wearing his silver hair in a buzz cut; she knew it was so he wouldn't have to fuss over it. He had beautiful thick hair and had been fortunate not to lose any of it, but she wished he kept it longer. He was such a practical man.

133

"Harold?" he said with a puzzled expression.

"Yes, a gentleman I've been dating," she said.

Now he looked seriously annoyed. "You're *seeing* someone?"

Joanna knew they could see her blushing, which only made her cheeks grow hotter. Why was Norman giving her the third degree? They hadn't even worked out whether they were still married or not. She had put it on her agenda of things to do—broach the topic with him now that he would be occasionally dropping by to visit the girls. Was he interested in her? She had no idea if he might still have feelings for her, and right now he appeared conspicuously jealous. She had thought he wanted peace, to work toward a friendship of sorts.

Freya stood up, and Joanna could see the little girl who got frustrated and angry and was ready to hex anyone who stepped on her toes. She was pushing her wild red hair this way and that. "Yeah, Mother, what's that all about. *Why* are you dating? I mean, you and Dad are still married, aren't you?"

Ingrid wasn't much help; Joanna thought at least her oldest would jump to her defense. Instead she gaped at her hands that lay limply in her lap.

"Am I suddenly under attack?" was all she could think to say.

Norman took a breath and sighed. "I just thought that we were going to give this a try, you know, being a family again."

Joanna studied all three of them expectantly watching her. She shrugged. "I really had no idea that was on the agenda for tonight!" she said. "Why don't you and I go in my study, Norman, and have a talk while the girls make dinner. There's something I want to show you in there anyway."

Norman rose, following Joanna; then Ingrid and Freya's eyes locked as they smiled gleefully at each other.

chapter twenty-three

Wanted: Dead or Alive

ᔇᔆ

Freya stepped into the greenhouse to search for Killian. She saw him at the far end, crouched by the Venus flytraps. He was feeding them with a pair of long metal tweezers, placing insects inside the jaws of those odd light green flowers with long teeth, until each flower mouth clamped shut over the squirming ant or cricket.

He hadn't heard her enter, so she watched him for a while, admiring his fine profile, the curve of his lips, the perfectly straight nose, his body lean and languid in his flannel shirt and torn jeans. He found solace here, she knew, lost himself in nurturing the plants, adding new ones, a little world he could control, make just right. His face looked troubled, the bend of his shoulders heavy. Her impulse was to run to him, hold him, reassure him, but she knew she couldn't. She moved along the path by the lily pond, calling out his name.

He turned to her and smiled. "I missed you."

"Me, too," she said.

"I'm glad you came." He walked toward her, and they hugged, but she could feel the sadness in his hold, the tentativeness of it, all the confidence he had always appeared to possess was gone. The binds that had held them together even while they had been apart had begun to fray. She heard a noise outside and started and stepped away from him, listening. It sounded like cans falling, clanking against each other. "Don't worry, probably a deer. Maybe a raccoon. They're always getting into the trash and compost."

"I came to tell you something," Freya said. There was a small bench between two palms nearby, and they walked to it. The air in the greenhouse grew cloyingly thick, and Freya found it difficult to breathe. She sat, staring into Killian's face while he remained standing. "Freddie told me he could prove you were the one who destroyed the bridge. The thing I was searching for on the *Dragon* . . . I looked and looked and couldn't find it." She stared imploringly.

Something flickered in Killian's eye. "What was it?" he asked.

"His trident. I need to know if you have it. Do you?"

He stared at her silently, his face clouding over. "I don't, Freya, but . . ."

"But what?"

Killian began unbuttoning his shirt, his expression deadpan. "There's something you need to see . . ."

Freya laughed. "Haven't I seen it all?" She was grateful to him for attempting to lighten the mood.

Killian wasn't laughing, though. "I don't think you've ever noticed. Or maybe it just didn't register." He removed his shirt, pulled off the T-shirt beneath it, let both drop, and then stood bare chested before her.

"You want to show me your perfect six-pack?"

"No." He turned around.

His summer tan had almost entirely faded. He instructed Freya to look at his back, where she now saw a smattering of freckles across the shoulders. It continued across his spine. At first glance, the freckles appeared haphazard, but on closer inspection, she saw that if she connected the dots, the lines would form the shape of a trident. Now she saw it clearly and remembered what Freddie had told her: *Whoever stole it will bear its mark.*

Killian bore the mark of the trident.

Freddie was right. Killian was guilty.

chapter twenty-four

Do You Believe
in Magic

I t was halfway through Counseling Services hour, and a lineup of North Hamptonites sat in the waiting area outside Ingrid's office. A tall, pallid, anorexic-looking blond stared glumly ahead, tapping a toe on the floor, an elderly lady and gentleman chatted, and a woman with a frosted graduated bob (who obviously got her hair done on the other side of Long Island) filed her nails, a tot in the chair beside her playing a video game on an iPhone.

Inside Ingrid's office, redolent of burnt sage, the curtains had been drawn, a pentagram sketched in chalk on the floor, five white candles lit at each corner of the star within the circle. A young man, Sander Easterly, stood inside the star in his grease-stained mechanic's coveralls. He was a tall twenty-one-year-old and so thin as to make his chest appear concave, or perhaps it was that he slouched, ashamed of his height. He had jet-black hair, blue eyes, and a prominent case of acne.

He told Ingrid that his face had started to break out midway through high school and how he had gone from popular kid to pariah. There had been myriad visits to doctors and dermatologists; he had tried every type of prescription, traditional and experimental, as well as all the infomercial panaceas touted by an endless parade of famous faces with flawless skin. In short, nothing had worked. He had been called horrible names and continued to be—"pizza face," uttered by a small child, the most agonizing. A math and science whiz, Sander was a lover of Stephen Hawking and Brian Greene, and had been offered a scholarship to study physics at a highly reputable Massachusetts university but had been held back by his "handicap." He had remained in North Hampton, working as a mechanic at a local garage. He had never fallen in love, but that was okay, because love, as he saw it, was a fable. Ingrid felt a deep sympathy for him, even though she knew her own handicap had been fortunately invisible.

She faced him, eyes closed, mumbling beneath her breath, asking for guidance from gods and spirits alike. Then she found herself zipping through the underlayer, her body hurtling through darkness, as if she had fallen into a wormhole, an Alice tumbling down to Wonderland kind of feeling—scary but thrilling. She came to a sudden stop and floated there. She saw Sander in what appeared to be the not-so-distant future, doing a salutation to the sun on a beach. Was it in North Hampton? He was perfect, really, so beautiful, his black hair lifting in the wind, just a few scars left over from the acne that had plagued him, giving him character, as they say. There was a book in the sand, and she had just enough time to glimpse its cover—*Bhagavad Gita*—before she was speeding down again, as words whispered past her. There was another catch in the wormhole, as if a parachute had opened above her and yanked her up, and now she floated down as gently as a feather, spying an arena below her dangling feet. As she descended further, she saw an older, confident Sander speaking at some sort of international conference. Her eyes popped open.

"It's all going to be fine," she said. "I am going to release you."

Her hands fluttered around his head, neck, and then above his chest. She saw his pounding heart, a black tar resembling mechanic's grease enveloping it. *A black heart*, she thought,

139

momentarily frightened, but the ooze hadn't seeped into his soul yet. Her hands squeezed the black goo from the organ as it contracted and expanded. She worked until she could see each artery, the thick superior vena cava and aorta. She shook her hands above her head, sending the viscous substance back from whence it came. A light shot out from his heart, and as it did, Ingrid experienced her own kind of deliverance.

"There you go. You can step out of the circle now, and I am going to write down a few things for you—a prescription, but not like any you've ever been given before."

Sander smiled at her, stepping out of the pentagram. "I feel lighter," he remarked.

"That's good!" At her desk, Ingrid wrote down a list on her pad that included yoga, the book *Bhagavad Gita*, the words *string unification*, the name Melody, and a list of herbs and tonics. "Freya, my sister, can probably supply you with some of these herbs if you stop by the North Inn. Or you can try Whole Foods if you're not a 'bar person.'" She handed the list to Sander.

"Whole Paycheck? Actually, I very well might hit your sister up. Thanks so much, Ingrid. I don't know if I am a believer, but I'm willing to give it a shot. I've heard great things about you."

Ingrid walked Sander to the door, where Tabitha and Hudson waited outside.

Tabitha gave Ingrid a huge grin. "Gentleman to see you! He's looking at the new arrivals display."

"Your man?" whispered Hudson, raising an eyebrow.

"Okay, got it!" said Ingrid, and the two shuffled off, although *waddled* might have been a better description for Tabitha. Ingrid looked at her lineup. "I am really truly sorry," she said. "But you are all going to have to come back tomorrow. I have some unexpected business to attend to."

The line had gotten longer, and some people were standing,

because there weren't enough chairs. They let out a collective "*Aw!*" The frail-looking blond, who would have been next, rushed up to Ingrid, pleading in the quietest voice. Ingrid wondered whether it was because if she spoke any louder she might crumple from the effort. She had the kind of face that wasn't particularly arresting at first glance, until Ingrid noticed the perfect symmetry, the beauty in its simplicity and ingenuousness, like a single line drawing. *This girl could be a supermodel,* she thought. But she said, "Again, I apologize. Come promptly at noon so you'll be the first in line. What's your name?"

"Melody," the young woman said in that same wispy voice.

"Oh!" said Ingrid, surprised to be hearing the name so soon—or even hearing it at all—that it seemed like an echo of the whisper she'd heard during her trance with Sander. The marvelous synchronicity of it gave her goose bumps. "Yes, please come back. I'll be sure to see you first thing at noon tomorrow, Melody."

Her clients filed out of the waiting area with hangdog expressions, and Ingrid returned to her office, where she opened the curtains to let the light flood back in. She put her placard in the drawer, snuffed out the candles, put them away, and then used a chalkboard eraser to remove the pentagram from the floor. There was a knock at the door. Ingrid rose, brushing the chalk off her skirt, and went to open it.

"Hi," said Matt, standing in the doorway in his usual beige sport coat and tan slacks.

"Come in," she said, beaming. "Nice to see you."

"Yeah, me, too. I mean, great seeing you, Ingrid."

She closed the door behind him, and they faced each other in the middle of her office. He placed a hand on her shoulder and kissed her on the lips, but they both jumped at the screech, followed by a voice booming from his hip. He hadn't turned off his walkie-talkie.

"I'm on Seashell Lane and Vine. Have not spotted suspect yet, over."

"Hang in there, Holding. I mean, Holding, *hold* your position, over."

"Very funny, McCluskey! Over."

Matt pulled the walkie-talkie out of his holster and turned it off. "Sorry about that!"

"You had it on in the library?" she asked.

Matt looked at her sheepishly. "Kind of. Sorry! Actually, I'm here on business."

There was a lot of getting used to with a person you liked so much. Ingrid remembered all the online lingerie shopping she had done the other night, and she blushed, as if Matt might be able to read her mind. "Have a seat," she said.

Apparently, there had been another burglary in the North Hampton area, and Matt wanted to know the latest on the band of homeless kids Ingrid had mentioned earlier.

Without batting an eye, Ingrid lied to him and said they had most definitely left town. The pixies were, of course, still plaguing her up in Joanna's attic. They had promised to be good, but were they up to their pranks again? Had they been involved in these thefts? She was going to have to sit down with them again and have a chat. They had seemed to be behaving themselves, but she really had gotten nowhere with them. She'd been unable to help them remember where was home, and now she believed they might be suffering from some sort of spell that kept them from knowing. She really needed to get them home.

Ingrid winced but attempted to reassure Matt, saying that she had seen to it herself, put them on a bus and sent them home. "Gone. Bye-bye. Adios. Sayonara," she said.

Matt rubbed his eyes. "You're sure?"

"I made sure I saw them get on the bus. Then I watched it

leave," she reiterated. She felt horrible but manage to force a smile.

"Okay," said Matt. "It's the strangest thing, Ingrid. We're dealing with a highly skilled thief or group of thieves. Like all the recent burglaries, this one showed no signs of break-in—no busted locks or broken windows. And it's not just the small stuff, like jewelry, that disappears but large items—paintings and sculptures. Some of it quite priceless."

"Oh, my!" remarked Ingrid. If the pixies were the ones behind the burglaries, surely she would be able to find the loot somewhere in the house. Something like a painting took up space. She would sift through the attic and see if they were hiding anything up there and return it immediately. The pixies never stole for money, however. They only took things that caught their eye, whether it was a marble or a Picasso; they had no understanding or concept of money. They just liked beautiful things.

"I missed you," said Matt. "Did I tell you that or was I just thinking it?"

"Thinking it," said Ingrid with a laugh.

He smiled. "Want to do something this weekend? I'd really like to." He appeared to be hinting at something.

"Sure," she said, wondering if he was thinking what she was thinking.

chapter twenty-five

Black Magic Woman

~ஐ~

A blood moon had risen, casting a soft, eerie light into the woods. The wind swept leaves across the clearing, where five torches surrounded the burial mound beneath the large oak tree. Joanna had worked since dusk, gathering stones to make a circle around the torches. Such rituals worked best during nocturnal hours.

She placed a bowl of water at the foot of the mound. The torches, rocks, and water represented three elements, and for the fourth she had brought a Tibetan singing bowl, whose vibrating harmonic overtones would stand for air and also wake the spirit from the dead. After the ritual of *utiseta* (sitting at the crossroads) had been completed, she would recite a simple Norse incantation to tease the spirit out further.

Inside the circle, she kneeled by the water, her singing bowl and wand in her lap, the basket of unleavened black bread and chalice of grape juice at one side. She had decided on an amalgam of practices, to improvise, letting her witch senses guide her. She took a piece of black bread. *Decay.*

"Return to the flesh," she said, placing the bread in her mouth. "Return to the blood." She took a sip from the chalice.

She swallowed, dipped her hands in the bowl of water for purification, then ran her wand around the rim of the singing bowl, drawing out its sound, and the hum spread through the forest. The leaves of the trees shivered as a sudden gust swept through the woods.

She put the singing bowl and wand down and stood for the incantation, feeling the air grow electric inside the circle. She loved this feeling, the intoxication and power of magic. She was careful to pronounce the words correctly, enunciate each syllable.

When she opened her eyes, she saw a green wisp of light wriggling out of the earth like a worm. It began to grow on top of the mound, first turning into a glowing orb, then stretching like a flame, until it became as big as she was, and she saw the outline of the wraith.

It was a young woman with a pale round face in a white cloth cap trimmed with lace that was folded back above her wide forehead. She wore a blouse with a large white shirt collar, buttoned to the neck and ripped at the shoulder, a gray bodice, and a dark apron tied around the high waist of a long maroon skirt. Above her rose-petal red lips was a small round black mole. She reminded Joanna of Vermeer's *The Milkmaid*, although she was not as thick or solid-looking as the milkmaid, thinner but curvy. She hovered there above the grave, with her pouting lips, her shoulders bending toward Joanna. She was breathtaking, really.

Joanna stepped closer. The wraith was speaking, but she couldn't hear her. As Joanna moved in, the girl's hand darted out, seizing her by the throat. Her grip was so strong it felt as if she had turned to flesh and blood, and Joanna struggled to breathe as a smell of decomposition wafted across her face. Her arms flailed.

"Find me!" said the girl close to Joanna's ear.

Then she vanished, like a dream ending abruptly but still holding her in its grip. Joanna gasped as the chokehold released and she fell onto all fours, half outside the circle, her body racked by coughing until she could breathe again.

145

chapter twenty-six

Stray Cat Strut

ر‌ے

Freya carried two enormous bags of trash to the Dumpsters in the car park behind the North Inn. It was after midnight on a weeknight, and the very last barfly had drunkenly scuttled out. It had been Freya's turn to lock up; no one ever liked doing it, especially alone.

"Oh, Kristy," she muttered to herself. "Why'd you have to go and have babies so young?"

She looked up and saw a full moon. No wonder it had been off-kilter in the bar tonight. She had thought it was all her fault, fixated as she was by the image of the trident on Killian's back, which she was still trying to understand. She had been distracted, couldn't focus, and her magic had gone limp: none of the potions had their usual fizz or aphrodisiacal tang, the drinks were oddly flavorless and bland, and today a customer had even remarked that she'd never tasted anything so bitter.

Freya lifted the heavy lid of the Dumpster, dejectedly tossing one bag after another inside it, bottles clanking, then swiped her hands on her jeans. They were dirty anyway, splashed with all kinds of liquor, reminding her of the indigenously named Long Island iced tea. She hugged her thin leather jacket as she started out toward the Mini, feeling uneasy. It was a chilly November night.

She hit the unlock button on her key fob, and her car bleeped back at her among the cars of the lodgers staying at the North Inn in the B&B section. She recognized the red Mazda of the girl who worked the night desk. To the right of the Dumpsters was a dimly lit alley that led to the back of the French beachside restaurant everyone in town, including Joanna, had raved about—although she and Killian had yet to try it. As she walked past the alley on the way to the Mini, she saw two shadows moving. They were walking toward her. She ducked behind a car and peered through the windows.

She would recognize him anywhere: Freddie, her twin. The glow around his face and golden hair lit him up like a firefly. But who was he with? A tall, broad-shouldered man, standing across from her brother but hidden in shadow. She could barely make him out. He was sporting a captain's hat—that much she could tell—or was it a police officer's hat? Freddie and the shadowy figure shook hands then parted ways, the man now moving toward her. Still, Freya couldn't get a better glimpse of him from her vantage point, and she needed to follow Freddie to see what he was up to. He had taken off in the direction of the French restaurant.

Ducking, she wended through the parked cars, as she heard the mystery man get into one of the cars behind her and peel out. It all happened too fast to catch the make of the car or a license plate, and she'd been too intent on following her twin. She scrambled down the alley, hugging the wall, hiding in the shadows, then caught up with him.

Now she watched him in the parking lot of the French restaurant. She scuttled low between the cars until she got as close as she could. He was with a young woman, but she could only make out her tall silhouette and long hair. She had her back to Freya. When the girl turned around, Freya had to duck lest she be seen.

But she heard something Freddie said: "It won't be long now." Then a door slammed shut. Freya quickly peeked again.

Freddie was coming around the car to get in the passenger seat, and then the two took off.

What had her brother gotten himself into? He was boldly walking around North Hampton, meeting strange characters in dark alleys, when he claimed it was paramount that nobody know he was back.

chapter twenty-seven

Stand under My Umbrella
(ella . . . ella . . . ella)

~25~

W hat's that noise?" Freya stepped out of her room on the second floor of Joanna's house, running smack into Ingrid tightening the belt of her white peignoir.

Ingrid's eyes fluttered behind her glasses. It was early, and she had barely splashed water on her face when she'd heard the noise and was about to run up to the attic to tell the pixies to pipe down. "What noise? I didn't hear a noise," she replied, making a point of saying it in a loud voice, hoping the pixies would hear her and zip it.

The sisters stared at each other. Above them came another loud scudding sound as if something heavy were being dragged across the floor from one end of the attic to the other.

"That noise!" said Freya, pointing toward it.

Ingrid tried to move discreetly toward the stairway to block it. "Oh, that's nothing. I think Oscar and Siegfried went up there to play earlier this morning."

Noises resounded again—something crashed, followed by a pattering of feet.

"You mean to say that my cat and your griffin are playing house up there? And that they've grown human feet?"

"Yes, exactly," said Ingrid emphatically. "They're practicing shape-shifting."

"Funny, because I just saw Siegfried curled up on my bed," retorted Freya. At the sound of his name, Siegfried darted out from Freya's bedroom and came to rub himself on her calf. She looked down at the purring black cat, squinted dubiously at Ingrid, then smirked. "Okay, spill it." She knew this wasn't fair. She had plenty of her own secrets, but she couldn't help it.

Ingrid placed one hand on the banister and the other against the wall, lifting her chin, clearly barring the stairs. Freya, in her short black kimono, pressed her body against Ingrid's, trying to push past.

"All right, all right, I'll show you!" Ingrid relented, letting Freya through. "I can explain!" Ingrid called to Freya's back, quickly following her up.

Freya swung the door open, Ingrid on her heels.

The attic had been rearranged so that the furniture, no longer haphazardly scattered, created what resembled a dormitory room with various sleeping areas. There were no more piled-up boxes. Instead, clothes hung on metal rolling racks, which Ingrid had never seen before. The pixies had bathed. Ingrid noted they cleaned up well and were easy on the eyes, with their pointy, delicate features and shimmering skin.

Sven lay on a daybed in his area, reading an Agatha Christie novel while smoking a cigarette, an ashtray on the bedside table next to his pack of Kools. Irdick was in his own makeshift cubicle, swinging to and fro in a rocking chair. Kelda and Nyph, children's costumes pulled over their dark clothing, sat on a double bed, playing the popular seventies game Mastermind. Val was taking a break from pushing a steamer trunk into a corner and was now straightening his Mohawk with his palms. They had all stopped whatever activities they were in the midst of to stare at the two witches who had barged in on them.

"Why didn't you tell me you were hiding fairies?" asked Freya, squinting at them.

Ingrid sighed, walking over to Sven to snuff out his cigarette in the ashtray and confiscate the pack of Kools. She turned to Freya. "They're not fairies. They're pixies and they're lost. I've been letting them stay here until we can figure out how to get them home, only they don't remember where home is," she said in one breath. "So they're sort of like refugees."

"She's letting us crash in her crib until—" Sven began, but Ingrid cut in.

"I just said that, Sven. And there is—as *I've* already expressed—a no-smoking policy in here. If you want to smoke, do it outside!" She pointed to a window, knowing that was how the pixies came and went, rather than down the stairs and through the house, adept at scaling roofs and walls as they were.

Freya gaped incredulously at Ingrid. "Does Mom know you're harboring fugitives?"

"They're not fugitives. They're refugees! There's a difference." Ingrid glared at her sister. "They haven't done anything wrong, I mean, not recently. They've been *relatively* quiet and well-behaved until this morning. Kind of." She scanned the room, giving each one the evil eye. "You know what I'll do if you don't do everything I say, don't you?" she whispered.

"Yes," they all said in unison, adamantly nodding their heads. "Frogs."

"Ribbit," Val joked.

"We promise to be good!" Kelda threw in.

"Your promises don't amount to much," Ingrid remarked.

She went on to explain to Freya all that had happened from the start with the pixies, how they'd asked her for help by stealing her away to a seedy motel they were squatting in, and how she had been searching for a spell to counteract their collective amnesia, had tried several, but none had worked.

"Motel? What motel?" Freya asked suspiciously.

"You know—the one off the highway, that's sort of sinking."

Freya nodded; she knew it well but didn't tell that to Ingrid. She realized now that she'd seen Ingrid on the night she was describing. She'd thought Ingrid had been with Matt, but no—she'd been helping out these "refugees."

Ingrid told her about the latest on the burglaries (while surreptitiously keeping an eye to see how the pixies would react), how Matt knew about the pixies but thought they were just a band of homeless kids, and that she'd been forced to lie to him because he would never understand any of it. He, um, didn't believe in magic.

"He doesn't believe in magic?" Freya asked. "What does he think you are then—just a librarian?"

"He'll come around," Ingrid said. "That's not the problem right now."

Ingrid interrogated the pixies—as Freya watched, impressed by her sister's surprisingly adept police techniques—but they denied any involvement in the current string of robberies and told her they would be happy for her to search the place if she felt the need.

"Well, you could be hiding the loot elsewhere," Ingrid retorted. "For example, where did those come from?" She pointed to the clothes racks, then crossed her arms and tapped a foot.

"We found them here and mounted them. We thought they would provide better spatial economy than the boxes," said Nyph.

"Plausible with all the stuff Mother has kept here over the years," commented Freya.

"Can you please keep this a secret?" Ingrid implored her sister.

"Sure," said Freya.

"You know Mom's not fond of pixies—all those cautionary tales she told us as kids about pixies doing horrible things to children. I don't think these guys are that kind, though, even if they are a handful. But I don't think Mother will make the distinction."

"Horrible things to children!" repeated Irdick from the rocking chair, then grinned stupidly.

"Maybe they're just a little annoying?" said Freya.

Since the pixies came and went through the windows, the sisters agreed they should lock the attic door in case Joanna tried to come up. They would tell Mother they had misplaced the key if she asked. Ingrid would continue to bring the pixies food in the mornings and evenings, although the pixies claimed there were better eats to be found elsewhere, like behind the French restaurant where they'd been scavenging the Dumpsters. But that nice French waiter had noticed and was now feeding them, so Ingrid really didn't have to bother with dinner anymore. Freya promised Ingrid to look into an amnesia-lifting spell, or perhaps a potion was in order, some sort of antidote.

Ingrid saw that something was troubling Freya, and she had to ask. "You look worn out. What's up?" She placed a hand over her sister's forehead.

Freya wanted to blab all her secrets to Ingrid, let them pour out and sob like a little girl on her older sister's shoulder. She *was* worn out. It had been a relief to have finally told Killian that Freddie was back from Limbo, but now it looked as if Freddie was right, that it *was* Killian who had sent him there, and now she had to hide that, too.

She wished she could confess everything to Ingrid, whom she missed terribly and whose sage advice she craved. She wanted her ally back. But it was too dangerous. Ingrid would side with justice, no matter who was at risk. If Killian did it, he would have to pay the price and take the punishment.

So instead she said, "Just work," and shrugged it off with a glum smile.

153

chapter twenty-eight

Season of the Witch

ᨀ

Joanna received an e-mail from Norman; the subject line read "Runes." When he was last at the house and they had gone into the study to discuss the status of their relationship, she had told Norman everything about the spirit and the message on the grave. She had used all the letters of the runes' names, believing that there might be an anagram hidden within them along with that number, perhaps a date, but the process had driven her mad, and she still hadn't decoded the message. If there were something she had overlooked, Norman would see it. Ingrid hadn't come up with any answers, either. Her oldest appeared altogether elsewhere these days, and mysterious packages kept arriving at the house that kept causing Ingrid to blush.

Joanna clicked on the e-mail, eager to get Norman's feedback, especially after the frightening *utiseta* experience on the burial site, when the wraith wrapped her fingers around her neck and implored Joanna to look for her. She still had no idea whether this spirit were a benign or malignant one. Maybe Ingrid was right. The message could be an evil one. The girl *had* threatened her, or so it had seemed, but it was possible that having only limited time to manifest in mid-world, the wraith had struck out, grabbed at Joanna wherever she could, to convey the urgency of her plea. Perhaps she had meant no harm. She read Norman's letter.

<<Dear Jo:

I would have written sooner but have taken on such a heavy load this semester I've barely had time to breathe until now. This is not to say that you haven't been on my mind every second.

First, I need to say I am deeply sorry to have made such a scene re this Harold gentleman. Of course, by now you have come to have your own life, and I understand that. We have been separated for several centuries (since 1692 to be exact), and I realize that life does go on.

However, I must make this clear: my feelings for you have not changed, nor ever will. The truth of the matter is I am still in love with you, darling, and I do harbor the hope that someday you might be willing to give our marriage another chance. I hope you won't fault a man for dreaming. It truly would be lovely to be a family once more, but foremost, I wish to capture your heart again. I am not sure how to go about that, and if anything, I have already fudged it by letting jealousy get the best of me: "the green ey'd monster, which doth mock the meat it feeds on." Yes, my feelings got out of hand. You are a free agent. I cannot dictate your heart, as much as I wish I could. My behavior was, to say the least, deplorable. I hope you'll forgive me.>>

155

Well, this was a slightly different approach from the one Norman had taken in her study, where he had continued to grill her about Harold. It had taken a while to calm him down. He had not made any declarations of love then but instead used the argument of doing what was best for the girls, as if Freya and Ingrid were still small, helpless children. She *had* thought it ridiculous of him and didn't understand why he was making such a fuss. It pleased Joanna that now Norman was not only being more honest with her but also with himself. His letter touched her.

She couldn't help but be flattered that this man who had known her for millennia was still in love with her. He was passionate, and she could forgive him for such a minor outburst of jealousy. Actually, she came to realize—a sudden epiphany sitting there at her desk—she had already forgiven him for everything: not having exercised his powers during the Salem trials in 1692, which would have been futile, anyway. If he had gone against the Council, they would have all been punished in the end. There had been no way of avoiding any of it. Not only that but also Ingrid and Freya had forgiven their father, so why shouldn't she? It made no sense to hold on to a useless grudge, which had the power of turning a good witch bad, white magic to black. Joanna was a well-intentioned witch, and she should have known better.

Last summer, Norman had gone to the Oracle to make sure that she and the girls wouldn't be punished for having breached the Restriction. He had gotten that seemingly ineradicable law lifted in the end, which was no small feat. His heart had always been in the right place, and now she saw that clearly. Even while they had been apart, she had felt his presence, a safety net she knew was always there to catch and cradle her and the girls if ever they fell. Norman had never left her, though she had been the one to oust him. She loved him for his loyalty, she loved him for all of it, and perhaps she, too, had never stopped loving him. She pushed her hair onto a shoulder. Gilly alighted on her desk.

"Aw," she said, feeding her some seeds. "You want us back together, too, don't you? I know what you're getting at, sneaky little raven. But Norman and I must take it slowly. I've grown used to being a single old hag. What to do?"

Gilly pecked mindlessly at the seeds in her palm.

"Yes, I'll think about it. You know I will." She continued to read his e-mail.

<<Second, you have probably figured out the message by now. On the train ride home, I had quickly scribbled it down: *hagalaz, ansuz, wunjo, algiz, manaz, A, laguz,* then *157.* Correct? Do you see it? And there is a separation between the first three runes and the second

three, so that you have to go by the Norn spread reading. If so, this is a clever little spirit, Jo. Not only does she (yes, I believe it is a she) [*Norman was right as usual*, she thought] urge you to travel to her in the runes, she left you a clue as to who, or rather what, she is. Let me know whether you and Ingrid have figured it out yet. If not, I will tell you. I would hate to spoil the fun.>>

Joanna had spent enough time trying to figure out who this wraith was and she had gotten nowhere, so she immediately wrote Norman back.

<<Dear Norman:

I am sorry to have been angry for so long. I have come to understand the decisions you've made and must confess I have been excessively harsh. Feelings, which aren't always rational, have their own life span and sometimes, for whatever reason, need to be lived out. It was a horrible day watching our daughters hanged at Gallows Hill in Salem. But I understand now that it wasn't apathy on your part. There was nothing you could do.

Let's start fresh. We can begin to work toward being comfortable with each other again. I miss your friendship. It would be wonderful if you could come for Thanksgiving dinner next Thursday, and we can discuss all of this further in person.

Yes, I want to know what you discovered about the message. Please let me know ASAP! It is urgent. I made contact but am still at a loss, so any additional information would be helpful.

Jo>>

She hit the Send button, then stared dazedly at the screen, hoping that Norman's reply would be instantaneous. It was early evening and classes were most likely out by now. Was he in his tiny monastic cell, an invisible line connecting them from laptop to laptop?

"Hello, Mother." Ingrid stood in the doorway of Joanna's study. "I heard you talking to yourself."

157

Joanna stared at her pretty daughter in the doorway, her blossomed flower, and laughed. "I was just having a chat with Gilly. Nothing to worry about. I haven't become a crazy witch yet."

"Any progress on the spirit?" Ingrid strode to the love seat against the wall and sat down, crossing her long, slim legs.

Joanna admired how her daughter could wear heels all day long and into the evening. She had a wonderful, understated European style, Ingrid. She recounted everything to her oldest, about how the spirit had told her to find her. She included that Norman had written, saying he had cracked some sort of code in the runes and that she was waiting for his reply, which she made quite obvious by glancing at her computer's screen every few seconds.

Ingrid was irritated with her mother for not having consulted her before performing the ritual as Joanna had promised she would. "You know how tricky and deceptive Helda is. There are all sorts of clauses and subclauses to her damned Covenant. That document is as labyrinthine as the nine circles beyond her gates, and she keeps that book locked away so no one can actually read it—classic obfuscation. I hate to say it, but your sister is a bitch!"

"Oh, my!" said Joanna. "Language, Ingrid."

Ingrid barely acknowledged the comment, only continued. "Well, the only way to find out how that Covenant works is through trial and error. Helda pulls it out only when it's convenient to her. How are we supposed to know every clause if we can't read the thing? And, of course, she has provided for every type of situation. I think there's actually a caveat for simply conversing with the dead, isn't there, Mother?"

"Yes, there is. Darling, there is a reason for all of Helda's laws. Everyone would be immortal if they weren't in place," said

Joanna, distracted. She was looking at the screen of her laptop and clicking the mouse. She had just received a reply from Norman. She began to read it aloud, skipping over the sections addressing their relationship, which Ingrid certainly didn't need to be privy to:

<<As you know, for every rune there is a corresponding and equivalent phonetic value. This is an acrostic. Just use the corresponding letter for each rune and, with the Scrabble *A*, it will spell a word. But the *algiz* tile is off—instead of standing for a *z* or *r* sound, it stands for *a*, the initial of that rune's name. You got the *157.* I think you will figure out what to do from there and have the proper materials to work with.>>

Joanna stared down at the runes spread that was still on her desk as Ingrid came to peer over her shoulder and call out their Norse names. Joanna scribbled them down on a pad as she went, along with their corresponding roman letters:

hagalaz ------> *h*

ansuz --------> *a*

wunjo --------> *w* or *v*

algiz ---------> *z* or *r* but *a* per Norman

manaz -------> *m*

A -------------> *a*

laguz --------> *l*

"The 'Hávamál' poem!" cried mother and daughter in unison.

"Stanza one fifty-seven!" said Joanna, rushing over to her bookshelf. "I was making the puzzle so complicated, looking for an anagram." Joanna scanned her shelves, then pulled out her leather-bound copy of *The Poetic Edda*, a collection of ancient Norse poems. Composed of 165 stanzas, "Hávamál" was a gnomic poem attributed to Odin, written as if he were imparting its wisdom himself—the word *hávamál* meaning "the high one's words." The poem was broken down into five sections: in the penultimate one, Rúnatal, Odin discovers the runes as he hangs wounded from a tree, while in the last section, Ljóðatal, Odin enumerates a list of spells. It was in this last section of the poem that Joanna found stanza 157, and she held the book aloft, reading aloud to Ingrid:

> *A twelfth I know:*
> *If I see in a tree*
> *A corpse from a noose hanging,*
> *Such spells I write and paint in runes,*
> *That the being descends and speaks with me.*

"Oh, my goodness, Mother, could she be a witch who was convicted and hanged?" exclaimed Ingrid.

Joanna thought of the girl and what she was wearing. "Yes, of course, it's a witch who needs my help. One of us, a goddess," added Joanna. "But where is she? Where would I find her and why hasn't she regenerated? Why is she roaming around as a spirit? What's wrong?"

They both spoke over each other. Joanna's dragon-bone runes had been familiar to the wraith because she was one of them— and obviously she knew *The Poetic Edda* well. The grave with the blank headstone had very likely been her hanging as well as burial site. She was from the region. A convicted witch, excommunicated from the church, would be denied a proper burial on hallowed ground. A convicted witch was a dead one, hanged, buried in a shallow grave, usually with no headstone, often without even a record of death, leaving no traces, as if she'd never existed. However, someone had taken the care to provide a headstone for her, a bold and risky act, which suggested she had been loved.

"Dad said she was a girl, but how did he know that? We knew because you saw her," Ingrid said excitedly.

"The Norn spread," said Joanna. "She could have placed the runes another way. But she set them in clusters of three. Maybe Norman is guessing that she is one of the Norns since they're female."

"The girl said, 'Find me!' *Where* is what I want to know," Joanna said.

Ingrid exhaled a lengthy sigh. Decoding messages from the dead was perhaps a fun pastime, but wherever this was leading was apt to be dangerous. "Earlier when I asked you about whether there were consequences to speaking with the dead, you started to say yes, then got distracted."

Joanna peered up at Ingrid, bunching her lips. "Getting information from the dead is a minor infraction. If you take something from that side, Helda takes something back from this side—quid pro quo."

"Well, these quid pro quos might possibly add up if you don't stop here, Mother." Ingrid stared questioningly at Joanna. "Are you going to make contact again?"

"Oh, I am. This girl needs me. I have to help her. It's my calling, darling. I just need to figure out where to find her. Worry not, my child!" This was the thing about the Beauchamp women, the common thread that ran through all of them, hubris: they were each stubborn in their own way and sometimes too confident for their own good.

Ingrid knew there would be no dissuading her mother, but she tried nonetheless. "But I am worried!"

"*Bah!*" said Joanna. "I will do a protection spell to counteract all that. It's nothing. She smiled at her sweet, concerned daughter. "On a lighter note, your father is coming for Thanksgiving. Maybe we can get Freya to cook! Wouldn't that be marvelous?"

Ingrid laughed. "Go ahead and deflect, Mother! You're incorrigible." Once again, Ingrid asked Joanna to promise to come to her for help, despite the fact that her mother had broken the last one. "Double promise this time!"

Joanna winked. "I double promise!"

chapter twenty-nine

The Lying Game

ᴏϲ

A streak of lightning ripped through the blanket of gun-metal clouds, then big, fat, hard drops began to pelt the Mini. The windshield wipers thrummed as Freya tried to peer through the downpour lashing at the window while she gripped at the steering wheel. Along the sides of the small road, cattails and reeds swayed wildly in the squall. It was nasty out there—cold, windy, and now this heavy rain. She pulled into the lot of the Ucky Star and put on the navy slicker she kept in the back-seat. She tugged the hood over her pouf of red hair that became irritatingly static during a storm, grabbed the shopping bag of food on the passenger seat, then made a mad dash toward Fred-die's door, splashed by the sheet of water cascading down from the walkway above. The place looked like a sinking ship.

Freddie let her in. The flimsy walls and windows rattled in the wind, and she heard a *drip, drip, drip* in the bathroom. A leak like that would drive her bonkers. Freddie took the shopping bag and helped her take off the rain slicker, then placed it on a hook by the door. He was in jeans and a turtleneck, a blanket slung over his shoulders. The heaters didn't have much effect, and the room's scent carried a tinge of mildew. It was extremely humid in here.

"Thanks for the food, Freya. I really couldn't do all this holing up without you." He came in for a hug, but she didn't see it, eluding his grasp as she wandered over to the desk.

"I can't stay long. Just here to check up on you. See what's going on, what you've been up to." *All this holing up*, she thought skeptically, picking up a pen on the desk, then throwing it back on the pad. It did look tidier. She gave him that. "So you've just been *holing* up."

"Yeah . . . exactly," he said, nervously picking at his fingernails. He seemed agitated, as if he wanted to say something more but decided not to. "What about you?" he said, his words coming out in a big rush. "Has Killian said anything to you . . . anything that might help me?"

"No! Of course not!" Freya said, suddenly suspicious.

They stared at each other, as if they were trying to get a read, attune their twin senses, but each came up against a wall.

Freddie shrugged. "Anyway, it's not like I can leave. You know that, Freya. I can't risk the Valkyries finding me. Until I know what to do, I absolutely cannot set foot outside this room."

So her brother was blatantly lying to her. She had unmistakably spied him in the alley behind the North Inn. She had never known him to lie, not to her. It wasn't like Freddie to tell a fib; he was too sincere, as earnest as the sun. Although lately, he'd been more of a mercurial twin than a bright and constant one. And what if she were wrong? What if this weren't Freddie at all? She thought of Bran and his deception.

"What's wrong, Freya?" Freddie moved toward her, but she began to back away.

"Nothing's wrong, Freddie. I'm just in a hurry." She had turned around and was already collecting her rain slicker from the hook. "I have to open the bar. I just wanted to say a quick hi and drop off that food." She was thinking of her last moments with Loki. Could he have returned? Might this be him in another disguise? Had she been deceived again?

When she had fallen for Loki's ploy and their love was con-
summated, he was bound to her, obliged to obey her forever. She
had made him give her the ring that allowed him to move between worlds, then return through the hole inside the *Yggdrasil*,
the Tree of Life that also connected all the worlds from whence
he had come. But before he had slipped back into *Yggdrasil*, he
had muttered something in a language she didn't understand.
Had he said he would return then? Perhaps Freya would be
stuck with Loki forever, the god of mischief chasing her throughout eternity, the albatross that never let her rest. *"You are more like
me than you think, dear Freya."* Had he returned as her twin to
prove that to her this time?

She reached for the slicker and felt her arms being clasped.
Freddie—or Loki—swung her around. Their eyes locked. If she
looked hard enough would she see that unscrupulous soul peering through these large green eyes? Instead she saw her reflection, and Freddie let go of her.

"What's gotten into you, Freya?"

Was he trying to manipulate her, tug at her heartstrings? Loki
knew her well. He knew how strong her love was for Freddie.

"I'm sorry. The storm has made me jumpy, and I really have
to get to work," she said.

He narrowed his eyes at her. "Are you sure you haven't found
anything? Nothing? Nothing at all to make you think that your
little brother might be right? That there might be something
about Killian that you're not telling me?"

"God, Freddie, I told you already. I haven't!" She certainly
wasn't about to tell him—whoever he was—about the trident
mark on Killian's back. She wasn't sure of anything anymore,
only that she needed to get out of there.

chapter thirty

Like a Circle in a Spiral

᭝

I think there's a forest and houses above maybe?" Kelda crouched to tie the laces of her combat boots. She had permanently appropriated Freya's black leather mask and looked up at Ingrid through it.

They were up in the attic, and Ingrid had passed around the amnesia antidote Freya had made for her, and now she and the pixies were waiting for it to take effect.

"Does that ring a bell for anyone else?" asked Ingrid. "Anyone?" She held her wand in one hand and tapped it against her palm. Actually, she felt a bit like a schoolmarm, the wand a ruler, the pixies gathered around, staring at her with too much reverence. Well, except for Sven, always the loner, presently sprawled on his bed.

"I think it starts with an *A*," said Irdick. "But it makes my head hurt to think about it."

"What starts with an *A*?" asked Ingrid.

"The place where we're from starts with an *A*, Erda," Sven grumbled from where he lay, an arm swung over his eyes. He hadn't joined them, claiming it made his body too achy thinking about any of it, but Ingrid suspected he was hungover.

"Okay, okay, that's great!" said Ingrid. "We know you can't use money, that the name of the place starts with an *A*, and you live in trees?"

"It's a c-c-c-city," said Val. The front of his Mohawk swooped over an eye.

"There are noises below, other pixies working," said Irdick. *"I think . . .* Ouch!" He put a hand to his forehead.

Ingrid scratched at her head with her wand. "I'm confused."

Nyph came over to Ingrid and tugged at her sleeve. "This antidote isn't working, Erda."

Ingrid started with a sudden realization. "How do you know my name is Erda? How do you know my ancient name?"

Nyph pushed her silky brown hair out of her face and shrugged. "I don't feel well," she said.

"What else?" Ingrid asked, scanning their sharp little faces that stared blankly back at her. This potion of Freya's was clearly not effective, and if anything it was making the pixies ill.

chapter thirty-one

All Ablaze

❧

Now that Joanna was certain the wraith was a dead witch, one whose features recalled Johannes Vermeer's *The Milkmaid*, she decided to use that as a jumping-off point. On the bookshelf in her study, she looked for her book on golden age Dutch painters, where she knew she would find the painting in question. She opened it to the picture, then gazed at the oil on canvas: the arresting touches of cornflower blue in the cloth that draped the edge of the table and the belt of the milkmaid's apron, illuminated by sunlight pouring from a window.

She glanced out at the Atlantic. It was an unusually bright and warm November day, white ripples undulating on the calm surface, all the way to Gardiners Island. It was too cold to garden and Joanna turned back to her work.

The book cited that the exact date of the painting's origin was unknown but placed it at circa 1658. The witch had been dressed in seventeenth-century clothing, but the painting perhaps helped narrow down an approximate time frame.

The settlers had brought the styles of the Continent to the Americas. Still, there were deviations between the wraith's style of dress and the milkmaid's. The fabrics of the wraith's clothing were a palette of somber colors. Her dress, modest in style, covered her nearly completely, which Joanna knew had nothing to do with weather: her hair hidden by the cap, the collar of the blouse beneath her bodice tightly encircling the base of her throat, her sleeves reaching to the wrists (unlike the milkmaid's, which were pushed above the elbows), and her skirt falling past her feet. Any hint of flesh besides face and neck, or parts of the body that might be deemed sensual (chest, cleavage, ankles, or feet) were cloaked. Joanna was familiar with this strict and austere dress code. This girl had been living among English Puritans, just as the Beauchamps had once themselves. The seventeenth-century settlers of Long Island were of the same stock and breed as those who had driven her girls to their nooses at Gallows Hill in Salem.

Joanna gleaned that the girl was about eighteen years of age, of lower station, suggested by the plainness of her dress—a servant or farm woman, the latter common on the east end of Long Island, a region whose economy thrived on sheep, agriculture, and whaling. Perhaps she was married. If she were and because of her social rank, she would go by the title goody (short for good wife or mistress of the house) rather than misses, which was afforded only to the elite. Joanna knew the history. She had lived it.

In 1629, King Charles I granted the Puritans, a persecuted religious splinter group, a charter to establish an English colony in Massachusetts Bay. The territory stretched along the East Coast of North America, including parts of the states of Massachusetts (Salem and Boston), Maine, New Hampshire, Rhode Island, and Connecticut. Falling within this colony was also Maidstone (East Hampton), an obscure little town called Fairstone (North Hampton), and the Isle of Wight (Gardiners Island). Though Fairstone was not listed in any public records, Joanna knew of it, for it was mentioned as the original name of North Hampton in the deed that had come with her house when she had purchased it.

The Puritans' goal, arriving on the buckled-shoe heels of the Pilgrims, was to create a utopia, a community to inspire—or enforce upon—all, a City upon a Hill, a Model of Christian Charity, as one John Winthrop, a settler and Puritan figurehead, had put it.

This new and pure society would be based upon the Bible. In other words, it was a theocracy with no separation of church and state. And as the Book of Exodus states, thou shall not suffer a witch to live.

The Puritans abided in blind faith in the Bible, or at least portended to. Some truly believed witches harmful and feared they might be bewitched, converted into witches themselves (*As if it were such a bad thing, or even possible!* thought Joanna). They saw witches and warlocks as women and men who lustily consorted with the devil (*As if we would ever!*), signing his book in blood.

Such notions, Joanna knew, were born of fanciful and prurient imaginations but were also backed by the prior three hundred years of witch persecutions in Europe. Others arriving on this new turf used witch-hunts as a means to their own selfish ends: to get to their enemies, divest them of their properties (which would go up for public auction once the accused were convicted and hanged), or to point out the rankling nonconformist, the village beggar or madwoman who got on one's nerves, the woman who wasn't as docile and subservient as a good Puritan wife should be, and the girl who was too willful and independent minded.

Witch-hunts, in essence, became a way to establish a pecking order within this so-called perfect society. Those who had crossed over to this side of the Atlantic but didn't subscribe to the belief system had to grit their teeth and conform to the social codes of the majority, lest they be branded witches or warlocks themselves—whether they were or not.

Even before the Salem trials of 1692, accusations of witchcraft ran rampant in New England. The first hanging of a witch in North America took place in 1648 (at least, the first recorded one): Margaret Jones, in fact a real witch living undercover as a Puritan midwife and practitioner of medicine in the Charleston section of Boston. Joanna's dear friend and mentor's profession didn't go over well. Of course, Margaret had returned to mid-world under a new name. She now lived in LA in a rambling house in Topanga Canyons, where she taught yoga, herbal remedies, and helped with a home birth now and then. She had garnered quite the following.

This was the irony: a witch or warlock always returned. Mortals hanged for witchcraft, on the other hand, never got a second chance. Thousands of innocents had been lost in the witch purges from the fifteenth century on.

Joanna strode to her bookshelf and searched for books on seventeenth-century witch-hunts in North America, specifically ones in the environs of Long Island.

chapter thirty-two

Will Always Love You

～ℯ～

They met in their favorite place, their safe harbor. Freya could not fight the pull. It was carnal—his lips, his sweet breath, like cucumbers and yogurt, the silk of his skin, the feel of his sinewy limbs, the unhurried grace with which his body received hers. It was an unseasonably beautiful day. Above the translucent dome of the greenhouse was a mackerel sky, blue slowly seeping through the scallop of clouds. They sat on the edge of the lily pond, Killian running his fingers through the water, his eyes on Freya's.

"There has to be a reason . . ." she said. They were talking about the pattern of the freckles on his back.

He drew his hand out of the lily pond and placed a wet finger on her lips, then let it slide down to her chin. "*Shh,*" he said. "I am enjoying being here with you." The light brought out the golden peach in Freya's hair, cheeks, and lips, a delicate orange-pink. He sat there calmly with her.

There is no way he is guilty, Freya thought. She felt this through and through, to her core. Of all people, she would be able to tell. If there had been any violence in Killian's past, she would have seen it in a vision, where she saw the rawest of emotions, those polar extremes—love and rage.

There had been those moments of doubt, sure, when she'd

believed she saw something terrible and blank in his eyes, but she now believed they had been induced by Freddie's nonstop haranguing. When she looked at Killian now, she saw only kindness. She wasn't under a spell, either—not like the time she had fallen for Bran—when Loki had bewitched her, clouded her vision, rendered her unable to detect his evil. She had allowed herself to be deceived then, but she was certain she was not deceived this time. Her eyes were wide open, and she saw Killian for who he was: a good man, goodness incarnate. No matter what the mark on his back said.

She felt restless, even though Killian was calm. He appeared resigned to his fate, to the fact that he carried the trident mark. But she needed to find out what really happened that fateful day of the bridge's collapse. She needed to exonerate Killian. There had to have been some mistake.

"We need to fill the holes in your memory and find out exactly what happened," she said. "I tried to make an amnesia antidote, and I tested it—but turns out it doesn't work. But maybe there is some other way."

Killian laughed. "You tested it?" He watched her face so closely it seemed as if he were attempting to capture each twitch and crease it made, searing these little expressions indefinitely in his brain.

"On a patient at the hospital," she lied. She wasn't about to launch into a story about Ingrid's pixies; she had other concerns. "Needless to say, the potion was lame. But what if . . ."

Killian took Freya's hands in his, his countenance grave. "Darling, there's nothing you can do. If what Freddie says is true, I will take my place in Limbo. I must be punished for my actions whether I remember them or not. If I'm guilty, I'm guilty. I shall atone if I'm at fault. No one else should have to bear the punishment that is rightly mine."

Freya couldn't bear the thought of this, of being forever separated from Killian. If he were responsible, there had to be a reason for it. There was no way she would let him go to Limbo, and
in a childish attempt to stave off the Valkyries, she threw her
arms around his neck and pulled him close and tight, as if at any
moment they might appear and tear him away from her.

chapter thirty-three

Like a Prayer

ᘒ

Y ou don't sound sick to me. You're lucky I picked up the
phone. Next time you call in to claim a sick day, try hanging your head upside down from the bed. It's the best trick in the
book for feigning a cold," said Hudson.

"My head *is* hanging upside down. You told me to do just
that, but obviously, it isn't the best trick," Ingrid replied. "Next
time, I'll pinch my nose and throw in some coughs." She laughed,
rolling over onto her stomach, then sat upright on her bed. She
was playing hooky today and had planned it all out in advance
with him yesterday. "I'm nervous," she whispered.

"Just close your eyes and think of England," said Hudson,
who was not at all being helpful.

"Thanks a lot." She inspected her hands, then toes, the nails
painted a faint pink.

"Good luck!" said Hudson to her silence. "Break a . . . hymen?"

"You're disgusting." She stood and caught a glance of herself
in her bedroom mirror. For a second, she didn't recognize herself.
Her hair was in an updo, a few strands falling down her face and
the back of her neck. She had put a touch of black eyeliner over
her lids, Audrey Hepburn style, as well as used a tiny bit of blush
and lipstick to bring out her natural color. She wore a snug tan
wool dress that reached a few inches above the knee.

"Hey, Ingrid!" Hudson boomed from the phone just as she was about to hang up.

"Yes?"

"Love ya."

"Love you more!"

"No, love you m—"

Ingrid hung up the phone. She adored Hudson but it was time to get moving. Her hands were drenched with sweat from nerves, and she wiped them on her bed. "Very sexy," she said to herself.

She donned a pair of black stockings and her black heels, threw on a trench since it was unusually warm, grabbed her purse, and clipped quietly down the stairs. She tiptoed past the study, where she saw Joanna, nose deep in a pile of books—she wasn't about to explain why she was taking the day off—and silently slipped out the door.

IT WAS A MODERN HOUSE, much fancier than what Ingrid had expected, an elegant cement-and-glass rectangular box, sandwiched between two thin horizontal white platforms, up on a winding hill, teetering off the cliff on two stilts. The manicured lawn, still a vivid green, was shaded by three large eucalyptus trees. A path of flat round stones led to the door, and she hopped from one to the other as if crossing a stream. She rang the buzzer.

Matt, barefoot and in jeans and T-shirt—looking adorable and rumpled—opened the door, freckles splashed across his nose and cheeks. He grinned. "Sick day?"

"Yes," she said, smiling.

Matt grinned back at her. "What a coincidence—I'm sick, too, Ingrid!" he jested.

He had phoned in to work pretending to be ill as well. He

had called Ingrid shortly after his last visit at the library to tell her he couldn't wait till the weekend to see her, and a brilliant idea had struck him: they should both play hooky together before the weekend. "How fun would that be?" he had said.

"We can't do that!" she had replied, appalled, but the idea struck her as deliciously wicked. She was always such a goody-two-shoes and had never missed a day of work before. Why not? She needed to live a little for a change.

Matt let her in and led her into a spartan living room with a terrace that faced the sea: blond wood floors, a glass coffee table with a vase containing a single white calla lily (the tall, slim flower that curled up on itself with its slightly open cup at the top), three brown Barcelona chairs, a steel lamp with a long arching stem, its shape resembling an elegant mushroom, and a sleek gray couch. The only section of the room that wasn't minimalist was the floor-to-ceiling, wall-to-wall bookshelf, brimming with books of all sizes, spilling into piles on the floor. The room was full of sunlight and smelled of the sea.

177

"Wow!" she said. "On a detective's salary?" she asked, then put a hand to her mouth, feeling her face flush.

"Well, it isn't exactly Frank Lloyd Wright's Fallingwater." He shrugged.

"Not at all. It's simple and beautiful and . . . clean . . ." said Ingrid, craning her neck to look around. "I'm just surprised."

"I'll give you the speech," he said.

"The speech?" asked Ingrid, wondering if Matt gave all the women who came to visit "the speech."

"Explain how I live here," said Matt.

"Oh, right," replied Ingrid.

"My younger brother's an architect," he said.

"That's it? That's a short speech," she teased.

"I paid for his schooling. He's my best friend," he said simply.

Ingrid could see there was a story behind it, saw in his lifeline the sacrifices Matt had made to help his brother achieve his success. The fights with the old man, who had wanted both of his boys to join the force.

"You must love him very much." Ingrid smiled.

"Ah, enough about him, or the house. It's good to see you," he said, placing his hands on Ingrid's shoulders.

Though Ingrid was touched by the story behind his house, and the beauty of his domicile, his sudden proximity made her anxious. She gave him a brisk smile, then made a dash to the glass doors to the terrace. She felt a bit trapped in this glass box.

It was such a clear day she could see Gardiners Island. Unbuttoning her trench, she stared out at Fair Haven and saw something peeking out from its side, shining like a gem. The greenhouse, she thought, and wondered if Freya was there with Killian now. Her sister had told her she was off to find him in the morning.

For a moment Ingrid felt awkward and terribly inexperienced, especially now that Matt seemed so confident in this house that looked out on the Atlantic from on high. She was a girl, and he was a man, a grown-up, while she still lived, embarrassingly enough, with her mother. She was immortal but she was the child. She had taken the day off to spend with him—in bed. This was it. She felt somewhat ridiculous, like a thirty-two-year-old teenager.

He came up behind her and slowly eased her trench coat off a shoulder. "They call that a mackerel sky, when the clouds look like the pattern on the back of a—"

"Fish. Yes, I know, I read novels, too, Matt," she said.

He laughed, then kissed the side of her neck he had uncovered. Ingrid turned around. He took her purse and helped her out of the trench. Her face had turned pink. She looked down at his bare feet. They were large, perfectly formed, squarish at the toes. She found everything about him perfect.

"If this is being 'sick,' I like it. I think we should get into bed right now and recover." He gave her a mischievous grin.

Ingrid started. "About that—"

"Come on, let me give you the tour," he said, taking her hand, throwing her trench and purse on one of the Barcelona chairs. Ingrid was relieved. He stopped in his tracks and looked at her with a boyish excitement. She could tell he derived a lot of pleasure showing off his house. "I forgot to ask—you want a drink?"

"I never drink during the day," she said.

"Me neither. It's better like that anyway. Come!" he pulled her by the hand.

What did he mean it was "better like that"? Did he mean sex without alcohol? Did he think they were going to have sex? Well, that was why she had come, wasn't it? All that stuff about being ill and bedridden was obviously a metaphor for sex. *Duh!* She was thrilled to give herself to Matt, but there was the prospect of breaking the news about her situation to him. Could she tell him? If she didn't would he be able to tell she was a virgin? Could guys figure out stuff like that? She remembered Hudson's reaction, how serious he had looked when she'd told him, as if virginity were a disease after a certain age. What if Matt thought she was weird, that there was something wrong with her? That no one had found her attractive enough to sleep with until now? That wasn't true of course. She'd had many offers. She'd just turned them all down. Hold on, maybe there *was* something wrong with her.

Matt showed her the kitchen, all steel with white stone counters and a white tile floor, the dining room, with a Saarinen table and chairs—everything sleek and sparse, with immaculate, clean lines. Ingrid began to feel more comfortable and took the lead, walking up to a closed door. "What's in here?" she asked.

Matt rushed over, pressing his back against it. His demeanor suddenly changed. He looked—upset? Certainly edgy. "It's just a room where I store stuff, it's . . . messy."

Ingrid laughed. "Now I *really* want to see it," she said teasingly, trying to reach for the door handle. He caught her wrist. The gesture wasn't hard or violent, but it was firm. He pulled her toward him, took her face in his hands, and kissed her. She melted at his touch, his breath rushing against hers. Something about his kisses made her feel more alive than she had ever felt. He smelled good, like freshly cut grass, an ocean breeze, like life itself.

"I thought you said no secrets," she reminded him, although she had plenty of her own.

"I'll show you, just not today. I promise." His voice was full of breath. "Come on, let's go upstairs." He was so damned cute, Ingrid couldn't help but smile. He took her by the hand and guided her to the master bedroom. At this point she couldn't utter a word, so she let herself be led into the room, which was so bright, the sunlight uncovering every corner. There was no hiding here. He threw himself on the bed. There was little furniture: a low-slung king-size bed on a white platform, an orange chair shaped like an *S*, a desk.

Matt was propped up on the pillows, observing her, his arm muscles bulging with his hands behind his neck. She noticed the tint of red in his brown hair, highlighted by the sun. She stood there, her arms dangling at her sides.

"You're too far away," he said. He seemed more self-assured than he had ever been with her. She envied him for that. Perhaps it was because he was in his element here, in this house built from love and pain. "You're driving me crazy, you know."

She smiled. She loved him. She did. It was undeniable. She was crazy about Matt. It was corny, but she liked this little game, and yet she wasn't sure whether she was ready to make a full-on confession. That scared her the most, more than the sex.

She steeled herself. "How can I help?" she asked, her voice suddenly husky.

"You could start by taking off your clothes." He gave her a huge teasing grin.

"Here?"

There was something very fun and exciting about all this. She felt like a kid. She had never done anything like this before, had never been undressed in front of anyone, other than, embarrassingly again, her mother and sister. She trusted Matt. She wanted to do it. She had bought and worn lingerie for the occasion, and the slinkiness under her dress made her feel sensual, but her hands were sweating again. She ran them along her hips and waist to get rid of the wetness.

"Hmm. That's nice," said Matt.

"Oh!" she said surprised, unaware she was being sexy. She reached for her side zipper and pulled it down.

Matt smiled encouragingly. "Come closer," he said. "My vision's blurry."

"No touching yet," she said.

"No," said Matt, shaking his head, looking very serious. "No touching."

She let her dress fall to her ankles and stepped out of it, moving closer to the bed. She was left wearing a short slip, with a garter belt to hold up her stockings. Freya had picked everything out, had bullied her into wearing nothing underneath the slip.

Matt gave a low wolf whistle. He seemed to really be enjoying himself, leaning back, watching her. Ingrid felt his gaze like a physical caress.

He rose from the bed, kneeling beside her and, hands trembling, began to gently undo the garters and peel off her stockings one by one. She let him. He pulled the pins out of her hair, letting it fall on her shoulders. Then she let him pull the straps of her slip off her shoulders so that the wisp of silk fell to the floor. She turned away, using her hair and her hands to cover herself.

She had to tell him. She didn't know how. The words were caught in her throat, as if she had swallowed gravel.

Matt stepped back. "Turn around," he said. "Let me see you."

She did as she was told, bracing herself. She had never been undressed in front of a man before. Had never let anyone get this close to her before—not just her body, but her heart . . .

"Come here," he growled, as if he couldn't wait a second longer, and he pulled her down to the bed, his strong arms circling her waist. He kissed her stomach, sending flutters through her body.

She pulled his T-shirt over his head, laid down on the bed so that his body covered the length of hers. She could feel his excitement as he pressed against her. And still he was kissing her, all over. Now her heart was thundering in her chest and she wanted to feel him—all of him—against her. She slipped a hand underneath the waistband of his jeans and he groaned against her. With her other hand, she helped him pull his pants down and he kicked them off. He was so hot, his body molten, that Ingrid felt as if she would melt. There was nothing between them now and she gasped, her knees shaking violently, as he leaned closer . . . closer . . .

"Are you crying?" he asked, looking down at her. "Am I doing something wrong?"

Ingrid pushed herself up on her elbows, horrified. "No . . . it's nothing. It's . . ."

Matt was looking at her so strangely, and she was overcome by an overwhelming feeling of shame and embarrassment. Was *she* the one who was doing something wrong? After all, she had no idea what she was doing. She'd never been with a man.

"Wait a minute, you *are* crying!"

Her face was wet, and she was mortified by these sudden

tears that wouldn't stop. She scrambled for her dress and ran out of the bedroom, grabbing her trench. Matt was right behind her, confused, his face and body red.

"Hey, come on, where are you going?" He reached for her shoulder.

She wanted to say something, to explain, but all that came out was a huge embarrassing sob. He had done nothing wrong. It was all her. She was a virgin. She couldn't tell him; it was much too shameful to admit. How could she continue to pretend to be anything but what she was? She just couldn't tell him. She buttoned up her coat over her slip, grabbed her dress and purse. She was ashamed for being such a wimp, for all of it, and she hated herself.

"Ingrid." He stood in front of her, naked, his whole body flushed red, looking ever so hurt and vulnerable. "Please tell me what's wrong."

"I have to go," Ingrid managed to get out, then hiccupped. "I'm sorry."

"Okay," he said, and then she was gone.

183

chapter thirty-four

Burning Down
the House

ᕬᕫ

Joanna was still in her study, engrossed in research on the North American witch-hunt era. Most books focused on Salem, mentioning other witch-hunts like cursory afterthoughts. During the Salem trials, the circle girls, Ann Putnam as leader, had achieved what had been tantamount to rock-star—or reality-star—status. Their hunger for fame grew exponentially as their accusations spread. Even today, their celebrity eclipsed other contemporaneous tragedies.

Joanna had gleaned, however, that before Salem, between the years 1645 and 1663 alone, eighty people had been accused of witchcraft in the Massachusetts Bay Colony, and of those cases thirteen women and two men had been executed. And these were only the recorded cases. The problem was that records of witch trials in the more rural areas were often poorly kept, if kept at all, thereby vanishing altogether from the annals of history.

Joanna finally came upon a story that had taken place nearby, lo and behold, the same year as the date given for *The Milkmaid*— a coincidence? Or her intuition?

"In February of 1658, sixteen-year-old Elizabeth Howell of the Isle of Wight (now named Gardiners Island), daughter of Lion Gardiner, accused fifty-year-old Elizabeth Blanchard Garlick, a wet nurse and healer of Seatalcott in the east riding of

Yorkshire on Long Island East Hampton of having bewitched her. These allegations came while Howell, who had recently given birth and likely was suffering an infection, lay in her sickbed, delirious with fever. There, she claimed to see the apparition of Goody Garlick in a corner of her room as well as a dark shape in the other (assumed to be Garlick's familiar, a black cat). 'Goody Garlick is a double-tongued woman. Because I spoke two or three words against her, now she is come to torment me,' cried the young Howell, who then accused Garlick of being a witch. Howell died shortly afterward, but her deathbed accusations were enough to launch a charge of suspicion of witchcraft against Elizabeth Blanchard Garlick, wife of Joshua. Other allegations from townspeople followed, most of them spurred on by one Goody Davis, who was reported to have had a cantankerous relationship with her ex-neighbor from the Isle of Wight. Depositions were gathered by the town's authorities."

Since 1645, more than a dozen cases of witchcraft had been tried in the New England courts, but this was a first for East Hampton, and the local court, having no experience in witchcraft trials, was at a loss. Because East Hampton, then Maidstone, fell under the jurisdiction of Connecticut, Elizabeth Garlick was sent to stand trial in the Court of Magistrates at Hartford on May 5, 1658. The jury found insufficient evidence to prove Garlick's guilt, and she was sent home with a letter from the courts admonishing her fellow townspeople and requesting that all "carry on neighborly and peaceably without just offense to Joshua Garlick and his wife and they should do like to you."

Still, Elizabeth Blanchard Garlick, whether a veritable witch or not, was not the witch Joanna was after. First off, she was older than the wraith she had seen; second, she had been propitiously acquitted. But this passage elucidated something else for Joanna.

East and South Hampton may well have fallen under the jurisdiction of Connecticut then, but North Hampton itself existed inside the disoriented pocket, on the seam, and most pertinently outside any greater jurisdiction. Whatever had happened in North Hampton would not be in any records, for there were none of the town itself. Even today, it wasn't on any map, or if it were, only as an accidental pinprick, a cartographer's faint memory or dream, a dot, a smudge. North Hampton would always be its own independent and invisible—rather than indivisible—little country.

Joanna's witch was from North Hampton or, more accurately, Fairstone, as it was called in the seventeenth century. She had lived here. She had been tried by the local magistrates and given a verdict by a jury made up of her own neighbors and accusers. She had been hanged from the oak that stood above the burial mound in the woods.

What Joanna had also gathered from the case of Goody Garlick was that around 1658, a fervor had begun to stir in the briny air of East Long Island, the first wave of a witch-hunt.

A sudden realization hit Joanna: something had happened in Fairstone, something important that the witch needed to communicate to her. Joanna would need to travel back in time to find out what it was. It wasn't her specialty, but she could perform it. Norman's brother Arthur was the time-traveler of the family. She also had to ensure that she arrived before the girl was dragged to the oak beneath whose long, gnarly branches a hole would have been dug.

The cell phone lying on her desk buzzed, making Joanna jump. She picked it up and read Harold's name on the screen. She didn't exactly feel like being interrupted, especially not during her epiphany, but it was her friend Harold, and she answered the call.

186

"Hello, my dear!" boomed his hearty voice.

"Harold! How are you? Good of you to call."

"What are you doing next week?" he asked. "My daughter, son-in-law, and Clay will be out of town; they are off to spend the day with his side of the family. I was wondering if you might be free?"

Joanna ran a finger down a paragraph on Long Island history while talking at the same time. "I am but why don't you come over to the house instead? Thursday is perfect since Freya's cooking. She's a marvelous cook. It'll be divine!"

Harold cleared his throat. "Thursday? Are you sure?"

"Of course," Joanna said, distracted. "Thursday."

"Well, that is very generous of you. I would love to join you. I'll bring some wine!"

"I'm in the midst of a project. Talk later?"

"Of course, my dear," said Harold.

Joanna hung up and continued to read.

chapter thirty-five

Like a Wheel
Within a Wheel

༤

The diner on the county road outside North Hampton was a classic oblong, 1950s-style eatery with black-and-white-checkered floors, red vinyl booths, swivel stools along the counter, blinds on the windows, and cheesecake topped with preternaturally red strawberries inside a glass case. It was aptly, or unoriginally, called Diner, loudly conveyed by the gargantuan neon sign across the front.

It was replete with the usual crowd one found in such places, often themselves in disoriented pockets: the weekend or prom-night teens, the honeymoon or wordless couples, widows, families with screaming infants, truckers, die-hard preppies with shirt collars flipped up, women with bejeweled fingers and Liz Taylor hair (in the latter years), or anyone who had, no matter the time of day, a hankering for flapjacks drenched in hot maple syrup with eggs any which way.

Jean-Baptiste sat in a back booth in a perfectly tailored hand-made suit with a red silk pocket square, his cashmere coat slung over the back of the banquette. He was wearing sunglasses even though it was pitch-dark outside. Freya spotted him right away—it was hard not to notice him—and slid into his booth.

"You're looking good, Freya," he said in a velvety baritone with a hint of southern lilt. He peered up at her from behind his dark, rimless Ray-Bans and gave her his understated wry smile. Just one corner of his lips that normally turned a tad downward peaked up ever so slightly, and the pronounced grooves at the sides of his mouth creased a little more deeply, indicating his pleasure at seeing her.

"I was just thinking the same about you, Jean." She stared silently at his handsome face, the faint grizzled mustache and goatee, the perfectly smooth bald head, his lovely amber-brown skin. Jean-Baptiste Mésomier brought to mind the word *suave*, as well as other sibilant ones—*smooth, sexy, savvy*, and so forth.

"Hungry?" he asked.

"Sure, I could go for the short stack special with the works. Just got off of a long shift," she explained.

Jean took a noisy last sip of his milkshake, the way kids do— not so smooth, but somehow he got away with it—then called the waitress over, and Freya ordered.

When they were alone again, Jean lowered his head to look questioningly up at Freya from behind his shades, his expression grave. "I'm wondering what warranted getting a crotchety old man like me out of bed to fly all the way from New Orleans to the Hamptons in the middle of the night. Glad I know the short-cuts, by the way. If it weren't the goddess of love and beauty herself calling, I would have much rather snoozed."

Freya chewed her lip. "I'm sorry. I should have come to you."

Jean let forth a stentorian laugh that startled Freya, but she found herself laughing along lest she offend the god of memory and have her brain entirely swiped.

"I'm just fucking with you, kid. Truth be told, I've been rather bored lately, and I'd give up the alphabet—well, maybe just numbers—to gaze at your pretty face for a few minutes whatever the time of day or place."

Freya smirked. She hadn't seen Jean-Baptiste in several

lifetimes, and she had been a toddler whom he'd bounced on his knee then. He looked the same. He wasn't someone anyone could easily forgot, unless he wanted you to, of course.

"As I said in my text, but I couldn't get explicit"—here she lowered her voice—"it's about the *bridge.*"

He looked at her askance, cocking his head. "The Bofrir?"

Freya nodded.

Jean let out a whistle, staring incredulously at her. "You know we can't talk about that. What's done is done, and there certainly isn't any goddamn thing this old man can do about it. The bridge was destroyed; our magic is weakened as a result. Period." He lifted his eyebrows, his forehead creasing with several sideways *S*'s, and suddenly he looked tired and much older. "I don't know what else to say, kid."

Freya pushed. "I want to know everything you know about that day, Jean, every detail."

Jean told her, but it was the same old story: Fryr, her twin, and Loki getting caught, Loki serving his five thousand years in the frozen depths, and Fryr biding his time in Limbo. It had been Fryr's trident that had destroyed the bridge after all, ultimately consigning the Vanir and Aesir to Midgard, save for Odin and his wife, Frigg. "Someone had to pay," Jean said. "And Fryr looked awfully guilty."

The waitress returned with a stack of steaming pancakes topped with a strawberry and served with eggs sunny-side up and perfectly browned sausage links. But Freya and Jean ignored the food. The waitress blew at a strand of hair falling in her face, straightened her apron, and then clip-clopped away.

Freya gave a sigh of frustration. "Well, I don't think that's how it happened, Jean," she said, finally turning to the heaping plate before her. She poured a thick stream of maple syrup on her pancakes, then dug in, talking while she ate. "I think the

Valkyries might not have investigated thoroughly into the matter. I'm not saying they were lazy, but everything was so rushed when it happened." She rambled on, thinking out loud while she shoveled large chunks of pancake into her mouth. Yes, it was Freddie's trident they'd found, she admitted, but what if he'd been set up? Framed? What if someone wanted to make it *look* as if he'd done it? Who could have done that? she hinted. Who do we know is capable of such *mischief*?

Jean smiled as if he pitied her. "It can't be Loki. He served his time. Five thousand years is no small pittance, my dear. They were young boys. It was a dumb prank."

Freya shrugged. She still had questions. Jean patiently listened as if indulging a small child. If anyone knew anything, Freya thought, it would be the god of memory. He kept the records of history that the Council had determined were fit to be archived. Once a major event got the seal of approval, it was stored inside that large bald head of Jean's, in the endless Byzantine corridors of his brain. But Freya also believed that he could help her get Killian's memory back. She believed he possessed the power to help him recover the truth about his past, or at least could steer her in the right direction so she might retrieve it herself.

"Freddie says that when he and Loki got there, the bridge was already destroyed," Freya said.

The expression on Jean's face was something between a smile and a frown. "If that's true, then these questions you are asking are very dangerous. The bridge held all of our powers. They were entwined within it from day one," he said. "When it fell the gods were permanently weakened. Since Loki and Fryr appeared hapless and guilty, Odin believed that the power of the bridge disappeared into the universe—that it dissipated into the ether. But if what you're saying is true, then whoever destroyed that bridge is incredibly powerful, since he, or *she*, has those powers now, the powers of the entire pantheon. That is, if you're right and the boys didn't destroy it and someone else did. You don't want to go messing with that kind of god, Freya."

She leaned closer to him from across the table and whispered fiercely. "I know someone who might have been there, Jean. A potential witness. Another god, but I can't say who. Somehow he can't remember what happened that day—just bits and pieces. His memory is gone, or it might have been stolen from him, to keep him quiet. I need to help him remember, so we can know what really happened that day. My brother is innocent, and he's been punished for a crime he didn't commit."

For a moment, Jean appeared perturbed and said nothing. Finally he motioned her even closer so he could speak directly into her ear. The old warlock was relenting. "There is a way to help this . . . *person. This witness who has memories of the Bofrir's destruction.* But to even attempt it is forbidden and dangerous," he said. "You don't fool around with this stuff; this is black magic we're talking about here. If you'll forgive the pun," he said with a smile. "But I'm serious. This is the real voodoo daddy. Could put you and this friend of yours in a lot of danger. Are you sure you want to go down that road?"

A chill slithered up Freya's spine. Jean was no longer joking or amused. He was dead serious, if not a little scared, which frightened her, too. If even the god of memory was intimidated by it, then what on earth was she doing messing around with that kind of devilry? But she knew she was also willing to do whatever it took to prevent Killian from going to Limbo.

chapter thirty-six

Live Freegan or Die

Ingrid had to rise at dawn, before Joanna woke, to make the
pixies breakfast in the morning. Their demands were very pre-
cise: soft-boiled eggs in individual eggcups, butter, ripe brie or
some kind of gooey cheese, dried salami, orange juice (Kelda told
her they preferred fresh squeezed, but this wasn't a five-star hotel for god's sake), chocolate (which made them hyper, Ingrid
had noted, so she had eliminated it from their diet), and Joanna's
homemade bread and pies as well as whatever else could be
brought up to their lair.

She was glad to have the pixies to attend to. It kept her mind
off what had happened the other day with Matt: every time she
remembered it, she felt herself blushing throughout her entire
body. Yet the memory was sweet, too—and hot—remembering
the delicious feel of his skin against hers, and how much she had
liked looking at him and letting him look at her that way. What
was her problem? She'd been ready. She'd felt ready. She'd
wanted him so much—but instead . . . She couldn't think about
it any longer. There was a reason she'd earned the nickname
Frigid Ingrid. No wonder he didn't even bother to call her.

She tiptoed past Joanna's room, carrying the heavy tray,
Kelda and Nyph meeting her in the stairway to help her as soon
as she unlocked the attic door. The pixies, extremely active during nocturnal hours, tended to be famished in the mornings.

Ingrid didn't understand why Freya's potion hadn't worked on them, nor had any of her own spells or charms, little knots and pouches of edelweiss petals placed under their pillows. She still had no clue as to the whereabouts of their home save for the scattered cryptic details they had given her: tree houses and underground workers, something beginning with *A*. Ingrid didn't put it past them to have made it up just to placate her.

She set down the tray on the makeshift dining table, a door propped up with crates, and the pixies excitedly gathered around, fighting over who got what.

"*Shh*, not so noisy," she admonished. Irdick was behind her, pulling at her peignoir. "What do you want, Irdick? Don't tell me this isn't enough food. You've just got to be fast like everyone else or you don't get your share."

"It's not that, Erda. Something else," he said.

Ingrid raised a brow at his apple-round face.

"So last night, we were Dumpster diving like good freegans . . ."

Ingrid laughed. "Freegans?" She was amused. "You guys have really assimilated."

At the table, everyone had stopped grabbing at the food, and they were all looking expectantly at Ingrid. Sven gave a smoker's cough before rasping, "Freegans shmeegans, Irdick is trying to tell you we *saw* someone."

"Who?" asked Ingrid. Then they were all talking at once, and she couldn't make out anything they were saying. She cleared her throat, and the pixies quieted. They were finally learning to be more obedient and this pleased her. It was like training puppies. They were coming along. "Okay, could one of you explain this clearly to me?"

Nyph raised her hand as high as she could, crying, "Me, me, me!" as Kelda stared up at her through the black mask.

Ingrid placed a hand on her waist and cocked a hip. "Okay, Nyph, shoot!"

The pretty raven-haired pixie's dark eyelashes batted, suddenly shy now that she was being singled out. She licked her lips then spoke. "We saw someone we thought looked extremely familiar, so we hid in the alley and watched him."

Ingrid was taken aback. "Who was it? Someone from your home?"

"No. It was the one who s-s-sent us away," said Val. Everyone looked to him. Val dipped a piece of bread in his egg yolk and took a bite. "We did a favor for that guy, whoever he is, then he banished us from our home. At least that's what we think happened. We recognized him."

"Hmm," said Ingrid. "What did he look like?"

"He's tall, big guy, good-looking," said Kelda.

These were vague descriptions, not helpful at all. "Can you please be more specific? What color was his hair? How tall? How big? Like, hefty? Or just overweight? What was he wearing?"

They all began shouting at once, and all of them had different opinions. Some argued the man had blond hair, while others said it was brown. It was dark outside, they all agreed, but they had definitely recognized him as a person they used to know. But now they couldn't remember at what exact Dumpster they had spotted him, which didn't help Ingrid at all.

Ingrid sighed, but at least she was getting a little closer to solving this enigma, however frustratingly piecemeal and slow the information came together. She needed to find out who exactly this man was, find out exactly what he'd done to the pixies to make them forget, and maybe she could finally send them back home.

195

chapter thirty-seven

Blasphemous Rumors

♄

After that one unseasonable sunny day, the temperature plummeted, and a morning mist now rose from the ground in the woods. Joanna had dressed warmly in rubber boots with thick socks, a wool hat, and a scarf. She stood at the foot of the burial mound and looked up into the sprawling oak. Was this the very same tree where her witch had hanged before being snipped down to plummet into her grave? Sometimes several witches were hanged from one tree at once, dangling from the boughs for days as putrefaction set in—setting an example for those who might think to consort with the devil.

Hanging was less violent than burning, but neither could be called humane, and now the memories of Salem and her own girls' hangings returned, as much as she tried to push them away: the townspeople jeering and celebrating, couples kissing and groping as the hangman fit the nooses around each of their necks. Some in the crowd were raising their fists, while others cried out in ecstasy or with smiles on their faces as the condemned swung off the platform. This was a part of *humanity* that Joanna would rather not have witnessed. It was the wrong way around; those with blackened hearts were in the crowd, not on the gallows. She wiped away a tear, remembering Freya's defiant stare and Ingrid's broken sobs. Joanna loosened the red scarf at her neck because she suddenly felt as if she were being choked herself.

There were several ways to die from a hanging. The neck could snap, but this didn't necessarily mean death came instantaneously. If the drop wasn't high enough and the spinal cord was not fully severed, the hanged could remain in the air, kicking and fully conscious for several minutes while asphyxiation took place.

If death wasn't caused by the neck bones breaking, or just plain decapitation if the body was catapulted with enough force, it was the occlusion of the carotid arteries and jugular veins that did it, causing edema followed by cerebral ischemia, or the heart slowing down enough to cause cardiac arrest.

Some claimed that the hanged experienced sexual excitement, but this was bunk, a myth, Joanna knew. There was only agony and suffering and humiliation. Men sometimes appeared to get erections, but that was only due to gravity, the blood surging to the torso and legs. It had nothing to do with pleasure and everything to do with pain.

This hanging, if it had been done from this tree, given the short drop, would not have been the quick kind but a slow one to ensure maximum torture. Joanna had watched her daughters' faces swell, turn purple and blue with cyanosis, blood marks spreading across their skin, their eyes, as the life was snuffed from them. Splotches of red crawled over their skin as veins and capillaries burst. Freya's tongue had protruded from her lips, as if in a final act of defiance.

Though it was cold, Joanna's forehead beaded with sweat. She wiped it off with the back of a hand, trying to erase the memories as well. She realized then why the witch's spirit had grabbed her by the throat. She had been showing Joanna what it felt like when she'd died.

Joanna had come to the burial mound to seek a passage into

197

the timeline. She closed her eyes and chanted, reciting the incantation that enabled one to slip through the portal into the passages. She had to be specific: she had to return to the right time,
at least a few days before the hanging. She waited for the portal
to open, closing her eyes, but her feet remained rooted at the base
of the burial mound.

chapter thirty-eight

Dance till You Can't Dance No More

ᴖᴖ

On the *Dragon*, Freya gathered strands of hair from Killian's comb in the bathroom of the master stateroom. She had stopped by the greenhouse earlier to gather the roots and cuttings of herbs that Jean had told her she would need for her ritual. She'd placed them inside a punctured Ziploc, along with a live cicada, which resembled a gigantic fly with its huge eyes and veined gossamer wings. Of course, the cicada had begun to sing, but that was exactly what she needed: a male. Jean had been adamant about that.

The ritual would also require a drop of Killian's scent, that delectable, intoxicating one she knew so well, but she wasn't quite sure how to go about extracting it. She carried a small glass vial, like those used for perfume samples, for that end and had placed it on the sink. "Be creative," Jean had told her. "Isn't that what magic is about?"

"Freya?" Killian asked, unexpectedly behind her. "Did you hear that?"

She started, quickly turning toward him. Luckily, the cicada had stopped humming. "Hear what?" she asked, feigning innocence as she slipped a bottle of his cologne into her bag. "I'm looking for aspirin," she lied.

"A witch with a headache!" He laughed. "Now you're being

secretive again, and we know that's no good." He pushed her hair out of her face and kissed her softly. Since they had been waiting for the Valkyries to descend upon them, they couldn't get enough of each other, treating each night as if it were the last. But Freya had also been busy, trying to figure out a way to stave them off.

"Hey, you." She smiled as their bodies pressed against each other in the cramped space.

"Hey, babe," he murmured, tugging her closer and cupping her behind.

She put her bag on the sink, her work forgotten for now. When she placed her hand at the crotch of his jeans she discovered he was already hard. It was as much a thrill as the first time.

Killian's lips parted from hers, and he looked at her inquiringly. "So are you going to tell me the truth?"

"I'm working on something," she said between breathless kisses.

"Anything I might help you with?"

"When the time's right," she quipped, unzipping him as he unhooked her belt and peeled off her jeans. "Right now you can help me with something else." She might get that drop of sweat sooner than she thought.

"Glad to," he whispered, grunting as he bent her over the sink and took her from behind in one swift motion.

Freya closed her eyes and moaned, holding on to the counter, as Killian leaned over her back, his hands on either side of hers, bucking against her, the force of his actions practically lifting her from the floor.

It was all part of assembling ingredients for her potion, she knew, but that didn't mean that work couldn't be any fun.

———

OKAY, THIS TIME I'M REALLY putting my foot down, Freddie. *This is it! I'm done!*" Freya said, feeling dizzy. Perhaps it was the slanted room. Or maybe in her haste to collect all the ingredients for the spell she had forgotten to eat? It was just a few hours ago she had left Killian on his boat. She had all the elements necessary to perform the spell, but she was getting cold feet. If it were as dangerous as Jean had claimed, she didn't know if she could go through with it. And if she didn't go through with it, then she would never know the truth and neither would Killian. Freya was now irritable, and she had arrived at the run-down motel to confront the source of her current frustration.

She sat at the foot of one bed to steady herself. "I'm really sick of it, Fred. You won't listen to me, and then you expect me to cater to your every whim, bringing you food, making sure you have warm blankets."

Freddie peered at her dejectedly, hanging his head. "I don't mean to be a mooch," he said like a little boy. "If I could leave here, I would. Plus, I miss Hilly. She won't see me until her dad gives the approval, and he won't do it until I get some job done for him. But he won't say what it is or how to do it."

"You know, enough of that silly flirtation. She's just some chick you met online! There are hundreds—thousands of them out there. Forget her if she's such a problem. Look," said Freya, "I think you're depressed. You need to be more active. Being cooped up in here is not helping you. Throw on a disguise, morph into something . . . I don't know . . . Why don't you go over to Mother's and help yourself. There's a *fridge* there. Something they don't have in gross, lopsided motel rooms."

"You don't have to be mean about it," Freddie said.

"Well, I'm just telling you. Mom and Ingrid are out tomorrow. No one will be home in the evening, either. Stop by and stock up.

I'm tired of doing it for you. I'll leave the back glass doors open for you. You can get in from there," she said, hoping he was still ignorant of the holiday calendar and the traditions most people observed. She had a plan in mind.

Freddie looked sad. "Okay, Freya. I didn't realize it was so inconvenient for you to help me."

"It's not, Freddie. Of course not. But I'm going away and I'm worried you'll be hungry and alone."

"I'm not alone. I have Hilly," he said.

"Right." She picked up her purse. "Remember to come by tomorrow," she said. And before Freddie could rise from his armchair, she was out the door and already peeling out of the parking lot in her Mini.

chapter thirty-nine

Frozen, When Your
Heart's Not Open

～

I ngrid set the alarm in the library, and then outside she locked the doors and the black gate with its gigantic key. She shivered, winding her scarf around her neck.

"Hey," a voice said from behind her.

She spun around, and there he was, the one person who had been hounding her thoughts as usual.

Matt held one of the wrought-iron bars of the fence that wound around the library, his head cocked, eyes doleful. Ingrid walked up to him as they looked tentatively at each other.

She stopped a foot away. She wished she hadn't been wearing her glasses, and that her hair wasn't up in its tight, efficient work bun. She hadn't worn any makeup, and she shoved her hands into her pockets, remembering how the polish was chipped from biting her nails.

"I know you probably don't want to see me. I didn't call because I figured you needed some space," he said. "I'll go away if you tell me to. I just wanted to see you and talk."

Ingrid picked up her head. She was surprised to hear this. He was the last person she wanted to hurt and hadn't realized she could have that kind of power over him. The wind pushed fallen leaves from the park down the street. She yanked up her collar. She moved in closer, whispering, "I'm sorry, Matt. It isn't you . . . It's me." She looked away.

He swung out from the bar, still holding on to it. "Oh, that old line."

"It's not a line. Will you let me explain?" she asked. "Walk with me?"

"Sure." They moved away from the fence to cross the street. They strode silently for a while. Ingrid passed the entrance to the park, and Matt grabbed her arm, pulling her toward it. She hoped he would kiss her then, but instead, he said, "We can cut through."

Ingrid gave him a dubious look, taken aback. "I thought . . ."

"Hey, you have a police escort," he joked with a thin smile. "Come on."

They made their way down the park's winding path, leaves crunching underfoot. Ingrid wished they were holding hands, moving through this cold darkness. She wished there wasn't any awkwardness between them and that things had gone differently the other afternoon. When she lay alone in bed at night, she tossed and turned, thinking about him. She imagined him stroking her back, kissing her neck, playing with his hair, or just lying alongside, staring into each other's eyes. Sometimes she wished for him so hard she would wake up in a cold sweat—or else gasping for air because her craving for him was so strong.

The denuded trees they passed looked like so many sad skeletons, the perfect backdrop.

"How was work?" he asked, attempting to make idle chat.

"Listen, about the other day, I have to tell you something, Matt. Something personal," she said. He couldn't exactly run away from her, leave her stranded in the park after having chastised her for walking it alone at night.

"You know you can tell me anything, Ingrid. First and foremost, I hope that we will always remain friends, no matter what."

What did he mean by "no matter what"? Did it have to do with that woman's number the pixies had given her? That was something that had actually slipped Ingrid's mind once she had chalked it up to their shenanigans. Did he *play the field*? Was he seeing other women?

He had stopped in the path, beneath a lamppost, and they faced each other. He reached out for her hands. Ingrid brushed back her hair, but there were no loose strands to pat back, so her hands fell into his large, warm ones. "Tell me," he said. "What's wrong? Why'd you run away?"

She looked him in the eye, and he nodded encouragingly. The pines whooshed around them. "I can't do it," she said. "I can't tell you. I'm scared."

"Don't be," he said. "It's just me."

She shook her head.

"You're pregnant?"

She laughed. "*Uh* . . . no."

"You already have a boyfriend?"

She shook her head.

"You're married?"

Again she laughed.

"Terminally ill?" he said, looking nervous all of a sudden.

"I'm a virgin!" she blurted out.

He looked taken aback for a while, and then he smiled, crinkling his forehead. His smile was gentle. "Well, there's nothing wrong with that."

She let go of his hands, breaking away, striding ahead, her cheeks burning. She quickened her step until she arrived at the playground, where she ran to hide in the shadows, sitting on one of the swings. Once again, she was mortified. *This* was why she was the world's oldest virgin. Because having to admit it was so painful, it was preferable to losing it.

She watched Matt's silhouette as it moved closer to her. She couldn't see his face. He came and sat on the swing beside her.

They both swayed ever so slightly, sideways and forward, their feet on the ground.

"Ingrid, it's really okay. I mean, it's not a big deal . . . I mean . . . it's sort of overrated, you know . . . not sex, but . . . What I mean is, it's very sweet, actually," he said.

"What? Saving myself for the *one*? It wasn't like that. It just . . . never happened. Plus, I'm over thirty. It's horrifying."

Matt smiled. "It's not really. It's cute."

She sniffed, Matt handed her a handkerchief from his pocket, and she took it. She pinched her nose with it, then lifted her glasses and wiped at her eyes. She turned to him. He was watching her intently, his hands on the chains of the swing. He was really much too big for it, like an overgrown boy.

She bunched up the handkerchief. "I'll wash this and give it back to you."

"Ingrid, we can take it slowly. I rushed it too fast. I want it to work out between us."

"You do?"

"Yes!" he said. "Listen, you want to know something?"

She nodded.

He swung closer and said very softly. "I wish you were my first. I wish you were the first girl I'd ever met. When you meet the right person, it's like nothing else—nobody else. No one in your past ever mattered. That's what it feels like, when I'm with you. You shouldn't be ashamed . . . There's nothing to be ashamed of."

She looked up at him and smiled. "Have there been many others?" she teased.

He shook his head. "No, not at all."

She exhaled. "What are you doing for Thanksgiving?"

"I was going in to the city to visit my brother. Why?"

"Will you come to dinner with my family instead?" she asked. "Would he mind?"

206

"Not at all. They'll understand. They'll be happy for me."

"Good."

"Now can I ask you something?" he asked.

"Sure."

"Will you walk over to that tree with me?"

"What for?"

She found out when they walked over. He kissed her tenderly, her back pressing against the trunk. He ran his mouth along her neck and cheek, breathing heavily, his lips trembling, so gentle, then rested his face against hers. His breath felt warm and safe. They stayed like that for a while, Matt leaning against her in the dark, wind-swept park, and though they remained immobile, she could feel all that was roiling within him.

And then he said it, something Ingrid had never heard from someone other than her family.

"I love you," he whispered in her ear. Then again, in case she hadn't heard the first time: "I love you, Ingrid Beauchamp."

chapter forty

Simple Gifts

꒰ꮡ

The house was redolent with the smells of Freya's cooking: sage, rosemary, melted butter. She had stuffed the bird with chestnuts, cranberries, sausage, and herbs from the greenhouse, mixed with chunks of Joanna's homemade wholegrain bread. The day before, Joanna had baked all the staple pies—pumpkin, yam, apple, pecan—so Freya could have free rein of the kitchen today. Freya's domain was the savory; she wasn't fond of baking, which was Mother's area of expertise.

Freya wore Joanna's red kerchief around her hair, along with a black Provençal apron with little white-and-purple flowers over a T-shirt and jeans. Sweat poured down her face as she whirled through the kitchen, juggling pots, pulling baking pans out of the Aga stove, throwing new ones in, washing dishes as she went, and barking, "Stay out!" at anyone who had the audacity to stand in the doorway and offer help, including Killian.

Freya knew she was bossy when it came to cooking, but that was the only way to ensure the purity of her magic. She really should open up her own restaurant someday, she thought, instead of whiling away her time in bars, although that would require learning to cook with a team, delegating, giving up control. Maybe. Tonight there would be all the traditional dishes: twice-baked sweet potatoes, haricots verts, garlic mash, blackened brussels sprouts with chunky garlic, homemade cranberry sauce, and thick brown gravy. Of course by the time it was all on the table, she would have no appetite, not until the next morning when she woke up famished and would have her own private Thanksgiving feast.

Killian, Joanna, and Norman stood by the fire in the living room, chatting as they sipped champagne. The table in the adjacent dining room, connected by an open archway, had been lavishly set for six. Ingrid was the one who had insisted on the romantic candlelight and the best china and silver. She was excited for Matt to meet her family as her guest instead of as a police detective asking rude questions. She was also hoping that her father's presence meant the family would be back together again. Speaking of, where would Norman and Joanna sit? Across from each other or side by side? They *had* been rather chummy this evening.

With a snap of her fingers, elegant place cards appeared on each plate, and Ingrid stuck them together just for the fun of it. She'd placed Killian and Freya on opposite sides at the head and foot of the table, although they probably wouldn't like that, not being able to touch each other every second or play footsies. But they were the most logical choice. It wasn't as if she and Matt were established enough to sit at those places.

She had folded the red cloth napkins on each plate into Japanese love knots, adding loads of magic inside each tie, performing a quick ceremony that asked for harmony that evening. She set down the votive candles in clusters of three. Joanna had been in charge of flowers, low autumnal-looking arrangements of Chinese lanterns, dark mauve-and-white calla lilies, red amaryllis, hypericum berries, and large green leaves. Ingrid had endowed the bouquets with her magic wand, so their fragrance would exude love and peace. This was going to be a real family dinner for Thanksgiving for a change, and Ingrid was thrilled. She'd had a long talk with the pixies in the morning, requesting they be out all afternoon and into the evening. All the familiars were up in the attic, sleepy and fed. She felt elegant with her pearl pendant, black dress with the thin red ribbon that Matt liked so much, a silk slip beneath it, and black suede pumps.

"So you have a date?" Norman asked Ingrid, who instinctively blushed.

"Dad! Please don't scare him off. He's smart. You'll really like him."

Killian clinked the ice cubes in his drink. "I approve. Detective Noble's been very generous about waving away my speeding tickets lately."

Ingrid laughed. She was giddy, the bubbles of champagne having gone to her head. "Has he now? He must want 'in' to this family." She winked, which wasn't something Ingrid usually did, but somehow it just happened.

"Oh, he is a dear boy, even sent some flowers to apologize about asking us in for questioning over the summer." Joanna gave her daughter a satisfied once-over, then swayed from side to side, pleasure animating her face.

Ingrid blushed prettily and Norman swung an arm around her shoulders, kissing the top of her head, which made Ingrid curl in on herself. She hated all this attention and suddenly resembled an embarrassed teen. "We'll see if he's good enough for our Ingrid," Norman said.

"Dad!" Ingrid groaned.

The doorbell rang.

"That must be for you," Norman said, patting her arm.

"Oh!" Ingrid said, suddenly nervous.

"You look great," Killian said. "Don't worry."

She'd been wrong about Killian, Ingrid thought as she rushed toward the kitchen. So wrong. She'd taken him to be one of those bad boys, flashy and superficial. But she saw now that he was more than his movie-star good looks. He was thoughtful, sensitive, and deep. She saw how much he loved her sister; she understood that particular glazed-over look now for she had experienced it herself from the inside out.

She hurried through the kitchen. "Not here to help, just passing through!" she called.

Freya glanced up at her from the stove's open door, her hand inside a fat oven mitt. "No worries, sexy. I'm almost ready to go upstairs and change."

Ingrid stood in front of the door before opening it. "Sexy," her sister had called her. Was that true? She tugged down the hem of her dress and pulled her hair onto one shoulder, then adjusted the pearl pendant at her neck. She coughed to clear her throat, then swung the door open.

Except the person standing at the doorway wasn't Matt. It was a tall older gentleman with a widow's peak and white-streaked black hair, dapper in his wool coat over a three-piece suit. He beamed at her, holding up a bouquet, then extended a hand.

"Hi. I'm Harold," he said in a soft, pleasant voice.

She shook his hand. "Ingrid."

"Ah! I know exactly who you are!" he said, his tone pure delight.

Ingrid experienced a strange sensation then, a sudden loss of gravity, a drop, a queasy-making kind of feeling. Where was Matt? Nothing could have happened at the precinct on the Thursday of Thanksgiving. Wasn't this a low-crime day? Matt was a senior detective, so he had the afternoon off, which he had confirmed via texts that morning. And who was this?

Harold coughed. "Joanna invited me," he said.

"Oh, of course! I've forgotten my manners! So glad to meet

211

you," replied Ingrid, thinking this must be Mother's gay pal. Every girl had at least one, why not Joanna?

Harold nodded and Ingrid stepped outside, closing the door behind her. She went down the steps, so she could take him around the house through the patio where everyone was waiting. She peered distractedly down the street as she moved along the path.

"Is there a problem?" Harold called to her back, still waiting by the door.

Ingrid swung around. "No, not at all! I was just . . . expecting someone and he was supposed to be here by now." She motioned with her head. "We have to go around this way to the living room. You know, Freya's *cooking*!" She said the latter as if Harold knew exactly what she meant.

Joanna nearly dropped her champagne glass when she saw Harold behind Ingrid coming toward the glass panes while Killian slid the door open for them. They stepped inside, Killian welcoming them with a "Well, hello!"

Norman raised his eyebrows at Ingrid. He wasn't expecting to meet someone his own age for his oldest daughter. But it made sense; Ingrid would want someone wise, settled, and established. The silly name suited him. Norman moved toward him, stretching out a hand. "A pleasure to meet you, Matthew Noble," he said.

Joanna, in her pearls and flowing red dress and silk scarf, rushed forward, aflutter, her face flushing as crimson as her outfit. She was racking her brain, trying to remember how this could have possibly happened. She had a vague remembrance of a phone conversation with Harold, something about his family being out of town and inviting him over for dinner. Had she actually invited him to Thanksgiving? It had been while she'd been immersed in research on Long Island witch hangings. She had been in a rush to get off the phone and back to her studies. She realized the horror of her blunder.

"Um," she said. "Actually, Norman, this is my dear friend Harold. And Harold, this is my . . . um . . . my sort-of husband . . . Norman."

"Awkward," whispered Killian, smiling at Ingrid, who returned a half smile, half grimace. In unison, they took a step back and observed.

So much for harmony, Ingrid thought. She had been primarily thinking of Matt while she had made her dining-room table incantations. *Shame on me for being so distracted.*

Freya ran through the living room on her way upstairs, pulling the kerchief off her head so that her wild hair came loose. "Ignore me. I'm a mess! Back down in a second!" But the only one who noticed her was Killian, who let out an appreciative snort as she trotted up the stairs.

Norman looked at Joanna, Harold looked at Joanna, and Joanna shrugged.

"Is this *the* Harold?" Norman asked.

"Sort-of husband?" Harold inquired, his face turning pink.

Joanna wrung her hands, her face turning from one suitor to the other. She had managed to bludgeon two of her birds with one stone.

"Yikes," whispered Ingrid. Mother wasn't going to get out of this one. The two of them continued to watch.

"Front-row seats," Killian commented under his breath.

"Indeed," said Ingrid, trying not to giggle.

"I can explain," said Joanna.

"I thought this was a family dinner," vociferated Norman.

"*It is!*" cried Joanna, scratching her hair, fluffing it out so that it genuinely appeared witchy. "Harold is like family!"

A log popped in the fireplace, like an exclamation point.

After a long silence, Harold strode toward the glass-paned door. "No, no, it's my fault. I'm so sorry to disturb all of you. It appears there has been some mistake. Joanna, please forgive me . . . I did not realize I was intruding on your family dinner on this holiday."

"Good riddance," Norman muttered as Harold swung the glass door open and stepped out, then slid the sliding door closed.

Joanna ran after him. "Harold! Please come back! I'm so sorry! Of course you're welcome to have Thanksgiving with us!" But it was too late. He had already stepped off the deck and seemingly vanished. She pressed her hands against the glass, then her nose. "Oh, dear," she muttered to herself. "Norman, this is all your fault!" she snapped.

"My fault?" her sort-of husband roared.

Killian put an arm around Ingrid, looked at her, and said, "Well, that was fun. But where's our good detective, sis?"

As if on cue, the doorbell rang.

"It's him!" Ingrid said breathlessly, running to get the door. She opened it to find the good detective standing on the doorstep with a huge bouquet of flowers in hand.

214

chapter forty-one

I've Got My Love to Keep Me Warm

⮹

They had gotten into quite a habit of pressing up against vertical surfaces. No sooner had Ingrid invited Matt inside the house than he cornered her up against the door, inching in close to kiss her. Her hands fluttered upward, coming to rest at his neck, pulling his face toward hers. It was wonderful, this feeling, this closeness, this warmth.

He peered into her eyes. "You're a good kisser, Ingrid." He bit his lip, looking down at her, then flicked his eyes back up, catching himself being entirely salacious.

She laughed. "*Really?*" It was about the best compliment she'd ever been given.

"Uh-huh," he said, nodding, widening his eyes at her. "I'm sorry I'm so late. I hope I didn't mess anything up. I got stuck at the precinct with some boring paperwork."

"You're right on time." Ingrid was actually relieved he had arrived later than intended, serendipitously missing the embarrassing parental drama. Perhaps that was how her table-setting magic had worked: they were still going to be six. Mother could be such a ditz, but she still couldn't believe Joanna had been so forgetful as to invite a date for Thanksgiving dinner when Norman would be there.

Matt held up a bag with a bottle of wine and the huge bouquet of orange gerbera daisies. "For you."

Ingrid took both, smiling. "My dad's here. I'm glad you'll get to meet him."

"Fantastic!" Matt said as if he enjoyed meeting the fathers of the girls he dated all the time.

"He'll love you. Don't worry." She took his hand and guided him through the kitchen to the living room. The atmosphere was still awkward, but Killian made up for it, coming over from the fireplace where he had chucked in a log. Norman rose from the dining table, Joanna from the couch, where they had been sulking separately.

Killian and Matt shook hands, then decided to turn it into a hug, patting each other on the back. "Good to see you, man!" Killian said, then narrowed his eyes. "Actually, should I call you detective?"

Matt laughed, brushing off the question with a hand. "Not tonight. I'm off duty."

Killian smiled warmly.

Ingrid stepped forward. "Dad, this is my friend Matt Noble."

"*Ah*, much better," Norman said, reaching out a hand, while Matt glanced questioningly at Ingrid, who shrugged. Norman cuffed him on the shoulder. "Ignore that. It's just . . ."

"Dad!" cautioned Ingrid.

"Never mind, nice to meet you, Matt! I'm Norman."

Matt laughed good-naturedly. "Likewise, Norman."

Freya was tottering down the steps in a tight red dress and high heels. Her hair was piled up onto her head, cascading down in a fountain of strawberry curls, her lips painted a bright red. She looked as if she'd never touched a pan. "Dinner's on. Who's carving the turkey?"

chapter forty-two

Prodigal Son

The sun had begun to set. The lights were turned off in all the rooms, the fire roaring and all the candles lit, lending an intimate old-world atmosphere to the house. The effusive praise for Freya's cooking flowed, as did the champagne and wine. It seemed as if Harold's visit was already a distant memory.

Ingrid had decided after all to place her parents at the opposite ends of the table. She sat Freya and Killian together on one side, and she and Matt faced them. Every time Matt slipped a hand on her thigh or knee, her face burned, and she was grateful for the dim lighting. Still, she quite liked the sensation. She had managed to clasp his hand once under the table while talking at the same time. It was probably the champagne.

At Norman's prompting (*So how did you two meet?*), Matt was regaling everyone with the tale of his bumbling courtship of the pretty librarian. Everyone laughed. Ingrid didn't want to cut in and break it to Matt that she hadn't actually realized how much she liked him until after he had started dating Caitlin. How fickle she had been! But those were the days when she believed in fending off heartbreak. Eventually she couldn't help but tell a bit of her side of the story.

"I kept making him read these god-awful-long books. You know, from that local author? The one who writes those eight-hundred-page-long ones—I mean, he writes well and should be read, but if only he weren't so hypergraphic, his books might circulate better. And those readings he does with a gun are a bit much."

"Oh, you're talking about J. J. Ramsey Baker," Freya threw in. "I fear that poor man might drink himself to death rather than shoot himself. He's a regular at the bar, a bit of a sad sack, always going on about some old friend from college who's shredded every single one of his books in the *New York Times*."

Matt cleared his throat. "I have to say, *The Cobbler's Daughter's Elephants*, Baker's last, did have its moments. There were pages of pure brilliance, so honest, but that one-hundred-page section on the protagonist's"—he cleared his throat—"*hair* was a bit much."

Everyone laughed. Then a slight gap in the conversation followed, and Freya leaned over and started making out with Killian, while the rest of the family tried to ignore them.

The door to the back terrace slid open suddenly, and everyone jumped save for Matt, who had instantly stood from his seat with a finger to his lips. He gestured for them to remain silent and seated. The floor creaked in the living room.

There was definitely someone in the house. Matt bent down, pulling up the cuff of his pants, where he kept a gun in a holster around his calf. Everyone at the table stared questioningly at Ingrid, who gave them a look and a shrug, as if to say, *Let's indulge him.* If someone had broken in, any one of them sitting at the table could cast a binding spell and instantaneously straitjacket the intruder.

Matt held his back to the wall, the gun cocked up vertically. He was right by the archway separating the two rooms. He swung around it, and everyone rose from the table as the sounds of a scuffle ensued. They all rushed into the living room, where Matt already had the intruder prone on the floor, pinned down with a knee. The intruder was male, a tall, lanky fellow, dressed entirely in black, his head covered with a ski mask. The detective yanked one of his arms around to his back and held a gun to his side. With his face pressed to floor, the intruder let out a muffled, "Don't shoot!"

"I thought you were off duty, Matt," remarked Killian.

"I did, too," he said grimly. Then to the intruder he said, "Get up!" The good detective got the man to his feet, nudging him with the gun, holding on to his wrists with his other hand. "Ingrid, can you please pull the mask off?"

"Sure," said Ingrid, clicking over in her heels. She was quite proud of Matt for handling it all so expediently without even using the gun. She grabbed the top of the ski mask and pulled.

Everyone gawked at the beautiful face, the head of mussed blond hair like spun gold glinting in the firelight.

"Fryr?" said Joanna, rushing to him.

"Fryr!" cried Ingrid, jumping for joy, clapping her hands.

"Bless the gods!" bellowed Norman.

"Um, we call him Freddie now," said Freya with a big smile. "Welcome home, twin! *Surprise!*"

JOANNA, BESIDE HERSELF, sat on the couch next to her son, weeping, laughing, grabbing his face in her hands, kissing his head, touching him over and over, trying to assure herself he was really there right beside her. *Her boy.* His absence had been a knife in the heart, and now he was here, and the stabbing feeling was gone. She wouldn't let him go ever. Norman flanked him on his other side, a hand on his knee, while Ingrid was saying, "I can't believe it! Fryr—Freddie—you're back!"

Freya watched all of this, Killian with his arms around her waist as she leaned against his chest. She was inordinately relieved. The family was complete, and she no longer had to carry the burdensome secret of her brother's return. Everyone she loved was here. It was just as she'd planned, except for Matt Noble's heroics, of course. But everything would be all right now. Surely, Dad would be able to help somehow. And once Ingrid and Joanna put their minds to something, they didn't let go until the job was done.

She had also decided she was ready to perform the spell on Killian to find out the truth of what happened that day. So what if it was dangerous? She didn't care. She only needed one more ingredient, which would call for Joanna's help—a drop of the black sap from a tree in the glom. She would find a way of talking Joanna into getting it for her, even if she had to lie. Killian had to be innocent.

220

Plus even if Freddie was still guilty, hadn't he been punished enough? Surely they could go to the Council and make an appeal for him. The family would discuss it all in private once Matt left, but she wouldn't tell anyone about the magic she was planning.

Freddie threw Killian mistrustful sideways glances, as if he thought Freya's fiancé might pounce on him any second. Matt, for his part, looked as if he was itching to arrest someone. A door creaked open upstairs, and Ingrid cried, "Oh, no, Oscar got out!"

Matt turned to her. "Who's Oscar?"

Ingrid shook her head. "Oh, no one, just a pet," she said anxiously, moving toward the stairway to the second floor to waylay the familiars. But a disordered thudding of feet was descending the stairs, and all the pixies had begun to bustle past her into the room.

In the black leather mask, Kelda lunged to the front, pointing a finger.

"My mask!" cried Freya. "I've been looking for that!"

"It's him! It's him!" Kelda shouted. "We heard his voice!"

"You aren't supposed to be here!" Ingrid scolded, standing

between the pixies and Matt, her arms stretched out, as if she could hide them from him.

Joanna stood up, shouting. "What are these *things* doing in my house! Pixies! They drown little children and eat them!" she cried. "Get them out of here. Immediately!"

Norman stood up and grasped Joanna by the shoulders and was whispering in her ear. "Calm down, darling. That's just a myth, something told in Asgard to keep the little gods from straying to the other worlds." He didn't want the mortal in the room to hear.

"It's him!" the pixies yelled in unison.

Ingrid turned to the pixies. They were dirty, their faces blackened from a day outdoors. "What are you talking about?" Ingrid asked, flustered.

"He's the one! He's the one!" they said, pointing toward the fireplace and couch, where Freddie and Killian were standing. It was impossible to tell exactly whom they were pointing at.

221

chapter forty-three

It's a Family Affair

❦

"W ho? What?" Ingrid asked.

Val pushed forward. "He's the one we s-s-s-stole the trident from. When we heard him, we s-s-suddenly remembered that part. He isn't the one who banished us. We were wrong about that. We were confused. Another guy made us st-st-st . . ."

"Steal?" asked Ingrid.

Val nodded his head. "Yes. Steal the trident."

Sven gave a cough, putting an arm around Val, and added, "Erda, as soon as we heard the guy, we knew it was him. The one we'd seen while we were Dumpster diving. We stole the trident from him. But he's not the one who kicked us out of our home."

"What are they talking about, Ingrid?" Matt asked. "Who's Erda? Is this the band of homeless kids who assaulted you? I thought you told me you put them on a bus!"

"Homeless kids?" Freya asked, cocking an eyebrow. "They're not kids. They're pixies."

Ingrid turned nervously. "I'll explain later, okay?" she said to Matt, whispering an incantation under her breath to strengthen the harmony spell.

"Okay." Matt scratched his chin with a thumb.

Ingrid addressed the pixies. "First of all, can you please show me exactly who you mean?"

Nyph, whose hair was pulled into a large knob on her head, emphasizing her ears, strode over to Freddie and tugged his sweater. "This one. We stole the trident from this one. Someone made us do it. But we didn't know why. We were threatened . . . I think I don't remember." She looked up at Freddie. "I'm sorry, we have nothing against you, someone made us do it."

"*Finally!*" he said, smiling because what the pixies were saying proved that he had been framed. Someone had made them steal his trident, and that someone was in the room right now.

Nyph was still hanging on to his sweater, gazing up at him with an enamored smile, as Freddie whirled around, pointing at Killian.

Freya and Killian took a step backward.

"Is this the guy who made you steal my trident?" Freddie boomed, pointing at Killian.

"What trident?" asked Matt, but no one paid him any mind.

The pixies stared at Killian and vigorously shook their heads no, then all began talking at once. "We've never s-s-seen that guy before," Val said.

"Who's he?" Sven asked suspiciously.

"I'm Killian," he said with a grin, obviously finding the pixies amusing.

"Killian's not the one who made us do it," Nyph confirmed. "It was a bigger man." She gestured with her hands, indicating someone broader and taller, and the other pixies agreed.

Freya was thrilled. Killian and her twin were innocent. She hugged her man. "I knew it!" She turned to her twin. "See, Freddie!" she said. "You're wrong! I told you!"

Freddie looked confused. "Are you sure?" he asked the pixies. "You're sure this isn't him?"

The shook their heads.

"Nope, not him, not him."

Freddie rubbed his eyes. He walked over to Killian and gripped his shoulder. "Sorry, man. My bad. I've been in Limbo a long time."

"It's all right," Killian said. "Don't even think about it."

Don't even think about it? Freya fumed. She was of a mind to give her brother a tongue-lashing after everything he had put her through. But she took Killian's lead. There was no anger in him, and she had to respect that. Besides, even if the pixies swore that Killian hadn't ordered them to steal the trident, that still didn't explain why he bore the mark. Until they found out who was behind this plot, none of them was safe.

Ingrid interrogated the pixies further about what the man in question looked like, but all they could tell her was that it was too difficult to describe him. It made their heads hurt. They promised her that when they saw him, they would know immediately as they had with Freddie. They would come to her with the information as they had now.

"You did well," Ingrid said, and she patted Kelda on the head.

INGRID KNEW THAT SITTING at the table was best for all and was eager to corral everyone over to it, including the pixies, who were so small they could squeeze in, when Joanna proposed bringing out dessert. Ingrid realized that the ritual she had performed while setting the table had turned it into a safe zone, so it was the best way to have Matt accept the pixies' presence without question for now. As long as everyone in the house remained seated around it, there was harmony, but as soon as anyone left it, chaos would ensue. She let Freya in on the secret, and the sisters quickly cleared the table and brought out the dessert plates, pies, ice cream, and whipped cream so that everyone could sit back down.

"There's much to celebrate on this Thanksgiving Day," Joanna announced at the head of the table.

Freddie sat beside his mother, a smile beaming on his lips. "So, guys," he said, "there's this incredible gi—"

Joanna quickly put a finger to his lips. "Hush, my darling son, I am making a speech—your welcoming speech, my love." She smiled at him, then ran a hand through his hair.

"Oh," said Freddie, his shoulders drooping. He was dying to tell everyone at the table all about Hilly.

Joanna rose from her seat and put her hands together as if in prayer. She was wondering how exactly to word what she needed to express without giving too much away to Matt. She couldn't talk about what had happened at the Bofrir or about Freddie having returned from Limbo, which would make the young man think she was completely bonkers, especially since from what she could tell, he was one of those who didn't believe in magic, which was going to be a problem since it did seem like he *was* going to be part of the family. She cleared her throat as everyone watched her, anticipating her speech. Norman lifted his chin to egg her on.

"My son has at last returned," she said. "And we have solved . . . *um* . . . an *issue* that has long troubled the Beauchamp family. We are all together once again after a *very, very looong* time. I give thanks to all the gods." Here she raised her hands to the skies, or rather the chandelier, then smiled at Norman, who grinned back, giving her a wink. She turned to Freddie, running the back of her hand along his cheek, gazing fondly upon him.

Freddie looked over at Norman. "As I was saying, there's this really beautiful—"

"Hear, hear!" cried out Freya, clinking a dessert fork against her glass. "That was an excellent speech, Mother! Short and sweet." Everyone clinked their glasses with her as she glared at Freddie, silently urging him to keep his trap shut about this

225

Hilly girl. It really wasn't the time and place for him to be going on about his latest coed conquest, and that would only open up a can of a thousand wriggling worms. They would have to explain Freddie's holing up at the motel for the last month, the websites her twin had become addicted to, and so on and so forth, all in front of Matt. She narrowed her eyes at her brother, and once again he deflated.

"Let's drink to the family! And *welcome*, Matthew Noble!" said Norman.

More champagne bottles were popped, froth pouring over glasses.

"None for me, thanks," Matt said, looking strained and confused. "My head hurts. I'm sorry. I don't feel well. I think I need to get going. It's been wonderful meeting you all." He stood up, looking dizzy, and Ingrid helped him to the door. She knew it was only the power of her harmony spell that was keeping him from saying what he wanted to say, and that he was most likely feeling ill because he was fighting it so hard. She felt terrible about using her magic on him and wished there had been some other way to keep the evening peaceful.

ACROSS FROM THEM, Freya and Killian were having their own little aside, talking sotto voce. "I have to admit," said Freya, "I was about to practice some very unsavory magic to get to the truth. I went to Jean-Baptiste and got a recipe and incantation from him to retrieve your memory. Not exactly our kind of magic. I'm glad I didn't have to do it."

Killian glared at her with disbelief. "Promise me you will never, ever do that again! You should never, ever resort to something like that, not on my behalf or anyone else's." He touched her neck. "What were you thinking? There's no way to escape justice, not among our kind. That kind of magic can backfire on us, badly."

Norman, adept at catching snippets of conversation from teaching hundreds of students at a time in large auditoriums, had not missed out on the latter exchange. "Freya, what exactly do you mean by the unsavory kind of magic?"

Joanna, fawning over Freddie, froze. "Freya!" she exclaimed.

Ingrid came back after bidding a quick and distracted good-bye to Matt so she could catch the rest of the conversation. She had second thoughts about having enchanted him and wished she could take it back, but for now she was glad no one had noticed his discomfort. "Black magic! Are you insane?" she chided Freya.

"Oh, no!" said Sven. "Someone's in troubs!"

The pixies laughed.

"This is not a laughing matter, guys!" said Ingrid.

Freya fluffed her hair, then tugged at the bustier of her dress. "Well, I *didn't* do it, did I now? Jean-Baptiste did warn me, but he's my godfather, and he gave me the recipe."

"Jean-Baptiste has a weakness for pretty girls. He'll give you whatever you want as long as you prod him a little. Of course he gave you the recipe, Freya!" said Joanna.

"But, but—" Freya protested. Killian caressed her bare shoulders, and she kissed his hand.

Ingrid crossed her arms, then felt a furry coziness at her foot and looked down to find a round little pig nuzzling her. "Gullin-bursti!" she exclaimed, calling Freddie's familiar by his ancient name. "Am I happy to see you! *Yes, yes!* It's been too, too long!" She tickled him under the chin, and he squealed happily.

Meanwhile, Norman and Joanna were questioning their children on everything that had happened with the pixies and with Freddie's return. The girls were relieved that everything was out

227

in the open so that the family could strategize. They needed to know who had ordered the pixies to steal Freddie's trident, because whoever did so was the real culprit of the Bofrir's destruction, and now the most powerful god in all the nine worlds. Whoever it was had already abused his or her power by making Freddie appear responsible. Once they knew the identity of the true criminal, they could go to the White Council and exonerate Freddie and Killian for good. Of course, it would mean Loki would be exonerated as well, but no one cared about that for now.

Every time Freya sensed Freddie was about to veer the topic over to Hilly, she shot him a cold, quieting glance before he could get the girl's name out. Bringing a meaningless person into the picture would only overcomplicate an already complicated situation, Freya believed. She pulled her brother aside and asked him to cut it out about Hilly; as things stood, Joanna was already upset with both of them—but mostly Freya—about Freddie having hidden out at the Ucky Star for so long without her knowledge. How would Mother feel if she learned her son had been casually dating and getting his kicks that whole time? "Just wait a while, Freddie. Don't rush it. Please! I know how you feel. You're in love and want to tell everyone, but let's just keep it between us for now until the time is right, okay?" Freddie grudgingly conceded she was right.

Joanna requested that the first order of business was moving the pixies out of the house, as the attic was no place for anyone let alone a bunch of excitable pixies. She seemed to have warmed to them and had stopped mentioning cannibalistic tendencies, but she was firm about not letting them stay. The pixies had caused too much trouble in the house to be able to remain; they had scared off Gracella for one. The misplaced objects were the spirit's doing, but it was clear that the pie eating and the missing food from the pantry and refrigerator were certainly the pixies' fault, and she wasn't going to stand for it.

The motel was suggested as an obvious choice for a good hide-out, Freddie having gone unnoticed there for such a long time. Ingrid agreed that bringing the pixies to the motel was a good idea. She would have to keep them safe from Matt, especially if it turned out that the pixies had actually been involved in the bur-glaries. It wasn't their fault they didn't understand the rules of right and wrong in Midgard.

"Still, if I find out you guys have been stealing when I told you to stop! . . ." she said, scanning their faces wrathfully.

"Frogs, we know," Sven said in a bored voice.

"When will you stop berating us, Erda? We really mean no harm," said Kelda.

Freya took her turn. "You guys need to get cracking on re-membering who ordered you to steal Freddie's trident!"

"Oh, sure! We'll get right on it, after we relocate!" The pixies grumbled loudly about how unhappy they were about having to move from the attic.

"They say death, divorce, and moving are the three most trau-matic events anyone can experience," Sven said with a sly look.

There was no getting anywhere with the pixies, and Joanna was losing her patience. She rapped her wand on the table, send-ing a shower of sparks. "Do as you are told or I'll send the whole lot of you to my sister Helda! Norman is going to drop you off at that motel on his way back to the university and that's final!"

For once, no one argued or questioned her judgment.

229

chapter forty-four

Would I Lie to You?

&

In the back office at the library, Hudson and Ingrid were on coffee break while a very pregnant Tabitha and the new intern, Jeannine Mays, a creative-writing graduate student who attended classes in the evenings at a nearby university and resembled a younger version of Tabitha with her long hair, ankle-length skirts, and sweet, laid-back manner, manned the library. They liked Jeannine even if she was forever pressing her latest manuscript on them to read.

Ingrid and Hudson were catching up. He had been away with his guy, visiting Scott's parents in Miami for Thanksgiving, where they had spent a week. This was it—the ultimate ultimatum. Scott had told Hudson that it was only fair that they spend Christmas with Hudson's family. Hudson better start moving on it, and if he didn't, Scott was moving out. Scott had told him it was time to come out of the closet, even if it was large and a walk-in, had a minibar and a television.

"So are you going to do it?" Ingrid asked.

Hudson gave her a slow smile, and Ingrid noted his lovely teeth, so pearly, like Matt's. "I don't have a choice, do I? But Scott's right. I have to grow up sometime. If you can tell your boyfriend you're a virgin, I can tell my mom and dad I'm gay. You've given me courage, old girl."

Ingrid smiled. "Well, I'm glad I could help." She sighed.

"What happened?" Hudson asked.

She shook her head.

"You can tell me," he said, cocking his head at her.

That was all the prompting she needed from her friend. She told him pretty much everything about the past week, leaving out the more inexplicable parts. It boiled down to this: she hadn't heard from Matt since Thanksgiving, after which, the very next morning, two officers had shown up at Joanna's, taking Freddie, her brother who had returned after a long voyage abroad, down to the station for questioning in the burglaries. She left out the part about the officers arriving with a warrant to search the premises since they'd heard her mother was harboring illegal immigrants in her attic. They had turned the house upside down but found no hidden loot or "illegals."

At the station, they had fingerprinted Freddie but saw no priors in the system. Then a fancy New York City attorney had shown up on Freddie's behalf, saying, "You're done with my client." The officers had instantly released him, but not without warning her brother that he remained a primary suspect in the burglaries and they would be keeping an eye on him. Freddie said he had no clue who had sent the lawyer, although Ingrid had sensed her brother was hiding something. But that was not the point. Freddie had reported to Ingrid that the whole time Matt had remained at his desk, watching all of this unfurl as if he were surreptitiously orchestrating it.

"You know what I think, Ingrid?"

She shook her head.

"You need to call him and ask him what's up. Do it right now or else it will drive you crazy."

"But—"

"But what? Because you're the girl, you're not supposed to

call him? *Please!* I thought you knew better than that. Put him on the spot. It's unacceptable that he didn't even call to thank you for inviting him over. That's just rude. Not to mention sending the police to your home!" Hudson ran a tongue over his teeth. "I was all for this relationship, but now I'm not so sure . . ." He grabbed their empty coffee mugs and pastry wrappings and walked to the door, turning back to her. "Call him, Ingrid! Do it now!"

"Bossy!" she said, then gritted her teeth. But she knew he was right.

A FTER PROCRASTINATING WITH SOME WORK, Ingrid returned to her desk and glared at the phone as if it were a ticking bomb. She reached for it but quickly pulled her hand back to primp her hair. Finally she went for it, sitting down, clasping the phone between her shoulder and cheek, and punching in Matt's cell.

He picked up on the second ring. Silence. Ingrid waited. Nothing.

"Matt?"

He coughed. "Yeah, Ingrid," he said brusquely. "What's up?"

"I just wanted to call and see . . . how you were," she said lamely. "I haven't seen you since Thanksgiving."

There was another long pause and finally Matt spoke. "You lied to me," he said quietly. "You said you put those kids on a bus."

"I know . . . I'm sorry . . . But there's so much you need to understand about my family," she said. "First of all, they're not kids, Matt . . . They're pixies. They're magical creatures from another world . . ."

Another long pause. "Ingrid, there's no such thing. The next thing you'll say is that you're a witch."

"But I *am* a witch," she cried. "I'm not thirty-two years old, Matt. I'm so much older . . . You have no idea. And I can prove

232

it! I put a spell on you so you wouldn't be upset about what happened at dinner . . . Remember your headache?"

"Enough of this nonsense," he said. "Red wine always gives me headaches. Look, I'm sorry about your brother, but the fact of the matter is there've been a bunch of unsolved robberies in the area."

"Freddie? He would never! You had no right to bring him in."

"He was dressed as a cat burglar."

"But that's just . . . a coincidence."

"In my line of work, there's no such thing," he said sternly.

Which means, in his mind, there was no such thing as witches and warlocks and pixies, either, Ingrid realized, her heart sinking.

"I trusted you. You said those kids were gone and they weren't. Not only that but they were living in your house. In the attic as I remember."

Ingrid didn't know how to answer to that. A droplet of sweat from her armpit slid along the inside of her arm inside her sleeve—so unpleasant, like a cold little worm. This was dreadful. Without thinking, she blurted out, "Well, you lied to me, too, Matt. I know you're seeing someone else."

"Seeing someone? What are you talking about?"

"Well, when we were at dinner, a little piece of paper fell out of that 'work' notebook of yours. It said 'Maggie' on it and had a phone number accompanying the name. Then at my house, you put your phone down for a second, and I noted that the last call had been to someone named Maggie. I might be . . . *inexperienced* . . . but I'm not naïve." She had done some fibbing, but ultimately it was all truthful, at least the salient parts: she had seen the paper and the name in his phone after quickly scrolling through his list of outgoing calls. It had been his last call.

"Jesus, Ingrid! You have no idea what you're talking about!"

"*You* have no idea what *you* are talking about, Matt!"

They were both speechless for some time. She could hear him breathing. The connection between them was stretching taut, about to snap. "Fine!" he said.

"Fine!" she snapped.

"You know, I don't think this is going to work out . . ."

"I guess not," said Ingrid. "Good-bye."

He didn't have anything to say to that, so they both simultaneously hung up. Ingrid stared at the phone again. She was more angry than hurt. Actually, she was furious.

Had she just broken up with him? Was that a breakup? She hadn't broken up with anyone before, but it felt like a breakup. She had made a horrible mistake with Matt. Why had she let herself fall in love with him? What a fool she was! A mortal could never understand her, especially one who was so closed minded to the possibility that there was more to life, more to the universe than what was in front of his nose. How could she ever have fallen in love with someone so . . . literal, so practical, so . . . mundane. Someone who didn't even believe in *magic*!

Besides, who did he think he was? Sending the police to get Freddie, not to mention search their house! She needed to shelve some books.

chapter forty-five

A Mother's Love

പ്പ

Her lovely boy now occupied the empty bedroom in the house that had caused her so much grief as a daily reminder of his absence. She had kept the bedroom orderly and clean—she so wanted it to be pleasant for him—and brought him breakfast in bed every morning so she could watch him wake; it was like seeing the sun rise as he opened his eyes.

Freddie had finally gotten out of that horrendous, torturous Limbo, that land of nothingness, and now he must live and enjoy the pleasures life offered, such as a mother's love. Oh, how he had suffered, the poor child! It was tantamount to being in love, a similar feeling (although the love a mother felt for a child was even more fathomless; it was constant, unwavering). One could throw anything at her now, and it would barely made a dent. She'd forgotten completely about blowing off Harold at Thanksgiving. As for the little matter of the local police, she hadn't been worried for a moment, knowing her boy was innocent and that there was nothing to be found in the attic. These were pesky problems that had been easily solved.

So she did not understand why her girls were acting so histrionic now. The children were gathered in the living room and Ingrid and Freya were practically hysterical.

Joanna sat next to Freddie on the couch, but he subtly inched away. Okay, maybe she was being too clingy? She needed to watch that.

Ingrid stood by the fireplace while Freya faced the glass doors to the deck, staring out toward Gardiners Island, which was presently enshrouded in fog. "Mother, you are acting so . . . What's the term, Ingrid?"

"Blinded?"

Freya turned to them. "Yes, and it's like you're drunk or something!"

Joanna did have a permanent smile on her face lately, so one might mistake her for being soused or tipsy—and she herself had caught herself humming once or twice, no real song or tune, just humming. "Drunk?" she said. *"No! I'm just happy!"*

Ingrid wiped a bit of lint off her skirt. "What Freya is trying to say, Mother, is that this trident business is very important. Whoever destroyed the bridge is extremely powerful and a threat to us, not to mention he or she could be lethal not only to Midgard but the nine worlds of the universe. It's our job to make sure nothing happens. We know you've been ecstatic since Freddie came home, and we need you to stay on course right now."

Joanna rose and threw a log on the fire. She pointed a finger at it, and flames instantly leaped up. She rumpled her hair. The girls were right; there were problems ahead. But couldn't she just enjoy having her son back for now? For just a moment? Besides, she did have something to say about this trident business, but she didn't know if her girls wanted to hear it.

"Freya, if you want my opinion, I'll give it to you."

Freya and Ingrid turned to their mother and stared at her questioningly. Freddie rose and stepped back a bit.

"I think Killian did it," Joanna said plainly.

"Excuse me?"

Joanna ran a hand through her long hair. "Why do you think

the pixies couldn't remember him? He put up a wall that night. He seemed so—what?—nonchalant, flippant? He didn't even flinch when the detective held a gun to Freddie's head. I mean, we didn't know that it was Freddie, but still! And you were going to practice black magic on his behalf. Whose influence is that? His!"

"Bu—"

"No. Let me finish. It's all very subtle, Freya. Don't you see? Killian is trying to turn you; meanwhile he's the one who has the pixies under a spell. We've never seen him practice magic, because he doesn't want to show us exactly how powerful he is. Which means he's probably so powerful he doesn't need to wave a wand; he just gives that hypnotic smile of his, and all his little soldiers line up and fight his battle for him." Joanna placed her hands on her hips. "Also, there's the matter of Killian bearing the mark of the trident. How do you explain that? Oh, don't deny it. I heard you whispering at dinner. He's guilty, Freya. The pixies will remember him in time."

Freya's jaw had dropped as she stared at her mother, incensed. "Mother, I can't even begin to address that . . ."

Freddie put a hand to his forehead and was shaking his head.

Ingrid held Freya by the shoulders now, steadying her. "Come on, Freya. Don't get into it. Mother doesn't know what she's talking about. It's not Killian."

Freya was huffing, and she let Ingrid guide her away. "Let's get out of here, Ingrid. I need a drive."

"Me, too," said Ingrid. And they moved toward the kitchen as Freddie glared at them pleadingly, but they both looked away from him.

"If that's how you girls want to play it, go ahead! Make camps. Go! But Freya, you know I'm right!" Joanna called to their backs. She headed to her study, where she slammed the door.

chapter forty-six

Sibling Rivalries

ᔆᕋ

F reya put the Mini in neutral, then turned the key in the ignition when someone began tapping at the passenger window.
Ingrid pushed the window button, and Freddie's head popped in.

"Please take me with you!" he pleaded. "Mom's wrong. Killian
didn't do it. He's innocent. I know it now. I'm sorry. She's acting
crazy and driving me mad. *Please take me!*" He was hopping from
foot to foot, shivering in just a T-shirt and jeans.

Ingrid looked to Freya as if to take her cue.

Freya shrugged. "Get in, but you have a lot of explaining to
do! I'm not sure I trust you—whoever you are!"

Ingrid opened her door and stepped out so Freddie could
get in.

"Jeez, thanks, girls. I love you! I love you!" He jumped up
and down, barefoot, having rushed out of the house after them.
He piled into the backseat, but he had to sit crouched sideways
because of his height and long legs.

"Maybe we should take Mom's car," Ingrid suggested.

"Let him suffer back there," Freya said. "There are a lot of
questions he needs to answer."

Ingrid got back in, moving up her seat to give Freddie more
legroom. "Aw, poor kid!"

"*Uh!* Don't feel sorry for him, Ingrid. Mom has done enough
of that," said Freya. "He doesn't need our pity."

"True," said Ingrid. "Can I show you Matt's house? We can drive there."

Freya threw her sister a puzzled look. "You've got to be kidding me! We're not going to stalk him. He acted like a jerk. Leave it for now. Maybe he'll come around." She put the car in first and pulled out of the driveway, heading inland toward the highway to Napeague, where she would go east toward Montauk.

Ingrid kicked at the floor. "I know. I don't know why I said that. It just came out. I don't want to have anything to do with him anymore." She looked down at herself.

"Good!" said Freya, squeezing her sister's knee. She was glad the channels of communication had been flowing between them again. She had longed for that for quite a while. It was so good to have Ingrid back, not to have to hide anything from her, and it was especially good to act as a confidante for her older sister's love troubles. That was a change! Ingrid had always been there for her in that regard, and now Freya could finally return the support, care, and kind words, as well as a little tough love when needed; it had always felt so uneven, always weeping on Ingrid's shoulder, leaning in toward her gentle, reassuring hands. Now she could offer the same.

Shame on Matt—Freya was furious with him. How dare he! No one should ever hurt Ingrid; it was appalling to even imagine. How could he have been so cowardly as to send the other officers to do his dirty work, arresting Freddie and searching the house. *The bastard.*

"Maybe it was my fault," Ingrid added. "I did kind of put a spell on him, but I hadn't meant to."

"It was just a harmony spell, Ingrid!" said Freya. "No harm in that. It was for the family. Come, come. We'll talk about it later. I promise. Let's take care of this Freddie business for now."

"All right, let's," she said, smiling sadly at Freya.

The sky had tinged pink and orange as the sun set behind

239

them. They needed to leave North Hampton, the pocket. It felt claustrophobic to Freya. Mother had made it so. Her accusation of Killian had been a slap in the face, and she was still smarting from it. She saw Freddie in the rearview mirror looking glum.

The car had already grown warm, and she cracked her window for a little air. Joanna had truly pissed her off. She glimpsed at Freddie in the rearview again. He always looked so innocent; it was hard to have any ill will against her twin. But still, she needed to know if he was truly Freddie and what he had been up to.

"First off," she said, "you lied to me. You said you never left the Ucky Star, but I saw you when I was taking out the trash at the North Inn. I saw you in that back alley. Now we know the pixies saw you outside, too."

"Yeah," sighed Freddie. "That was me. I only left the motel twice and only when it was dark at night. You and the pixies must have seen me on one of those nights. You see, if you'll forgive me for talking about it, I am very much in love with Hilly Liman—"

"I know that," cut in Freya.

"Who's Hilly Liman?" asked Ingrid.

Freddie inhaled a huge breath. "Oh, my god, Ingrid, she's *incredible . . .*"

"Enough!" exclaimed Freya, slapping the driver's wheel. "Get to the point, Freddie! Don't distract him, Ingrid." They had entered a forest, and the trees shadowed the road. Freya flicked on the headlights. A deer was running gracefully along the side of the road, then darted into the trees.

Freddie rearranged himself in the back. "Well, you see, Hilly's dad is . . . um . . . very protective of his daughter. And I really want to marry the girl!"

Ingrid swung around, leaning over her seat. "That's so great, Freddie!"

"Shh, let him continue. We really need to clear this up," said

Freya, reaching over to her sister to give Ingrid a gentle pat. Freddie had a way of distracting everyone from the point sometimes. He was kind of like the pixies.

He continued. "Mr. Liman, Hilly's dad, thinks I'm a slacker . . . a playboy . . ."

Freya laughed. "He isn't wrong, is he?" She was driving fast, and she took a sharp swerve on the road, and they all knocked about in the little car.

Freddie came back up and leaned forward. "Well, Hilly thought that if I got a good job, her dad would think more highly of me. One night she hooked me up with her dad's partner. It was supposed to be on the down low; her dad didn't even know about it yet. She drove me to the French restaurant, where the partner was having dinner. He met me in the back alley, we talked about the job, a kind of meet and greet, and then Hilly drove me back to the motel. I went back a second time to see the fellow to sort out some loose ends. He seems to like that particular restaurant."

"Okay," said Freya. "But what did you mean when you said to Hilly, 'It won't be long now'?"

"You heard that? Jeez!"

"I was spying!"

"She's pretty, isn't she?" asked Freddie. "Hilly?"

Freya exhaled a sigh of frustration. "Freddie!"

Freddie continued. "What I meant was the guy had offered me the job, and it wouldn't be long till I started working for him and that her dad would approve of me more, and Hilly and I could be together soon—without having to worry."

Ingrid spoke. "What kind of job?"

The little car exited the forest and the left side of the road gave way to a silvery beach. Freya pulled up on the shoulder and abruptly stopped the car, pulling the safety break.

The man was a sea captain, Freddie explained, and the job

241

entailed going on a last tuna run. Freddie had always been enamored of the sea and sailing, so he was quite excited about it.
The boat was leaving in a fortnight, but apparently there were
still some arrangements to be made, a contract of some sort that
required signing before Freddie departed.

The motor of the car clicked as it cooled. Suddenly this little
nook felt like a respite to Freya. All right, so Freddie had lied,
but only because he was in love and Freya of all people was very
familiar with that feeling.

"I have another question," Ingrid piped in. "Who was the lawyer who came to the precinct?"

"Good one!" Freya glanced at her brother in the rearview to
find him checking himself out in the mirror. Still vain old Freddie. If anything it just confirmed it was her brother in the car
and not Loki.

"Hilly sent that lawyer. Mom gave me her cell when they
took me away, and the first chance I got, I called Hilly, and that
lawyer helicoptered in from the city—just for me. Cool, right?"

"I guess," said Freya flatly.

THEY GOT OUT OF THE CAR. Freya and Ingrid threw on their
coats, while Freddie shivered. Freya checked the trunk, found
one of Killian's sweaters, and handed it to her brother. The three
of them walked toward the beach, Ingrid in the middle, and she
reached out for their hands. Once they were all connected, Freya
sensed the magic running through them like an electrical current. For a moment, she felt whole and carefree. She tugged at
them and ran ahead on the beach, still holding hands. She felt
like they were kids again, and all their troubles seemed to suddenly dissipate in the open air. It was going to be all right. Freddie and Killian were both in the clear. The pixies had seen to

that. Freddie had been set up, but not by Killian. Even Ingrid began to laugh as they ran.

They all plopped down in the sand, one after the other, laughing, and looked out at the glorious sky, pink bleeding into orange, slate blue above and, below, indigo waves splashing down with an unstoppable force.

Freya looked over at Freddie: he was trembling and looked vulnerable. She felt a twinge. She wanted Freddie to be happy. She wanted her siblings to both have love as she experienced it with Killian. They ran back to the car together, with a better feeling between them.

"How do you know Killian is innocent?" Freya said to her twin as she steered the car back to the road.

"I just do. What Mom said was totally bogus. It's not him. When I saw him at Thanksgiving, saw how happy he was to see me, I knew. It couldn't be him. He's my friend. He's loyal. He's one of us."

Freya nodded. "I've been trying to tell you that for months."

"But there's something I need to tell you about Killian . . ." he said, his face pale.

"Just spit it out, Freddie," Freya said. "Now that you've come around you want Killian to be your best man at the wedding?"

Freddie cleared his throat. "I know Killian is innocent, as I said. But I didn't before. I spied on you, too, Freya. I know about the trident mark. I overheard you talking about it, saw him showing it to you in the greenhouse. I don't know why he has it. He had to have had the trident in his possession at some point; that's the only way. When I saw it, I still believed in his guilt—"

"So you went and told the Valkyries . . ." concluded Ingrid.

Freya pulled over and stopped the car. She swung around to face him.

"I had to clear my name!" Freddie protested. "I was convinced he did it! He had the mark!"

Freya turned back and stared ahead at the dark road. She tapped on the driver's wheel, and Ingrid reached out to her but she brushed her older sister aside. "Get out of this car right now, Freddie!" They had so little time, and she'd been clueless. Why had her stupid brother waited until now to tell her? Damn him! If they couldn't find the real responsible person, Killian would be carted away to Limbo for sure. "Get out!" she cried.

"But—" said Freddie.

"Freya—calm down."

Freya glared at Ingrid, who reluctantly opened the passenger door and stepped outside to let Freddie out. He unfolded his long frame from the backseat and stepped onto the road.

Ingrid got back in the car. "Come on, you're being really harsh. We can't just leave him here!"

"For god's sake, Ingrid, he's a god! He can make the sun shine! Let him find his own way home!" Freya snapped, and she gunned the engine, leaving their brother behind in the darkness.

christmas

the most wonderful time of the year?

chapter forty-seven

Devil Woman

꩜

A crescent moon hung in the sky, as slim as a fingernail clipping. It was a cloudless night, bright with stars. Freya could see all of this from Joanna's study's window—the ocean dark as ink, the moon and stars' reflections glimmering there. Joanna sat at her desk, Freya on the love seat, and Norman in the armchair by the books. He was acting as mediator. A good thing, too, since the holiday season was upon them—it would be Christmas soon—but no one was in the mood to celebrate.

Joanna had been profusely apologizing to Freya for having accused Killian. She explained that Freddie's return had blinded her, but now she realized the error of her ways. "I'm sorry about Killian. I was just so worried about Freddie, but apparently now I'm suffocating him and my baby boy is pulling away from me." Joanna sighed.

Freya listened intently and frowned. "Do you realize, Mother, that you have brought the conversation back to Freddie once again?"

"Oh, I'm sorry!" said Joanna, looking over at Norman for help.

"Okay," said Norman. "We have that all cleared now. Your mother is very, very sorry, so let's move on. We have these impending Valkyries to deal with, and there is little time to waste."

He ran a finger along the spines of Joanna's books. Norman was not fond of conflict—or he simply didn't like it when his ladies got prickly with one another.

"Yes," said Joanna. "I want to make it up to you, Freya, and I think I have a solution. I think we need to try a new angle."

"What's that?" Freya crossed her legs, picked at a hole in her black jeans, and then pulled at the top of a high-heeled boot.

Norman clapped his hands, as if to mark a shift in the conversation. "Your mother thinks that perhaps this spirit that's been trying to contact her is a witch trying to help us. The *Waelcyrgean* believe there are several sorts of spirits. We were trying to understand which kind this is. We narrowed it down to two possible ones. There is the *vörðr*, or vorder, the warden spirit."

Dad had launched into professor mode, and Freya loved to watch him at work, how he sought to make whatever topic palatable to the younger folk.

He rose from his armchair and stretched an arm out, leaning against the bookshelf. "The word *wraith* takes it root from *vörðr*, and *ward* and *warden* are its cognates, actually." He smiled at Freya. She found her father so handsome, that shock of silver hair slipping over a lens of his black-framed glasses. Ingrid got her delicate, foxy looks from him, as well as her lovely soft pink lips and tall, slim, lanky body. "Anyhow," Norman continued, "the *vörðr* is very much like a personal watchdog, a tagalong, so to speak, or a guardian angel if you want to think in Christian terms; it watches over a mortal from birth to death. If it attaches itself to a god, it is present through all of that god's lifetimes."

Norman went on to explain that there was another type, and that one was called *fylgja*, which in Old Norse meant "someone that accompanies." "But this kind only checks in occasionally," he said. The *fylgjur* (plural) were portentous. Aware of one's fate, they sometimes appeared as an omen of death. However, when they appeared as a woman, as this wraith had, it usually meant that she was warning you and possibly your clan that you were in danger. "What I am saying here is that Joanna and I believe this spirit to be the latter. She wants to tell us something, warn us about something, and she is sending her spirit through time to do so."

Freya rose and walked to the window, where she made an impression on the vapor with her fist. Then she drew the letter *K*, like a teenager. "So what am I supposed to do about all this?" she said, turning to her father.

Joanna rose and walked over to her daughter, then stood behind her. She placed her hands on her shoulders, and Freya flinched, but then reached a hand to her mother's. She wanted to forgive her. She was still angry, but there was no use holding on. Her mother had apologized and said she wanted to help Killian now. They needed to work together, and if her parents thought they knew how to resolve this, then she was willing to do whatever it took. She trusted their knowledge and experience.

Joanna squeezed her daughter's shoulders. "Someone needs to go back in time and find this witch before she is hanged. She will draw us to the correct time and place and help us, and we might in turn be able to help her. I'm too old to make the journey. I tried, but the portal wouldn't open for me. It requires youth and vitality, which I am not sure I have."

Freya turned to her mother, her eyes shining. Perhaps it was because she had been straining to see Gardiners Island. Killian was there, and she wanted to be with him. "I'll do anything to help Killian. If you think this is how we need to proceed, I'm willing," she said. "I'll do it."

"Good, good!" said Joanna. "There is much preparation to be made, and we need to get right to it. I need to brief you, and you also need to change into the proper attire." Here a distasteful look crossed Joanna's face. "We'll dress you like a good Puritan, cap and all. I've already put the costume together."

Freya frowned. Such clothes brought back awful memories, and she had grown so very fond of her twenty-first-century clothes. There was something to be said about Lycra.

"We'll do the ceremony on the beach. It's a perfect night for it. Isn't that right, Norm?" Joanna said, turning to her husband, still by the bookshelf, and he nodded gravely at his wife.

THE WAVES WERE TUMULTUOUS, crashing hard upon the shore, and the wind lashed at her white cap and beige blouse, too tight at the neck, the large collar flapping in her face. Joanna had tied a shawl around her daughter's waist and sewn a pouch full of gold coins into her skirt. Inside a circle in the sand, Freya pressed the heavy dark mauve skirt against her legs, one hand clasped around the runes that the *fylgja* had placed on the grave. As part of the ceremony, Freya needed to be touching something the witch's wraith had made contact with to make it all work.

"Look up, darling," Norman shouted. "It should be relatively painless."

"In godspeed!" cried Joanna. "I love you, my sweet!"

Freya looked up into the darkness pierced by stars. Something was pushing through, like an enormous weight on the other side, dropping toward her, sagging through the cloth of midnight-blue sky. The wind began to spin around her as if she had been swept inside the eye of a twister, a centrifugal force, the sand lifting and hitting her in the face like birdshot. She bent over, protecting her head and cap with her hands.

"Painless, my ass!" she muttered, and the words seemed to be sucked out of her by a vacuum, pulling at the inside of her throat, clasping it shut. She felt as if every molecule of her being were being disassembled, pried apart, and it hurt, a physical pain, but also an excruciating emotional one, like losing someone deeply loved, a death.

FREYA AWOKE FROM A DEEP, dreamless sleep. Her entire body ached. Something wet lapped at her face. She felt heat, the sun beaming down hard upon her side and back. She smelled the ocean. She lay on something uneven, hard, and gritty, and what were those sounds? She heard bleating. Again she felt a swipe of wetness across her face. She opened her eyes. A black dog was panting at her, wagging his tail. She put a hand in front of her face to shield her eyes from the sun. She lay on an outcropping of rock, tall grasses swaying about, sheep everywhere. She was surrounded by them, grazing in the grass, stepping onto her stone. Then she saw the runes scattered on the rock and quickly scrambled onto all fours to gather them.

"Ragbone!" a boy's voice cried.

Freya rose to her feet, batting the sand off her skirt, setting her cap to rights. She unwrapped the shawl from around her waist and threw it over her shoulders, then was happy to feel the coins hidden below the waist of her skirt. The dog watched her, cocking his head. The boy, around eleven years of age—a shepherd she deduced—ambled toward her with his staff.

"Good morrow," he cried, and Ragbone ran to him.

"Good morrow," replied Freya, smiling. She looked about. She was at the edge of a field, right before where the beach began. She looked toward the sea. She saw an island. She couldn't tell whether there were houses there or not, certainly no Fair Haven, but the line of the shore was its same pointy shape, the promontory and long sandy finger pointing toward the *U* of Long Island. She looked toward the land. Gone was Joanna's house, built in

251

1710. Instead there were trees, overgrowth, and the occasional large, ominous brown wooden house looming in the distance.

The boy stood a few feet away, staring at her. "Where did ye come from, Missus?" he asked. "I have not seen ye round these parts."

"I am from another village." Freya pointed vaguely down the shore. "I was rambling along the beach; then I decided to rest. I must have fallen asleep, dear me! What village are you from?"

"Why, I am from Fairstone," he said, studying Freya, who was staring out at Gardiners again. "Have ye been to the Isle of Wight? I would very much like to go there someday. A very rich man lives there now, Mr. Lion Gardiner, he does. There is work aplenty there. He bought the island a year ago."

Bingo. It was 1640. Lion Gardiner and his wife had bought the island in 1639, settling here. This had been part of Joanna's brief. It was hot, probably August. These clothes were so damned uncomfortable and were making her itch. She loosened the shawl around her shoulders and smiled encouragingly at the boy. "May I ask what the happenings are these days in Fairstone?"

The boy gave her a pained look. "Well, Mr. Bidding gives me quite a beating if I don't do my work properly. Goody Bidding can be nice if she isn't giving me the lash. Their daughter, she is fair and a good spinner both of wool and tales. Perhaps—"

This was a rather loquacious boy, Freya gleaned, so she cut to the chase. "Is there a courthouse in Fairstone?"

The boy shuddered, then looked down at himself. Freya moved closer and put a hand to his chin, lifting it gently, reciting a calming spell in her mind.

He sighed. "There is a courthouse with magistrates and much arguing there over property lines and animal thievery. And . . ."

"And?"

"Well, Sally Smitherstone accused Goody Anne Barklay of being a witch, trafficking with . . ." He hesitated.

"The devil?"

The boy blanched, then glanced at his dirty bare feet. "Yes." He looked at her. "Sally said Goody Anne came to her in spirit form, seeking to bewitch her. Many of the women in Fairstone dislike Anne. She is quite beautiful, a Frenchwoman who married an Englishman—Mr. Barklay. They even call her a harlot." Freya was grateful she had happened upon such a chatty, precocious boy, and he kept going. "She was always nice to me, Anne. Some say that Sally wanted to marry Mr. Barklay. Anne is perhaps a witch, but not a harlot. She did not confess to witchcraft, so tomorrow she is going to hang at sundown at the oak tree on the hill. They say she has the mark."

"Where is Anne now?" Freya asked, and it came out too loudly. She put a fist to her mouth and bit it.

The boy pointed to the west inland. "She is in the jail cell some ways over there. They have her in chains for all to see."

Freya immediately took off through the field in the direction the boy had pointed. She had to lift her heavy skirts to get her legs going.

"Do you know Anne, Missus?" the boy called to her.

Freya looked over her shoulder at him but did not answer. She winced at each step, slowly wending her way through the bleating sheep.

253

chapter forty-eight

The Greatest Love
of All

༄

As soon as Ingrid had entered the slanted room on the first floor of the Ucky Star, the pixies started bombarding her with information. She had to keep telling them to slow down, and they finally calmed a bit. She had driven Joanna's car here to put more money down on the room and check up on them. It seemed that being back at the motel had opened the floodgates of memory. She really needed them to get to the point; the Valkyries could show up any minute. Freya was in a time warp, trying to figure out the mystery from that end. All the Beauchamps were busy trying to find a way to save Killian.

"We're from Álfheim and we're called *álfar*. My real name is Skuld," said Kelda. "Well, actually, I'm half *álfar*, half Valkyrie. The Valkyries look down on me as a half-breed. Anyway, I've always been more *álfar*-identified."

"Oh, I've heard of Skuld!" said Ingrid. "A famous warrior and witch." She looked at Kelda thoughtfully. It was obvious whoever had put a spell on the pixies had divested them of their powers somewhat.

Kelda smiled proudly, lifting her narrow chest. She certainly didn't seem like someone who would raise soldiers from the dead to return them to battle. Kelda was too sweet and so cute with her delicate, pale round face and black tough-girl clothes. She had gotten a Medusa piercing in Midgard, a tiny garnet nestled in the philtrum above her rosebud lips; it did look pretty on her.

Ingrid was grateful to be getting such specifics at last, but she was so preoccupied, not only about the looming threat of the Valkyries but also about Freya, out there time trotting. She wished she had been the one to go instead, keeping her little sister out of harm's way: Freya had returned to a dreadful, dangerous time for a witch. Ever since her sister had left, the many times Ingrid thought about her, she squeezed her eyes shut, sending a protection spell Freya's way. She hoped her powers were such that they would reach her, but she feared it might not be enough.

"Do you remember who made you steal Freddie's trident?" Ingrid asked. "That's the most important matter of business at hand. Then we'll work on getting you to . . . *Ahem.*" She sounded as if she was clearing her throat when she said the latter, because she had never heard of the place before and didn't quite catch the name.

255

"Álfheim," Kelda corrected.

"An *áss*," said Sven from the armchair.

"Excuse me?" said Ingrid.

Sven took a pull on his Kool and exhaled. "An *áss* made us steal the trident," he said, exhaling a smoky sigh.

"Well, I'm sure an *ass* made you do it," retorted Ingrid. "And that's a naughty word."

"No, what he means is the type of god," said Irdick from the desk on which he was perched, his feet swinging back and forth. "He's an *áss*."

"Oh," said Ingrid. "I haven't heard of that kind of god before. Interesting. An *áss*. Well, do you know anything else?" she asked.

"*Yeah*," said Sven bluntly, which was his way. He grabbed the bottle of booze on the floor and swigged.

Ingrid wished Sven wouldn't drink so much. Maybe she could

get him to attend an AA meeting while he remained in North Hampton. It was anonymous after all. Tabitha had told her she was a proud member of that group and had been gratefully sober for years now. She raised an eyebrow at Sven, waiting for him to continue.

"Ah!" he said after gulping down way too much at once. "The *ass*, whoever he is, kidnapped us from Álfheim to steal the trident, but afterward it left us to wander Midgard to cover his tracks. But, unfortunately, we cannot remember who the guy is or what he looks like. That still makes our heads hurt. It's kind of like a blackout." Val came over and squeezed Sven's shoulder, and Sven batted his hand off.

Ingrid was glad to have more substantial clues. Maybe the pixies would remember eventually. She would come back tomorrow. In the meantime, she would go to Joanna and Norman with all this information. Her father had taken to driving up to North Hampton and spending the night lately. He and Joanna would know what to make of all of this.

Though she had much to fret about, Ingrid was relieved to have a purpose. It helped keep her mind off her pathetic love life, even if it had lasted only two hot seconds. She had stopped thinking so much about Matt, her first and only love, and still hadn't heard a peep from him since the *breakup*. Well, perhaps she only thought of him a little now. Or was it more than that? She hugged herself. What was that noise? A rushing sound. It was chilly and so moist in here; the heat was on, but it seemed as if cold, wet air crept in from every little crack. "What's that sound?" she asked, pointing vaguely in its direction.

"That's a leak," said Val. "In the bathroom. It's gotten kind of bad."

"I'm going to have to ask them to fix that for you before it gets any worse," she said, distracted. She really needed to get home. Poor pixies. She kind of missed them being in the attic, having them close by, which was strange because it had been so stressful when they'd been at the house. She imagined that this was what it was like to have children. They drove her crazy, but she did miss them terribly once they were out of sight.

chapter forty-nine

Come Sail Away

꒰ꕥ꒱

Freddie took another trip into the city, this time to visit Hilly's father at his downtown offices, located on the southernmost tip of Manhattan inside a triangular glass building resembling the bow of a ship that faced the East River. Standing before the skyscraper, looking up, Freddie almost lost his footing with the vertiginous feeling. The silver-blue walls shone blindingly in the midday light. The man was up there on the forty-second floor. After having spent thousands of years in Limbo, nothing in this world daunted him, but Freddie found Henry Liman terrifying, and not knowing the purpose of his visit further increased his angst. Hilly had texted him the address and appointment time the day before, and Freddie had arrived early, knowing Mr. Liman would expect punctuality. He took the elevator up and found the offices of Her Majesty's Shipping Co.

In the lobby, with curving walls of bubbly, frosted glass that appeared liquid, was a clear pod—also shaped like the bow of a ship or perhaps the top of an anvil, and inside sat a young man wearing a wireless headset. Behind the pod, three glass cases inside the wood-paneled wall displayed antique ship models.

"I'm here to see Mr. Liman," Freddie said, in suit, tie, and polished dress shoes. This time he had borrowed the outfit from Norman, so it wouldn't vanish—despite Mr. Liman's love for magic tricks.

The receptionist requested Freddie's name, looking at him blandly, then pressed a button, and said, "Mr. Liman, Frederick Beauchamp to see you."

Freddie smiled nervously, dabbing his brow with the handkerchief Ingrid had given him for the trip.

With much disapproval, the receptionist glared at Freddie. "You're early. Have a seat, and Mr. Liman's assistant will be out to get you."

According to the loudly ticking clock inside the glass pod, it was only seven minutes before the appointed time. There was no pleasing Mr. Liman. Freddie clasped his hands behind his back and strode over to the ship models to pass the time. He did love a good old-fashioned ship.

The first was the *Fancy, Pearl, Victory*, and its black sails indicated, indubitably, that it was a pirate ship. The second, *Queen Anne's Revenge*, had a dazzling oversize wooden hull of several tiers, large white sails, and a square-nosed bow, adorned with wooden mermaids, horses, and gods instead of a single prow. This ship Freddie proudly recognized; it was rather well-known as the largest pirate ship to have existed. He had come across it in his online catch-up studies, becoming quite the autodidact on the history of seafaring. Edward Teach, Blackbeard, had captured her in the Caribbean in 1717, christened her with that name, and used her for battle at the apex of his of reign of terror.

"Mr. Beauchamp?" squeaked a meek voice. Freddie turned toward a gaunt, mousy fellow, also with a headset. "This way," he said. The assistant guided him along more watery curving glass until it gave way to a door, which he opened for Freddie, then nodded, signaling for him to enter alone. As Freddie stepped into the office, the sun shone so brightly from the windows ahead that he couldn't see at all, although he did immediately recognize the voice, which made the hair on his arms rise.

"All of my employees are male, but that doesn't mean you

should take me for a sexist. It's because of my wife," said Henry Liman. "*Hollis.*" He harrumphed.

Freddie had a hand up at his face to block the glare and was still trying to make out Liman. "I didn't," he said.

"Good," said Liman. "I wouldn't be sending Hilly—and Gert, too—to that expensive school if I were. Sexist, I mean."

Now Freddie could see that Henry was smugly smiling to himself behind an enormous, intimidating, gleaming dark cherrywood desk, also curved like a ship. There was certainly a theme here. He waited for Liman to ask him to take a seat and wondered if he would. "How is Hollis?"

"Fine. Everyone's fine. Take a seat," said Liman.

"Thank you, Henry," Freddie said, remembering Mr. Liman had insisted on being called by his first name.

"It's Mr. Liman."

"Mr. Liman." Freddie sat on the edge of the chair as Norman had instructed him ("Don't sit all the way back if he thinks you're a slacker"). There was less glare down here, and he could see Mr. Liman's face clearly now, his drawn pointy features, his thin black mustache, his sparkly eyes observing him curiously, the sun making an outline around him.

"So, it has come to my attention that you are going to be working for my partner on this—ahem—tuna run."

"Yes," said Freddy, eagerly inching even more forward, sitting with perfect posture for the man.

Liman swiveled around in his chair toward the window. He rose and walked down to the side of the room and pressed a button, and blinds slowly came down, making Freddie feel grateful, but he suspected it was all part of some psychological plan. Mr. Liman wanted him to feel that way.

"Although I gotta level with you; this isn't exactly a tuna run," Liman said. "More like a dangerous treasure-hunting expedition."

"Even better!" said Freddie.

Liman returned to sit at his desk. "Don't get ahead of yourself."

"Okay," said Freddie, wriggling in his seat, although the shade now was much better.

Liman picked up a long, slim, sharp-looking dagger, a letter opener, Freddie supposed, its chrome shining brilliantly. "I do have something to propose that you might find amenable."

"What's that?" asked Freddie.

He was studying the dagger, which he ran along his palm. "If the mission is successful, namely, if you can single-handedly retrieve the treasure, then I will give consent for my daughter's hand."

"Awesome!" Freddie had risen to his feet, beside himself, nearly trembling with joy. He hadn't expected this at all. Of course, he would retrieve the treasure, even if it were a thousand trunks of doubloons.

"It's rather light. I mean, not too big," said Mr. Liman as if reading Freddie's mind. "But a dangerous expedition nevertheless. If you are willing to embark on it, then you may marry my girl, but first you have to sign the contract."

Freddie was ecstatic and wanted to jump up and down, but he contained himself, instead letting out a deep breath. "I'm ready. Where do I sign?"

Liman gave him the once-over, then smiled to himself. He pushed at a sheet of paper before him, glancing at it, then looked up at Freddie. "We'll need a witness." He pressed a button on the desk. "Bleaker, is my partner here?"

"Yes, Mr. Liman," came the mousy fellow's voice from the desk.

"Please send the captain in," returned Liman.

THIS WAS THE THIRD TIME Freddie was meeting the captain, and when he strolled in, he was not in his whites and captain's hat as he had been last time Freddie had seen him. Instead, he wore a three-piece suit and emerald tie with a gold pin.

Freddie rose to greet him. "Captain Atkins," he said, extending a hand. Freddie realized he had seen him before—and not just at the alley. He had seen the good captain leaving his mother's house that Thanksgiving Day, carrying a large bouquet and looking a bit upset. He hadn't mentioned it to his family in the tumult of his return, but it crossed his mind now that he probably should. How did Harold Atkins know his family?

They shook hands, and the captain gave him an amiable, warm smile.

Mr. Liman cleared his throat and addressed him. "Harold, we need you to witness the signing of the contract in blood."

"Why, of course," said Harold, smiling at Freddie. "I'm delighted to have Freddie on board!"

"Blood?" asked Freddie.

"Standard." Liman picked up the dagger he had been playing with. "That's why I have this." He held the dagger up, handed Freddie an ostrich feather pen, and then came around the desk with the sheet of paper. Then Liman and Captain Atkins loomed over Freddie, who held out his palm, looking away.

chapter fifty

Devil's Haircut

つC

The guards were dragging Anne Barklay out of her cell on the outskirts of Fairstone, a low-slung set of barracks on the edge of the woods, more like wooden cages judging how small they were. The village proper was no more than a dozen or so sinister brown houses, one with a steeple and cross, chickens pecking about, pigs snorting in pens, people bustling, working, building more wooden houses, performing daily chores, getting water from the well, splashing it along in the dust, men in black broad-brimmed hats, women in white caps.

Freya stood hiding inside a thicket, watching, as they pulled Anne through the field toward the village. It was definitely her, as Joanna had described: the proud high forehead, round face, dark eyes, and large sensual mouth, dotted by a black beauty mark above her lips. Even her clothes were as Mother had mentioned, the gray bodice over the white blouse, a black apron, and maroon skirt, all of her clothes stained and frayed, the blouse ripped at the seam, so that her slim pale shoulder poked through. As Anne pulled from the guards, her white cap fell in the grass, and Freya saw that her head had been shaved.

This was what they did, a gruesome and rather prurient practice passed down since the publication of the *Malleus Malefi-carum* (*Hammer of the Witches*), which dated back to 1487 and had gone through several new editions from the fifteenth to the seventeenth century. It was a guidebook, so to speak, on how to identify, interrogate, try, and convict witches. One of the ways to peg an alleged witch entailed shaving her entire body, head, armpits, and genital area, in order to search for the "devil's mark." This so-called mark was supposedly a third teat from which the witch suckled her familiar. It could be anywhere on the body, and if it were found—like a birthmark—it was tested, probed, and pierced with a pin. If this caused pain and blood flowed, then the woman in question was not a witch; if there was no pain and no blood, then she was. Other forms of torture could also be used in order to draw out a confession.

Anne's bare feet dragged as the guards led her to the village. She was having trouble walking, most likely after having been kept in the small, cramped cell. She finally got to her feet, straining to keep up pace, holding her head high. They were far away enough now for Freya to run and gather her cap in the field. She would bring it to Anne as a show of her friendship. As she leaned over to pick it up in the grass, she felt a presence behind her, and a large hand, stained black around the fingers, grabbed at her wrist.

She turned toward the stranger crouched beside her in the grass: a man in a floppy black hat with an arresting face, large cat-like eyes, an almost indescribable color—perhaps the pale yellow-brown referred to as tiger-eye—a broad mouth, a five o'clock shadow along the chiseled jaw, and golden-brown hair nearly reaching his shoulders. He wore a loose shirt of jute, open at the chest. His skin was taught and tanned like a laborer's.

Freya almost let out a friendly "Hello!" but she saw nothing but ire in his eye, which stopped her short.

"What are you planning to do with me wife's cap?" he asked her.

She let out a sigh of relief. "Mr. Barklay, I am here to help. I want to see Anne free." She handed him Anne's cap, which he took and brought to his lips, inhaling it, and for a moment she thought he was going to burst into tears; his chest shook, then he got a hold of himself and rose to his feet.

He set out through the field toward the village, and Freya moved into step with him, walking in tandem. It was difficult to walk fast with all these skirts, their heavy weight. She would sink straight to the bottom of the ocean if someone chucked her in.

"Woman, she won't confess!" Mr. Barklay said to her. "There is not a thing you can do for poor Anne. These people have nothing but blackness around their hearts. It is they who are consorting with the devil. They have got it all backward."

"I can give you money. I have gold." She was reaching inside the belt of her skirt, ripping the seam Joanna had carefully sewn. "Perhaps we can come at night and get the guards to release her; give them money. I can take you elsewhere. I have the means," she said, thinking how much happier he and Anne would be in the twenty-first century.

He stopped in his tracks and looked her up and down, then laughed heartily. "You certainly don't look it. Who are you?"

Joanna had dressed her as a peasant woman so as not to draw too much attention. She pushed a fist at him, held it open, showing him a handful of gold. "I'm a witch," she said, taking a chance.

He laughed at her. "A witch! There is no such thing; even Anne will tell you so. Keep your money, woman. Anne is proud. Why do you think they are dragging her to the stocks in the town square? If only she would break down and tell them what they want to hear!" His eyes shone and he strode away hurriedly, but not before Freya had done a bit of sleight of hand, placing the coins in the pocket of his loose pants; they could get quite far with that once they got Anne out.

265

"I appreciate your trying to help. My name is John. Yours, Goody Witch?" he said, not unkindly.

"Freya Beauchamp," she replied, curtsying as she walked. "At your service, and I wish you would let me help you. I think Anne has an important message for my mother."

He glanced at her as if she were batty. Everyone had begun to shout in the village, and a chant of "Witch!" rose from the square.

"I have already lost too much time with you!" John took off fast through the field. "Anne must be hungry. I brought her food, and she needs water," he shouted back as he sprinted. Freya ran after him as fast as she could.

It seemed everyone had come out of the houses to gather in the square, where they had chained Anne to a large oak instead of placing her in the stocks. It was clear they wanted to make a spectacle of her body, displaying it in as lascivious a manner as they could, her arms pulled back so that her breasts jutted forward, the chain wrapping around her curves to reveal more of her form. Luckily she was shaded beneath the oak. It was about noon now, and the sun beat down. No one would notice Freya as a stranger with everyone outdoors—and the crowd was frenzied, too focused on Anne.

"She signed the devil's book with her blood!" someone shouted.

"She has the mark! See—above her lip!"

"No, that's not it. They shaved her! It must be somewhere else. Show us the witch's mark!"

"Show us the mark!" people began to chant.

John had pushed past the crowd and was asking one of the guards flanking the tree for permission to be with his wife.

"She dances with the devil at night, John. Why do you still want her? You are a fool!" a young woman cried. It must have been Sally Smitherstone.

The guard solemnly shook his head at John. Freya saw her

266

opportunity to show him she was on his side, and she struggled through the rioting townsfolk. When she got to the guard, she slipped him a coin, and after he looked down at it with a smile, he pushed John forward toward his wife.

John placed Anne's cap back on her shaved head, whispering in her ear. She gave him a pained smile and moved her cheek toward his. He poured water inside her parched lips.

"That woman! That woman is a witch!" cried a man from the crowd. For some reason, Freya turned to the voice, which had immediately made her skin crawl. It was so familiar. He was pointing at Freya, singling her out, not Anne.

"What do you say, Mr. Lion Gardiner?" someone shouted back at the accuser.

The man, with a black mustache and goatee, in a brown hat, his white collar pouring over a majestic black cape, stepped forth. It was obvious he was wealthier than those around him and held sway over these villagers. They had suddenly quieted at hearing his name.

"I saw that woman falling from the sky as I came in on the boat today from the Isle of Wight. I couldn't find her when I got here, but I recognize the clothes, plain as day. We must take her to the magistrates to see if she has the mark." He said this calmly, matter-of-factly.

"Witch! Witch! Witch!" the people chanted, now pointing at Freya.

No. Not again. Why had she volunteered for this? She felt faint, so light-headed. She had had nothing to eat or drink since she had arrived. She didn't know how much time had gone by since she had passed through the portal. There was no telling. A few seconds? Hours? Days?

She tried to get away, but her skirts were too heavy, and there were too many hands holding her down.

chapter fifty-one

Mood Indigo

ᴥ

Ingrid stood in the back of the library in the cordoned-off area, hovering over the mythology section of the reserved book collection, none of which anyone was allowed to check out. You had to ask for permission to enter this area, either from Ingrid, Hudson, Tabitha, or Jeannine, the new intern. Usually one of them supervised, trying not to appear too much like a vulture circling overhead.

She put her cell phone down. She didn't want to be out of touch with Joanna and Norman for one second in case they needed her. Freya had still not returned, and Ingrid had been growing increasingly worried about her sister traveling to that particular blight in time.

She perused the *A* section for books on Álfheim (one of the nine worlds, Norman had told her) and *álfar* (elf or elfin) and perhaps she would also find something on the *áss* ("I think it's their word for Aesir," Joanna had said, which did narrow down the type of god they were looking for). Ingrid found it amusing that most of these books were written by gods themselves, witches and warlocks turned scholars, like one Norman Beauchamp, PhD. She grabbed a few of her father's on the nine worlds, hither and thither. Mostly she needed to look at maps.

She ran an index along the books' spines, continuing to scan the titles. Her parents had filled her in on gaps, but she liked poring over the written words and images; she retained things better that way. She was a visual person and mental snapshots always helped.

The cell phone buzzed on the metal shelf. She glanced at it, juggling the books. Curious. It was Matt. Her heart pounded. She grabbed the cell and walked over to an isolated carrel and set the books down, taking a seat, bending down to hide her head.

"Hello?" she whispered.

"I'm calling to give you a heads-up," Matt said, his voice devoid of emotion.

"Um . . . okay," she replied, letting her own voice flatline.

"There's a tail on you. If you're still hanging around those homeless kids, they'll be found and deported if they're not citizens."

"Deported? What on earth are you talking about?"

Matt exhaled into the phone, and she had to pull it slightly away from her ear. "You told me they were foreigners. Remember? I wrote it down in my *notebook*."

Great. They were speaking in code. *Notebook* with emphasis—or was it aggression?—was a flagrant reminder of the piece of paper with the girl's name on it and of Ingrid's snooping around.

Matt continued. "You called them, quote, 'foreign,' close quote, and you said, 'They don't know this culture.' I have it written down."

"Impressive," Ingrid said flatly.

"Well, the chief read my notes because I'm in—"

Ingrid waited, then couldn't wait any longer. "You're in what?"

"Never mind," he said. "I just wanted to warn you, Ingrid."

She was about to lie again, proclaiming the pixies were gone, but she was tired of this game. She tapped her foot. "Okay," she said coldly.

"Okay," echoed Matt. She couldn't tell if it was an angry *okay*. Perhaps a little sad. No. It was just a plain, boring *okay*.

They both waited for the other to hang up, and it took so long, Ingrid started to feel a bit wistful, missing Matt, so before she actually softened and broke down by saying good-bye, she hit the End button and returned to the books she had set down in the carrel.

chapter fifty-two

Holding Out for a Hero

༄

F reya, Freya, wake up!"

Freya felt a hand tapping at her face. She lay supine, arms stretched out at her side, the long skirt a heavy weight on her limbs. All the aches and pains and knots in her neck were back, as they had been when she arrived in 1640. There was sand beneath her, and she could hear the waves crashing in the near distance. She opened her eyes. It was dusk, and she saw a face she recognized, a face she dearly loved. A smile spread on her lips.

Killian. He looked pale and drawn, leeched. She sat up and hugged him with all the strength left in her body. He kissed her face, her neck, burying his nose in her hair.

"Am I home?" she said hopefully.

He shook his head and removed an energy bar from his pocket. "Eat. Get your strength back," he said, ripping the package open, burying the wrapper in the sand.

Freya was glad to have it, even if she'd always dismissed them as cardboard before. She was famished. Her throat was dry. It was hard to swallow, but after a few bites, she felt her body begin to renew itself again; it would be enough until she had a decent meal. "How did you get here?"

"I felt something shift inside me . . . sort of like an alarm . . . I could feel that you were in danger. Now that we've found each other again, I'm attuned to your spirit. So I followed you through the portal into the timeline," Killian explained. "I had to do a few more shifts to get you safe. *My gift*, by the way, space and time, moving objects about, manipulating the passages, which means screwing around with the continuum—like reconstructing the greenhouse so fast."

He caressed her face. "Since the bridge collapsed I can't do it very easily, so I'm glad I saved most of what is left for this. We're not supposed to do this. It upsets the natural balance: chaos theory, the butterfly effect. A long time ago we had posted guards to keep the timeline safe, but they're gone now, so I had to be very careful. Why would Joanna and Norman send you back here?"

She explained everything to Killian in a hurried breath. "For you, Killian. We need to find Anne. She might be able to help us. *When* is it?" Color had begun to spread through her cheeks, and she had become frenzied, worried that it was already too late, that Anne had been hanged.

"It's the night of the day I found you except things are a little different. You never made it to the square. I don't think you ever met John Barklay," he said to answer her question.

"Fuck!" said Freya. "That means he never got to talk to Anne while she was chained to the tree. Never got to put her cap back on or give her water." She slipped a hand inside her skirt and the pouch of gold coins was still sewn into the seam. She had all her gold again, and that was disappointing. "This is so confusing," she said. "We need to get you in proper clothes, then find Anne. Can we go back in time a little more?"

"I don't want to risk it, I have to make sure I have enough power to get us back home. Whatever we need to do, we need to do now."

chapter fifty-three

Smoke on the Water

The treasure expedition was nothing at all as Freddie had envisioned. He had anticipated something exciting, walking about the deck with wind and ocean spray in his face, rigging, pulling, feeding lines, winching, cleating ropes, and such—the thrill of unfurling the sails, catching the wind in them, then harnessing it. Freddie loved to wear himself out physically, using his body to maximum capacity until it was sore and he collapsed from all the effort he had expended. Kind of like sex. That's how he had pictured it.

It was nothing like that.

First, they had taken all his effects from him, including the new cell phone Joanna had bought him. He'd barely had enough time to text Freya and his dad to tell them he had gotten the job. Then he and Captain Atkins, along with a rough-and-tumble crew of young men, had flown in a private plane to what Freddie had gathered was a Caribbean island; he overheard "St. Lucia," as much as they tried to keep him in the dark. After a drive, during which Freddie was blindfolded, they boarded an eighty-foot-long, three-mast schooner, which was beautiful, but then Captain Atkins kept Freddie confined to his berth under lock and key as they weighed anchor. It wasn't in an unkind way, though. The captain said it was for Freddie's own good. He wasn't to know the exact spot where the treasure was to be excavated until they arrived close to it. The only view Freddie was afforded during the trip was through a little porthole where he could see water rushing and frothing past, but that was all. He did enjoy the occasional swell, about five to six feet high he judged—a calm sea.

The schooner had been rocking in place for a while when Captain Atkins finally came to Freddie's berth. He handed him a wetsuit to don and told him to come up to the deck once he had it on, then he left the door unlocked.

The view of the island from where they had set anchor took Freddie's breath away, a towering volcanic peak partly covered in rain forest with nary a sandy beach but craggy black cliffs lifting from the turquoise-green waters—the jagged peak like a black diamond, the trees clusters of emeralds. It was a perfect day, the sun warm but not overbearing, a soft tropical breeze, just hints of clouds in the cerulean sky. Captain Atkins and a scruffy-looking crew member helped Freddie into the scuba gear.

"You can scuba, right?" the captain asked. "You are trained and certified I presume."

"Absolutely," he lied, but he wasn't worried. "Breathing underwater? No problemo." Not only was he a natural swimmer, a natural athlete with excellent hand-eye coordination—he was also one with all that was sun and sea.

Harold smiled. "Well, not to worry, we have this nifty little thing." The captain placed what resembled a watch on Freddie's wrist. "It's a top-notch, state-of-the-art dive computer. Even someone with zero experience would be able to follow rate of descent and ascent on this thing. Plus, we are giving you Nitrox in case you need to stay down there longer than anticipated. I'll explain it all. No worries—you're a strong boy. You're going to love it, but don't let yourself get too distracted by the colorful seascape." He gave Freddie a pat on the back, then nodded at the

274

scruffy guy with an Italian accent, letting him know they needed to be alone. "Come sit with me for a bit, Freddie. We need to look at the map."

Finally, it was time to dive. Freddie swam following the instructions to a T. The prize was Hilly, so he was anxious to complete his mission and do it well. Beneath the water, the rock of the island continued for seventy or more feet deep. There was an array of caves and yawning craters beneath him, all encrusted with DayGlo coral reefs and orange elephant ear, netted barrel, and green finger sponges. It was like another land, the colors so vivid. He hadn't ever seen anything like it before, not in all the other eight worlds.

He glimpsed a reef shark peering out from between rocks and kept going, then followed a hawksbill turtle, going in the correct direction according to his compass. He saw adorable sea horses and frog fish. It was wonderful to be back in the ocean again. This could certainly become a hobby for him and Hilly once they were together, he thought. He wished she were here now, sharing it all silently.

That was the thing; it was so peacefully quiet in the ocean depths. The twenty-first century was great, but it could get so loud, especially New York City—where Hilly said she wanted to work at a magazine once she graduated from college—always some noise somewhere. If it wasn't cars and horns honking, it was a jackhammer or pile driver making one clap hands over the ears. Maybe Hilly and he could move to the Caribbean instead. He wondered if she would be agreeable to that.

Every now and then, he checked the diving watch to make sure he wasn't descending too fast. He felt a pocket of warm water, a geothermal vent, pushing bubbles at him and swam through them, against its current. This would lead him to the tunnel swim-through where he would hopefully find the treasure.

He found it inside the recess where Captain Atkins had told him it would be, lodged between rocks: a long, slim gold-filigreed rectangular case. He pried it out, and it fell into his hands as if he owned it. It wasn't too heavy, just kind of long and unwieldy. He strapped it to his back, then began timing his ascent.

Soon Hilly would be his.

chapter fifty-four

Orinoco Flow

❧

Inside the carrel at the library, Ingrid had fallen asleep. Drool had pooled onto the page of the oversize book on which her head rested, mouth agape. She woke with a start, and looked down at the page with a black-and-white lithograph of a map of the Nine Worlds, *Yggdrasil*, the Tree of Life, at their axis, and saw a huge unsightly wet spot on it. She quickly wiped it off with her sleeve, looking around as she did so, but there was no one back here.

She'd had a dream. There had been so much water in it—clear, turquoise, not frightening but pure, inviting. It was so blissfully peaceful, just the lightest, quietest trickling and gurgling in the background. She had been reading about *Yggdrasil*, then studied its maps before she'd fallen asleep. She rubbed at her eyes. An enormous serpent coiled around *Yggdrasil's* roots perpetually gnawing at them, animals fed on its sap, goats and stags grazed on its tender shoots, and yet still it persisted, regenerating, evergreen, supplying life with its élan vital, both its humanity and aggression.

The Norns were devoted to the tree, covering its nicks and sores with white clay from Mimir, the spring of wisdom and understanding, giving it offerings, saying prayers, pouring water over its branches and roots from the well of fate. The water

277

dripped down from its enormous leaves and roots, falling down to earth, where it turned into dew.

The problem with the maps was that they all slightly diverged. For instance, Vanaheim, Ingrid's home world, was located on some maps directly beneath Asgard, which was at the zenith, above the tiptop branches of *Yggdrasil*, whereas others placed Vanaheim on the same horizontal plane as Midgard (earth), located at the center of the holy tree. But all the maps placed Asgard at the top and Álfheim (land of the pixies) somewhere between Asgard and Midgard, which made sense if someone from Asgard had plunked the pixies down in North Hampton. But only Odin and Frigg remained in Asgard.

Water, Ingrid thought. *Water. That is it*—the water from her dream. At least, it was one key she needed.

chapter fifty-five

Come to My Window

‿❧‿

Easier said than done: finding attire in the middle of the night in Fairstone to dress Killian in less conspicuous clothing than his sweater and jeans. He wore leather boots, so those would pass. The villagers appeared wary of leaving a stitch of clothing, even a pair of underclothes or a blouse, on the clotheslines in their backyards and gardens. The lines hung bare. Freya realized that in the twenty-first century she had come to take her vast wardrobe for granted, whereas someone in the seventeenth century, living in an agricultural and fishing village, could barely afford one outfit, let alone two.

Everyone was asleep at this hour. Since they were not to waste their magic, they had to find clothing the hard way and tried to sneak inside several houses, but the doors were bolted shut. Finally, on the outskirts of town, they found a shack, and inside they crept by a slumbering man, who only flipped over at the sounds of their entry, and they swiftly snatched the loose breaches and linen shirt he had set out on a chair beside the bed. They hoped the poor, unsuspecting heavy sleeper had something to replace these with, although most likely if he did have another set it was just his Sunday best. The clothes fit Killian, but he wrinkled his nose at the smell. As for a hat, they found one on a peg in a barn, along with a goatskin water bag, which they filled at a well, flinching at the groan and squeaks of the bucket rising.

Now Freya and Killian trudged hand in hand through the field toward the wooden barracks where they were holding Anne. The pulsing song of the cicadas drowned out their whispers. A watchman sat beneath the single torchlight, half asleep on a chair. Freya recognized the stocky, big-bellied guard as the very one who had accepted her coin in the square—except that hadn't happened anymore. Working a double shift. She knew he would be amenable to gold, so she stopped and ripped the seam Joanna had sewn once again and took out the pouch, handing Killian a coin.

The guard happily accepted the money. He was probably used to these nocturnal visits that greased his palm, a perk of the job. "Fourth one down," he muttered.

There was snoring coming from a pen; they saw forms crouched or curled on the floor in each, no more than four feet high. *These poor people, caged like animals,* Freya thought. They kneeled when they arrived before Anne's cell.

"Anne!" called Freya. She could see her stirring in the corner in dim moonlight. She was relieved to see the white cap back on her head.

"Anne," repeated Killian, a bit louder.

"*Oui!*" she whispered. "*C'est toi, mon chou, mon chérie? Tu es revenue?*" Her voice was raspy and weak. She moved out from the corner and wriggled forward toward the bars.

Freya coughed. "She thinks you're her husband who has returned for her," she said to Killian.

"Yes," he said with a sympathetic frown.

Anne's hands clasped the bars and her nose fell between them. Her eyes were crusted, her big lovely lips caked with blood, her face black with dirt. It was all Freya could do not to throw a hex on the whole populace.

"John!" Anne said.

Freya caressed her hand. "It is not John. It is Killian and Freya. We have come to help you, Anne."

She let out a sigh and her head fell down. "I don't want to confess!" she said in her French accent. "If I do, then next they will say John is amiable with the devil. I do not want my husband to hang."

"I know," said Freya. "We're trying to save both of you." She slipped a hand through the bars and helped Anne lift her head.

"Let me give her water," said Killian, and he lifted the goatskin bag so Anne could drink.

Freya looked over her shoulder. The guard had his arms crossed above his belly, his legs stretched out, crossed as well, and his head had lolled; he appeared fast asleep. "You called my mother from the grave where you are buried on the hill. You've been trying to help us, Anne, sending your spirit through the glom, and we want to help you. You are my mother's *fylgja*. I must bring you to her."

Anne stared at Freya, furrowing her brow. "I do not know what you are speaking of. Please tell John about the sick pig—the skinny one—he needs to be fed milk and grain. He came earlier with my cap. Where is he? John!" She seemed delirious. "I do not wish to go anywhere with you."

Freya looked at Killian, who shrugged. "Anne, you must listen to us. Please, or you'll die here."

"Then that is my fate. Leave me be," Anne said, closing her eyes, falling asleep against the bars.

chapter fifty-six

Homeward Bound

꒰ꗃ꒱

What Ingrid needed to do was find a branch from the Tree of Life to return the pixies to Álfheim, and she believed she knew exactly where she would find it. At Fair Haven, the portal in the tree's trunk had closed forever once Loki passed through. Passing through the center of *Yggdrasil* was forbidden, which is why the yellow brick road had been built as a highway to connect the remaining eight worlds. Only the bridge to Asgard was destroyed, that path lost forever.

According to the pixies, the yellow brick road had crumbled, but if she could find a branch on the Tree . . .

She closed the books scattered inside the carrel, their pages snapping satisfyingly together. She would have Jeannine put them back in their rightful slots; their intern was diligent that way. Ingrid had received a call from Norman and Joanna earlier. Killian had gone missing—he wasn't answering his phone—so Joanna had made the trek out to Gardiners Island to search for him, fearing the Valkyries had already come for him. Instead she had found a short, succinct note on the bed in the master cabin of the *Dragon* addressed to the Beauchamps, as if Killian had anticipated her: "I'm going through the passage. I will return Freya to safety. Yours, Killian." This had calmed and reassured Ingrid somewhat; at least Freya and Killian were together.

But now the pixies were in danger of being arrested and possibly deported. It was time to get them to their real home.

If Matt had put a tail on her, so be it. She could easily circumvent that. Who was going to play hardball now? Driving wasn't Ingrid's only means of getting to the Ucky Star. Although like Freya she had noticed that her magic had gone slightly awry lately, not as potent as it once was, and she hoped she wouldn't tumble from the sky on her way to the pixies. She darted to her office, grabbed her coat, wool hat, scarf, and gloves, gave a few instructions to her fellow librarians, then rushed through the back door to the garden, picked up a rake, and flew into the air.

SHE ALIGHTED WITH A THUMP on the second story of the motel, straightened her coat and hat, then clumped down the metallic steps in her sturdy heels, removing her gloves. She found the room at the corner and knocked. Val opened the door, and as Ingrid burst in, she declared, "I think I know how to get you home."

The leak in the bathroom had worsened considerably; it sounded like a downright waterfall in there. The pixies, who were eating around the desk, looked up at her in awe.

"It makes complete sense," said Ingrid, briskly pulling off her wool hat and removing her scarf. She shrugged off her coat, drew the wand out of its pocket, and then tossed everything on the twin bed, hanging on to the slim baton of dragon bone. She unbuttoned her cuffs, then pushed her sleeves up to the elbows. "This is where you arrived. This is where Freddie chose to stay. The portal to your home is right here—in the Ucky Star."

Kelda's mouth fell open, and the rest of them continued ogling her with flummoxed faces. Ingrid rushed toward the bathroom.

"No, no, don't go in there!" cried Sven. "You'll get your nice clothes wet!" He blushed, having lost his cool in his concern for her.

But Ingrid was already tugging at the bathroom doorknob, and the entire door, moist and rotting, fell off its hinges. The pixies raised their arms to help protect Ingrid as she crouched, and the door collapsed in a gooey mess beside her.

The bathroom was a deluge, water dripping from the ceiling and along the walls. The tub and sink (the toilet's lid was fortuitously closed), whose drains gurgled, overflowed, trickling onto the sunken white tile floor, where a pool had formed as clear and turquoise as the Caribbean sea.

"Don't you see?" said Ingrid, turning to the pixies with a smile. "This is sacred water dripping from a branch of the Tree of Life, from its very leaves. Now we just need to find the right door."

Ingrid kicked off her shoes before stepping in. The water reached a few inches above her ankles, like a wading pool. The pixies watched her from the doorframe. She pointed her wand at the walls, but it seemed to have a will of its own, like a divination rod, and tilted downward, aiming at the center drain in the tile floor. "It's here. Come help. We need to be fast. I need to send you home before the police find you; otherwise I might not be able to get you out later," she said, feeling her stomach drop from nerves and more than a hint of separation anxiety.

"What will they do to us . . . the lawmen?" Kelda asked.

Ingrid didn't know. If they believed the pixies were illegals, they would deport them back home—but where was that? The pixies could languish in a jail cell for years before they determined where to send them. "I don't know. I don't think we want to find out."

Irdick and Sven stepped in. The drain came out easily enough, its screws seemingly stripped. Kelda stuck her small hand inside the hole and pulled, and the tiles around the drain lifted in one piece. Ingrid was on her knees, drenched to the bone. They pulled out the tiles and scooped out goopy white stuff that resembled a doughy wet plaster. The pixies formed an assembly line, coming and going, dumping tiles and goo on the wreck of a bathroom door.

The water began to drain down some of the straight cracks they had uncovered; some were wide enough to slip a hand through and seemed to form a square. It was a hard surface that turned out to be made of dense dark wood: a door, about four-by-four feet, ornately carved with an image of *Yggdrasil*. They lifted it open by slipping hands inside one of the cracks, and as it opened water trickled down onto a flight of wooden steps that led to a branch. Ingrid lay prone to poke her head inside the trapdoor. First, she was struck by the clamorous din: birds twittering, insects humming, everything tapping, pulsing, and clicking. There were more boughs beneath this one, and they stretched and stretched for as far as the eye could see, with huge unctuous leaves dripping water and dewy white flowers that exuded a scent of gardenias, or was it camellias? A few of the pixies had squeezed in beside Ingrid on their bellies, squinting down, oohing and aahing.

"Okay, we need to get you down there onto the branch," said Ingrid. "Then you'll follow it home. I'll close the door as soon as I see you're all safely on it."

"No!" yelped Irdick.

"Can we do it another day?" asked Val.

"Pussies!" said Sven, puffing on a cigarette. He had switched over to the green pack of American Spirits, which he had rolled up in his T-shirt's sleeve.

"I don't want to go!" whined Nyph.

"Neither do I," said Kelda. "I like it here. We want to stay.

And we still want to help you find the man who made us steal the trident."

Ingrid pushed a strand of wayward hair back. "I know," she said wistfully.

"What the . . . ?" boomed a voice from inside the motel room.

Ingrid quickly rose to her feet—the voice had a kind of snap-to effect on her. She stared at Matt. She was filthy, wet, and shivering. She must have looked a fright, she thought. The pixies, sensing her alarm, had stood and gathered behind her protectively outstretched arms. "How did you find me?" Ingrid demanded. There was no way he had been able to tail her from the sky.

Matt shrugged. "A hunch, as they say." He came toward her, static and a voice crackling from his walkie-talkie.

It was too late. No one was going to go home anytime soon. The only place they were going—including Ingrid—was jail.

chapter fifty-seven

Earth Angel

✷

A nne had fallen asleep, holding on to the bars, one hand slowly slipping down.

"We have no choice," said Killian. "We've got to take her with us, even if she doesn't want to go. They're going to hang her this afternoon."

"So what do we do?" asked Freya, peering into her lover's eyes that sparkled in the darkness, reflecting the torchlight above the guard.

Killian instructed Freya to place a hand around Anne's left wrist. He took Freya's free hand, then Anne's right that had fallen outside the bars as her body slumped. They were all connected. "Hold on tight!" he said with a wink.

"Oh, no, not again!" said Freya, squeezing her eyes shut to brace herself for the pain.

THIS TIME FREYA did not fall asleep, moving through the time-line was much quicker and smoother, more like a jump cut in a French new wave film, like the scene from *Breathless* in which Jean Seberg's movements are spliced as she rides along in the convertible—the tiniest moment missing from one to the next. They were here in one position, then there in another, all three huddled together on the sand, Joanna and Norman rushing at them. Freya felt sapped from the experience. Killian's face looked paler, and a droplet of blood dribbled from his nostril, which Freya reached over and wiped, while they both held Anne, limp between them. It was early evening now, and the sky was a band of gray, then pink along sea.

"She needs food and water immediately," said Killian. "Or more like an IV bag."

"Yeah, I have one in my briefcase in the house," said Norman—an attempt at humor. "I'm so glad you're back." He grabbed them all in a bear hug, and Joanna came to kneel beside her daughter, caressing her head, kissing it.

"We need to get Anne inside," Freya said.

"Anne . . . how lovely. My *fylgja*." Joanna had tears in her eyes.

"Goody Anne Barklay," Freya said.

Anne's head rolled. "Where am I? Who are you? Take me home! Please take me back," she mumbled.

They carried her into the guest room by the study downstairs, made her comfortable in the bed. Joanna and Norman tended to her like seabirds to a nestling while Freya and Killian raided the fridge. After being caged for days on end and dragged into the square again and again, time-traveling had nearly done Anne in. They spoon-fed her broth and mashed vegetables, but mostly she needed to be hydrated, which would take time.

Killian and Freya had perked up but were still the worse for wear. They joined Joanna and Norman in the guest room once they had eaten and changed into their regular clothing.

"She looks like a Norn," Norman said to Joanna, hovering by the bedside. "The beauty mark above her lip."

"I am," rasped out Anne, her eyes straining open. "Norn. My name is Verðandi, so I chose Anne in Midgard."

"Verðandi," repeated Joanna, shaking her head in awe. *Verð-anne-dee.*

Freya sat at the side of the bed and took Anne's hand. "Do you know my mother? Did you come to Joanna in spirit form to warn us about something?" she asked excitedly.

"Yes," said Anne. "I lied to you before. I'm sorry. The guard, he has ears everywhere even though he feigns to sleep. Only interested in money, that one. He's bleeding my husband—every little kiss costs more." Her frail body shook. Joanna pressed a cool wet cloth to her forehead.

The information came slowly, Joanna and Norman filling Freya and Killian in with their own knowledge. Anne—Verðandi—was one of the Norns who tended to *Yggðrasil.* She was also a goddess of destiny as it is twined into the unfurling of time. Anne was the goddess of the present, her sisters the goddesses of the past and future, forming the triumvirate that controlled the fates of gods and men. Just as Joanna had guessed, Anne had placed the message on her own grave in such a way that Joanna might come to the conclusion she was a Norn.

Anne was indeed her *fylgja,* but she explained why she had been resistant to leaving the past with Killian and Freya. She had fallen in love with a mortal, she told them. "Me, I can always return to life, even if they hang me, but once John is dead, I will never see him again," she said. She licked her chafed lips. Despite her misery in Fairstone, she had wanted to spend every last moment of that wretched, ignorant time with John Barklay. Taking her away would endanger him. When she returned, he could be dead.

She had wanted Joanna to come to her directly; she had made contact with her and trusted her. She didn't know who else she could trust. Joanna was tied to her by an invisible thread, a thin tendril that tugged at Anne through time or when any of the

289

Beauchamps or their loved ones were in danger. She would always recognize Joanna, and Joanna alone, because she was Anne's spiritual ward, assigned to her since the beginning of time.

Anne told Joanna why she had reached out to her. Something had happened. She wasn't meant to be hanged; she and John were supposed to live their lives together. She had seen it. But something had changed; evil had come to Fairstone, had begun the finger-pointing, stirring up trouble, singling out and persecuting witches.

"It all started when a new family purchased the Isle of Wight and settled there. They are new to the community and have caused us much grief."

"Who?"

"Lion Gardiner and his wife," Anne said. "We know him as . . ."

"Loki, of course." Freya sighed. She would have recognized him anywhere she knew now. They called him Lion Gardiner but she knew him under different names: Branford Gardiner, Bran, Loki. "We can never seem to escape him—not in this life or any other."

chapter fifty-eight

White Wedding

ᔕᔑ

Captain Atkins and Freddie, the treasure in a cylinder slung over his back, silently glided up in the elevator to the forty-second floor and entered Her Majesty's Shipping Co. This time they did not have to speak with the receptionist, who immediately called Mr. Liman as they walked past the clear-glass pod and headed toward his office. Freddie heard the young man announce, "They're on their way, Mr. Liman."

Liman rose from his swivel chair behind the ship-size desk, rubbing his hands. "Hello!" Luckily, the blinds were down, the light soft and welcoming this time. "Freddie, I'd say you look like the cat who has dragged in the mouse and is about to deposit it at my feet."

"Looks like I've fulfilled my contract, Mr. Liman," Freddie proudly replied.

"Indeed you have," added Captain Atkins, standing behind Freddie, placing a hand on the boy's shoulder.

"Excellent!" said Mr. Liman, coming around the desk, appearing antsy to get his hands on the treasure that Freddie was slinging off his back. Mr. Liman took the cylinder from him and brought it over to his desk, punched in the combination to unlock it, humming to himself, then slid the slim, brilliant gold case out. "Excellent," he repeated, inspecting it, then running a hand along its smooth surface. "I'll open it later." He lifted his eyebrows and smiled at Freddie.

Freddie beamed. "So when can I see Hilly? I wish to propose to her formally, even though I don't have a ring yet—" Freddie cut himself short because Mr. Liman had begun to titter, but soon these soft, quiet paroxysms turned into bellowing, maniacal laughter that shook the walls of the skyscraper as if a supersonic jet were passing overhead.

Freddie's face twitched. "What's so funny?"

Mr. Liman picked up the contract, which still lay on the gleaming surface of his desk, and strode over to Freddie. "My dear boy, you *are* marrying my daughter as the contract states, but you must have not bothered to read the fine print. It isn't Hilly you are to wed but rather one of my adopted daughters, Gert . . . the eldest. You'll never be quite good enough for Hilly, Freddie." Liman handed the contract to Freddie, whose knees had buckled at the news. He felt as if he had been socked in the chest by a large, blunt object. "Not back then, and not now."

Freddie quickly skimmed over the contract and found the paragraph that undid him:

Following the execution of the duties described hereto in the Contract, Retriever will deliver unopened Gold Case containing Treasure to President and thereby will be obligated under the Contract, within a period of no longer than thirty (30) days, to (i) propose to, (ii) exchange vows with, and (iii) wed Gert Liman. Under no condition will Retriever evade above-mentioned obligations (i), (ii), and (iii), get cold feet, not show up at the altar for, or refuse to say 'I do,' or thereafter divorce Gerðr, or annul the marriage to Gert, or attempt to wed Hillary Liman instead of Gert, or conduct adulterous relations, whether emotional or sexual, in whatever form, at whatever point, with Hillary. If Retriever does not comply with the conditions set forth hereto, thereby breaching the terms of the Contract, Retriever will be subject to a fine described under Paragraph V and required to return to Limbo for a period no shorter than five thousand (5,000) years per Paragraph VI.

Freddie looked to the bottom of the page and saw the signature he had scratched with the ostrich feather pen earlier, using his blood as ink, only the color had changed to a darker one, resembling dead rose petals. "Who are you?"

Harold patted Freddie's shoulder as if this could calm him down. "There, there," he said. Freddie shrugged the captain's hand off.

"So you have forgotten me," said Mr. Liman, as if he were speaking to a child. "I'm just a humble god. It's not like the mighty Fryr ever paid attention to details. But times have changed, haven't they? Although in this, I think, your fate will always remain the same. Always in love with my girl, but I fear it will be unrequited for perpetuity. This is what happens when Joanna goes and communicates with the dead. Helda extracts a price and you have paid it. If you had only read the contract. You were too eager, dear boy, and you signed it with your blood." He tsk-tsked.

Freddie swung around to Captain Atkins and glared at him, feeling entirely betrayed. Harold made a sad, cringing face and shrugged. "My hands were tied. I had no choice. I'm so sorry, Freddie."

If anything, Freddie found the captain even more despicable than Mr. Liman. At least Liman had been a bastard from the beginning.

chapter fifty-nine

Bewitched, Bothered, and Bewildered

ᘡᕋ

Yep, same thing over at Mayor Frond's place. No damage. Over," came the voice from the walkie-talkie as Matt strode toward Ingrid.

Teeth clattering, Ingrid extended her wrists together (one hand holding up her wand), the pixies crowded behind her.

"What are you doing?" Matt asked.

"Well, I *was* sending these kids home," she said, still holding up her wrists.

More noise sputtered from the walkie-talkie, and Matt switched it off. He gestured to her hands. "I mean, holding out your wrists?"

"Aren't you going to arrest me?" she asked as he leaned into the gaping doorway.

He shook his head. "Why? Did you do something wrong?"

"Isn't that why you're here? To take them away?" she said as she cautiously let her arms fall to her sides.

He answered her question with one of his own. "What's all that noise?" he asked. "It sounds like birdsong."

A warm breeze wafted up from the door, but Ingrid was still cold. The pixies continued to huddle around her anxiously.

Matt walked past them toward the open trapdoor. He kneeled down, held both sides of the door, and peered inside. He had such strong arms, Ingrid noted. "What is it?" he asked, looking back at Ingrid. "It's amazing."

"It's where these homeless kids . . . these *pixies* live. It's a portal to their world," she said, knowing there was nothing to do now but tell the truth. He could either believe her, or he could continue to live under the delusion that magic did not exist. She studied his face, saw him grimace and then relax.

"Huh," Matt said. "What's it called?"

"Álfheim, the pixies are *álfar* . . . elves," she said.

"Well, then we should get them home, shouldn't we?" he asked.

"You're not here to take them away?"

"Why would I?"

"But I thought . . ."

He shook his head. "I didn't want to believe what was right in front of me. I knew there was something different about you . . . and I'm sorry for being such a pigheaded idiot." He sighed. "It's been hard for me accept that you're really a witch. It goes against everything that I know is true. But I know a higher truth now. I don't understand everything, but I believe you and I believe in you. I believe that you are magic."

"You're not an idiot," Ingrid said, a smile beginning to grow on her face. She watched as he got to his feet—a single jump out of the pushup without falling in. She had no idea he was this athletic.

"I am . . . I would be . . . if I let you go," he said, looking deep into her eyes. "Do you forgive me?"

"Always," Ingrid said, her eyes shining.

"So, you're a witch, huh?" he asked.

She nodded. "That's one word for it. My real name is Erda, and I'm from somewhere else, too. But unlike the pixies, I can't go home."

"I wouldn't want you to. You have to stay right here, with

me," Matt said. He moved to kiss her but was interrupted by a sudden loud racket as Sven cleared his throat, Irdick blew his nose, Val stomped his feet, and Kelda and Nylph clapped their hands and giggled. *"Aw!"* said Kelda. *"They're in love!"*

"What about them?" Ingrid asked, laughing.

He turned to the rowdy bunch. "They better get going before the police and fire department arrive. I wanted to make sure I got here first to warn you. This place is going to be crawling with all sorts of law enforcement in any minute."

"We're not in troubs?" asked Irdick.

"Don't push it!" Kelda warned.

Matt ignored them for now. "There's something else you need to know. Maggie is my daughter—the number you saw on the paper," Matt said, his words rushed. "That room I wouldn't let you see at my place: it's hers."

Ingrid nodded.

"I mean, I got my high school girlfriend pregnant, and she kept the baby. I wouldn't have wanted it any other way, really. I've never been embarrassed about her. It was just that I was worried what you might think or that you might not want to go out with me if you knew I had a kid. It was stupid of me. I know. I have custody every other week, and I'm out of town a lot so I can visit her."

"I want to meet her." Ingrid smiled, taking his hand. "I hope she'll like me."

Matt grinned.

"What about the burglaries? Did they catch anyone?" Ingrid asked.

He scratched his head. "The thing is, everything has been *mysteriously* returned," he said. "People keep calling the station to say their jewels have been found, or this or that is back on the wall or on its pedestal. I heard just now that the mayor's extensive art collection is back in place."

"Our present to you!" said Kelda, elbowing Ingrid.

"We gave everything back! We were just borrowing it to decorate the attic," Irdick explained.

Nyph leaned against Ingrid on her other side. "I hope you're not too mad."

Ingrid put her hands on her waist and looked at the pixies sternly. She had always suspected they had not given up their ways. "I'm very disappointed in you guys," she said. "But I'm glad you returned everything."

Sirens sounded in the distance. The police were on their way.

"We should get them moving," Matt said.

"Right," Ingrid nodded, a wave of sadness consuming her. Troublemakers or not, she'd grown very fond of the pixies.

One by one, she hugged them good-bye, disinclined to let any of them go.

"Do we have to?" Kelda asked plaintively.

"We want to stay," Nylph said.

"Well . . ." Ingrid looked at them. She realized there was no reason to send them home just yet, after all, they could help clear Freddie's name with the Valkyries, and Killian as well. Besides, the pixies had yet to reveal who had made them steal Freddie's trident in the first place, who was it that was behind the original crime all along.

"Hooray!" Sven said. "We can stay!"

"Stay or go—you've got to do something," Matt warned, looking out the window. A convoy was on its way to the motel: two fire engines, a half a dozen police cars, and an ambulance arrived in the parking lot. They would be in the room in a moment.

There was loud rap on the door. "Open up! Police!"

The pixies cringed. Matt grimaced and removed his gun from its holster. He nodded to Ingrid. "Take them out the back window. I'll take care of this."

She felt a flush of love for him then. She knew he would do

anything for her and would protect not only herself but also her friends. "No, no need." She removed her wand and waved it over the pixies, the broken door, and the bathroom.

The door opened with a bang, but when the police entered, all they found was the happy couple standing by the window, surrounded by five hopping frogs.

chapter sixty

Let's Do the
Time Warp Again

꩜

I t was dark and cold outside. With Joanna's careful magic
attending to her ills, Anne had revived. She had bathed, and
Joanna and Freya had given her fresh clothes. They sat in the
living room now: Joanna, Norman, Freya, and Killian, Anne on
the couch across from a blazing fire.

She liked it here, in this period, Anne said, had never been
here in the physical sense, but she had seen it through one of her
sister's eyes, and she looked forward to living in a much less op-
pressed time. But saying this made her think of John Barklay,
which made her eyes grow brilliant in the firelight. She wiped at
them. There was still so much she had to tell them before they
could solve her own problems. The thing about time, she sought
to explain, was that past, present, and future all coexisted.

"Not as linear as our brains make it out to be. We seek conti-
nuity," Norman interjected.

"Yes." Everything happened at once, and there were alternate
realities and parallel universes, a million different possibilities as
to the way one event could unfold, all happening simultaneously,
but then only one coming into effect, a rather noumenal concept
Freya had difficulty wrapping her head around.

"My sisters and I, we see it all at once when we are together.
Time is malleable and yet it flows, everything shifts and starts

anew, sometimes completely differently, but it has always happened." In other words, time was a kind of palimpsest, traces of the past peeking through the present, only to be written over in the future again.

Anne had recognized Loki in Lion Gardiner, and once he knew that she knew, she was in danger because she knew his secret.

"Loki can never be trapped anywhere; he was just biding his time. He can come and go as he pleases through the universe. He has done great mischief in the timeline. He was the one who started the witch-hunt fervor in America. It would never have happened without him. He fed the flames, stoked the fires, and saw to it that his enemies' power would be hampered by the Restriction of Magical Powers. It was all part of his plan for revenge," Anne told them. "He knows that, as a Norn, I saw the other future, the way it should have gone. That is why he had me executed. He wanted to punish me by taking John away from me forever, and he kept me from making contact with you, Joanna. He knows your clan is powerful and he fears you."

Joanna reached for her *fylgja*'s hand. She understood now what had happened. After Anne had been hanged, she had been trapped in the glom, a desperate, wandering spirit, unable to enter the Kingdom of the Dead or return to Midgard.

"Loki is not without help," Anne told them. "Even if he is not in your present, he has others working for him."

It all made sense now, Joanna realized. All those times she was trying to unlock the mystery, there was always an obstacle that stopped her—someone who was there, just at the right time, to interrupt her and keep her from finding out what she needed to know.

Joanna sucked in a breath through her teeth. "Harold!"

"I remember now . . . We used to know him as Heimdallr,"

Norman said. "But he is a weak one. He cannot have done this all himself. There must be someone else pulling his strings."

"There is," Anne said. "Buðli. He threatened Heimdallr's half-mortal family, his daughter and grandson, so that Heimdallr would do his bidding. Buðli is Loki's puppet, but a puppeteer himself."

"Buðli, I remember now. He once had a beautiful daughter, did he not?" Joanna asked. She turned to Norman. "Do you remember what her name was again?"

"Of course, who can forget Brünnhilde?" asked Norman.

"Hilly!" Freya cried.

"Who's Hilly?" asked Joanna.

Freya clapped a heel down as she stood next to Killian by the fireplace. "Um, that would be Freddie's new girlfriend, the bait, which he fell for hook, line, and sinker. He's gaga about the girl. He was supposed to do a tuna run but it turned out to be some kind of treasure hunt he said. He texted me earlier."

"Treasure hunt, what for?" Joanna asked, alarmed. "Maybe he's in trouble!"

Norman stood from his seat. He put a hand to his forehead to rub at its creases. "If so, it's not as if it hasn't happened before."

chapter sixty-one

Ring of Fire

୨ୖ

F reddie was in New Haven to deliver the news to Hilly. She
met him outside on the steps of the entrance to the freshman-
sophomore dorm, a Gothic building that appropriately resembled
a castle with its crenellated parapet and four round corner
towers—a replica of the famous ring of fire.

His memory had returned and he remembered now the years
of longing for Brünnhilde in other incarnations. It was patchy,
but he recalled the two other primary suitors, Sigurðr and Gunnar, who attempted to cross the ring of fire in order to wake her
from a spell of perpetual sleep. Gunnar, through magic and
trickery, had been the one to eventually win her hand, and that
marriage had ended messily with a series of wars among the
gods. Freddie hoped this time he might succeed in claiming her
hand—somehow!—although he feared he had already lost his
chance yet again.

The campus lampposts were illuminated, casting a soft light
on the lawns around the dorms, still green in early December,
scattered with fallen orange and parchment-colored leaves that
drifted about. Freddie and Hilly sat on the steps, forehead to
forehead, their faces sluiced.

Freddie cupped the crown of Hilly's head with his palm. "I
can still touch you as long as I have not executed clauses (i), (ii),

and (iii). A loophole. The contract states nothing about what I can or can't do before that," said Freddie, placing his hand on her cheek.

"I'm sorry, Freddie, but Dad must have his reasons. I told you he's old-fashioned." She sighed.

Freddie had nothing to say to that. He'd been hoodwinked by Henry Liman, his bastard future father-in-law, and now he had lost the love of his life. A girl rode by on a bike, along the dimly lit path. She rang the bell on her handlebars, which made a cheery sound that made Freddie feel even more dejected and miserable. She stopped and walked the bike over to them.

Hilly looked up.

The girl gave a nonchalant smile, barely registering the fact that Hilly was distressed and crying it seemed. *How cold*, thought Freddie.

"So," said the perky girl. "You meeting with us later, Hilly? You better! We have that important matter of business to attend to." She opened her coat and flashed a gray KKΓ (Kappa Kappa Gamma) sweatshirt underneath it. The university did not officially recognize the Panhellenic systems; they were not allowed to convene openly or set up residency on campus, but such sororities were still alive and well, enrolling around 15 percent of the undergrad student body.

The girl quickly closed her coat and gave Freddie the once-over, lifting her eyebrows at Hilly. Freddie wasn't sure what this meant. Did she approve and find him handsome enough for Hilly? Was that what she was getting at?

Hilly smiled at her sorority sister. "Absolutely, of course I'll be there. Wouldn't miss it!" They said good-bye, promising to see each other in an hour with the other sisters, and then Hilly apologized to Freddie for the interruption.

"Campus life!" She took his forlorn face in her hands and

stared at it. "I want you to know that I'll always love you, Freddie," she whispered, "if that's any consolation."

He pulled away, feeling frustrated at her passivity. For a warrior goddess she had no fight in her. He sat down and put his head in his arms. Hilly rubbed his back, making a circle with her palm, which irritated him. The gesture seemed somewhat flippant. She just didn't seem to care *that much*. He could hear her sigh as if she were antsy to get back to the dorm and be done with it all so she could make her silly sorority meeting—be done with Freddie's impromptu visit, his failure, his inability to snip her out of her chain mail armor. Perhaps she was just a cold shield maiden at heart. No one ever really changed.

"Listen," she said. "Gert really isn't that bad. She goes to school here, too, you know?" He did know that; Liman had mentioned it. He couldn't even remember what Gert looked like—horsy? With that braying laugh?

Hilly was still talking. "Why don't you let me text her, and you two can get to know each other. I really have a lot of homework to do and that meeting."

Freddie wiped his nose. He was irked that she was so ready to pawn him off on Gert—he felt pathetic—and he could already hear Hilly texting her sister even though he hadn't given her the go-ahead.

Fine, he would meet Gert. He had nothing else to say to Hilly. He didn't know what he had expected. He'd thought that when she found out the news they would agree on a plan to sidestep the contract, to run away and elope together, something dramatic. Not this pitiless farewell. Had Hilly ever cared for him at all? He was beginning to doubt it. He glanced at her direction. She looked bored.

"There she is," Hilly said, sounding relieved.

Freddie saw a tall girl sauntering toward them, books clasped to her chest. Her liquid-smooth hair, shining like the sun in the dusky light, fell to her hips, which swayed as she walked. Gert was all woman, voluptuous but solidly athletic. She came straight at them and placed a foot on the steps.

"What's up, you two?" she asked.

Freddie couldn't take his reddened eyes off her and felt as if he had just been rescued from a ring of fire, awoken from a deep slumber himself. Why hadn't he noticed how beautiful Gert was when he'd first met her? Had someone put a spell on him? Had Hilly? Had Mr. Liman? Gert was lovely and solid, and all he could imagine now was a wrestling ring, a match, every bit of fight coming out of both of them, giving way to a thousand gentle caresses and kisses to heal their bruises. It must have been Brünnhilde's magic that had stopped him from seeing Gert as she really was.

Hilly flipped her hair onto a shoulder. "Dad pulled a little switcheroo on Freddie, so now instead of marrying me, you two are getting hitched. You've got a month to work out the details."

Gert crossed her arms and smirked. "Huh, did he now." She looked at Freddie up and down. "I guess you'll do." She smiled.

Freddie rose to his feet and stretched. He did feel better. It wasn't *Ragnarok*. His eyes alighted on Gert's behind, substantial and shapely, which made him smile. Gert was perhaps slightly older than him—but maybe this was best. He was kind of done with fickle girls. "So will you." He grinned.

Hilly glared at Freddie, glared at that grin. "But I know you'll carry a torch for me forever . . ."

Neither Freddie nor Gert heard her. They were already walking away down the path, chatting, as Hilly swung around on her heels and quickly climbed the stairs, tossing her hair onto the other shoulder.

FREDDIE TOOK GERT'S BOOKS from her and carried them. "So what are you studying here?" he asked.

"Marine biology," said Gert.

"Really?" said Freddie. "Do you scuba dive?"

Laughter flowed out of Gert like water, bubbly and light. "I've worked for my *asshole* dad just so I can sail somewhere and put on a wetsuit."

"I think I want to move to the Caribbean," Freddie said.

She gave him a sidelong glance, then timidly replied, "Me, too!"

Freddie stopped in his tracks. Gert stopped. They faced each other. "I have a secret I've never told anyone, not even Hilly, but for some reason I want to tell you. Promise not to tell?"

"Sure." She shrugged.

He could see Gert better now, the light shining on her from a lamppost. Her mouth looked so kissable, cushiony, and soft. She resembled a mermaid on the prow of a ship. He bit his lip, staring into her eyes, and for a moment couldn't speak. He saw their color, a deep mesmerizing marine blue, and there was something so pure and guileless about them, not deceptive at all—the latter a quality that seemed to run in the Liman family. He felt comfortable with Gert, as if he could tell her anything, right off the bat. The more he stared at her, the more smitten Freddie became. Perhaps he wasn't meant for Brünnhilde after all.

"In my pocket," he told her, "I carry a ship. It can be unfolded and placed on the sea, and with it, we can sail anywhere."

Gert danced on the path. She twirled around and looked at him full of wonder and surprise. "Really?" she said. "That's about the coolest thing I've ever heard!"

chapter sixty-two

Flight of the Valkyries

～2～

Ingrid arrived at the house with Matt and the pixies, who were a little nauseated from being turned into frogs. She found the family gathered in the living room, told them what had happened, and was brought up to speed.

"It's him," Freya said. "Of course. It has to be."

"What do you mean? Who's 'him'?" Ingrid asked.

"What Anne said earlier . . . that Loki was only biding his time. Loki can move between the worlds. He took the power of the Bofrir for himself; he was the one who destroyed the bridge all along, then pretended to discover its destruction with Freddie. He was the one who stole Freddie's trident. He must have intended for Freddie to take all the blame, but something happened . . ." She looked at Killian. "Maybe it was because you were there. You stopped him somehow."

"I remember it now—just a little bit," Killian said. "I tried to change the timeline, to bring back the bridge, but I couldn't . . . But I had enough power to hold him until the Valkyries came. I'm sorry I couldn't save Freddie, though."

"Loki? Skinny fellow? That rings a bell," Val said.

"Loki! That's right! He the one who made us steal the pretty pitchfork and place it at the Bofrir!" Kelda said.

"We told you he was an ass." Sven smirked.

Freya nodded. Like Killian back in Asgard, she had been able to hold Loki for a while: as her lover Loki had been temporarily put under her spell, but he was too powerful for her spell to hold. While Odin's ring had made it easier for him to navigate through the universe, he did not need it to achieve his goal. Even if Freya had ordered him to destroy it while he was under her command, it had only succeeded in slowing him down, not stopping him.

"His power is growing," Freya said. "And ours are fading." It was as Jean-Baptiste, the god of memory, had told her—by sending the bridge into the abyss, Loki had weakened the powers of the gods, hoarding them all to himself. After the Restriction was lifted, there was a tremendous surge of magic from the Beauchamps. They had held their magic in check for so long, they had stored up a reserve, but now the well was about to go dry. She had felt her magical powers diminishing for a while—more than one customer claiming that her potions were bland and flavorless. Soon they would all be running on empty. She could especially see it in Killian's drawn face, how he had become weaker after the time shifts, how his nose had bled.

"Freya's right." Ingrid nodded. "The transformation wiped me out," she said. "I almost couldn't turn the pixies back to their real form."

"Well, that's good to hear," Sven muttered.

Anne spoke again. "Loki wanted Fryr and Balder to be forever at war. He was jealous of their friendship, and it was not only the Bofrir that he wanted to destroy that day. He is a serpent in our midst, nibbling at the roots of the Tree of Life, seeding doubt like a poisonous snake."

"He must have put the trident on the *Dragon*," Killian said.

"Of course—so that you would have the mark." Freya nodded. "And Freddie would be convinced of your guilt." She shook her head. "What I don't understand is that I turned the *Dragon* upside down and never found the trident. Freddie told me it would be there."

"It wasn't," said Killian. "I was wondering what you were searching for, so I searched myself—after you tore my boat apart."

"Of course it was not there." Sven smiled. "I remember now. We took it. Loki made us do it. Then he sent us to Midgard to steal it again."

"So that was you guys!" Freya said. "I heard you!" She remembered waking up one night on the *Dragon*. She had sensed a presence on the boat, an intruder.

"There was just one problem," Irdick said. "We dropped it."

"Into the sea . . . and it disappeared. We all jumped into the water but couldn't find it," Kelda said. "We have no idea where it is."

Killian pushed himself off the mantel of the fireplace. "We've got a lot to do, and I don't know if I have enough in me to do it, but we need to get Anne back to her rightful time. Maybe if we do it together, it will help push her through the passages."

Joanna pulled her hair back. She was concerned about her *fylgja*. Anne had done so much for them. "We need to send her back before this whole witch-hunt began, before Loki even caught sight of her. We'll give you gold, Anne, and you and John can get away, start a new life somewhere safe, far away from the Isle of Wight. You'll have your time with him."

Anne looked up at her, a smile on her lips, the fire's soft light flickering on her face. "It would be lovely to start again with John . . ."

They walked to a spot on the beach near where John Barklay's house had been and formed a circle around Anne and helped her into the portal. After the *fylgja*—the goddess of present, Verðandi, the healer of the Tree of Life—vanished into the passages, they collapsed in the sand. Freya woke and saw Norman and Joanna coming to, but Killian was still out. She had no idea how long they had been passed out on the beach. It was cold and damp.

She dragged herself to Killian and took him by the shoulders. "Wake up, darling! Please!" She shook him and his head rolled. His eyes wouldn't open.

Freya's parents rushed over. Norman felt for Killian's pulse. "It's slow," he said.

"Do something, Mother!" Freya pleaded.

Joanna had begun to rub Killian's body to warm him, as she said an incantation, and they all frantically did the same.

"We need to get him back to the house," said Norman.

They began to lift Killian's limp body, Norman swinging an arm over his shoulder, Freya doing the same at her lover's other side, as Joanna strained to pull him up.

"Stop right there!" came a voice. They were surrounded by several tall strongly built young women, each wearing a gray KKΓ sweatshirt. One of them looked slightly familiar to Freya, and she wondered where she had seen her before, then she realized. It was Hilly Liman.

Brünnhilde was a Valkyrie, and so were the rest of her sorority sisters.

"We're here to take him to Limbo," Hilly said, pointing at Killian. "He bears the mark of the trident. He destroyed the Bofrir. He will be held in Limbo for eternity."

"No!" Freya yelled, but she was pushed back as if by an invisible force and thrown to the ground.

"You have no right!" Ingrid said. "He deserves a trial. The White Council shall know of this."

"The White Council is the one who ordered us here," Hilly said with a smug smile.

"Where's Freddie?" yelled Joanna.

"Who cares?" said Hilly. "That son of yours is a total dweeb.

He'll never, ever have me. He didn't even make it into the tales of my last rescue from the ring of fire."

Joanna was helping poor Killian stand upright, but it was all she could do not to run straight at the girl and rip out her eyes.

FREYA CRAWLED OVER TO Killian and clung to him with all the force she had left in her as the Valkyries began to pry him away from her grasp. She was dragged in the sand, holding on to him, screaming at them to leave her and Killian alone, as they pulled at his near-lifeless body, her parents and Ingrid running after them.

Soon Freya was alone, weeping and howling at the sky where they had swept Killian away. She collapsed into her mother's arms as she gestured to the sky, like an infant trying to grab at something slightly out of reach, as if she could still get a hold of her darling who had been violently torn away from her.

311

chapter sixty-three

Pocketful of Dreams

❧

Norman paced the living room in the large colonial house. The whole family was present, including Matt Noble, who was comforting Ingrid. The pixies tried to make themselves useful, offering drinks and food. Freya was pacing furiously. She was no longer heartbroken. She was *furious*. "What can we do? We've got to get him back. He's innocent. When I get my hands on those girls, I'm going to—"

The knock on the door interrupted her sentence.

"I'll get it," Matt said helpfully.

Freddie walked in with a tall blond girl who had a sensible air about her. "Hey, guys, what's up? This is Gert. Gert, this is everyone."

"Freddie! Thank gods! You're all right!" Joanna said, rushing to embrace her boy.

"What's wrong? What's happened?" he asked, looking around.

They told him. Killian had been sentenced to Limbo, but there was no guarantee he had survived the trip, while the Beauchamps were teetering at the edge of their own abyss, their powers fading—their line threatened to extinction.

"There is only one way we can help Killian and end all this," Ingrid said. "We need to find Loki. He's out there somewhere; we need to find him and bring him to justice once and for all."

"The trident—if we can find the trident, it will lead us to the bastard," Freddie said.

"The pixies said they lost it in the sea, but if they weren't able to find it, then it must have slipped into something else . . . like a black hole," Freya suggested.

"Or something else," Ingrid said. She began brainstorming, making associations. She looked to her father. "What makes one forget?"

"Well, there's Lethe, the river in Hades in Greek mythology, which causes its drinkers to forget the past," Norman said.

"Yes!" said Ingrid, again recalling her dream in the library. It held a portent that made everything appear to coalesce for her. "Water. The silence of forgetfulness. That's why the pixies forgot everything: they drank from the silence!"

Joanna began reciting the Thomas Hood poem: "There is a silence where hath been no sound / There is a silence where no sound may be / In the cold grave—under the deep, deep sea."

"'Deep in the silence!' Deep under the sea!" added Freddie. "I was there. They needed me to retrieve the trident—of course. It was inside a gold case, which I didn't recognize. I had forgotten what it felt like to have it in my possession—crap! I gave it to Liman. It's probably halfway to Loki by now."

Everyone let out a grunt in some form or another. It looked grim. But Ingrid hadn't lost hope. She was tenacious and knew there was always a way—and some problems just fixed themselves, as hers had with Matt. Also Ingrid was in love, and a witch who had fallen in love for the very first time was a particularly optimistic witch, and there would be no stopping her. She could still feel there was magic within her.

"I know how we can get the trident!" she exclaimed. "The pixies can steal it back. After all, they were the ones who stole it in the first place."

chapter sixty-four

Time After Time

~~

The pixies volunteered for the mission with glee. "We like stealing things. We can find it—wherever and whenever it is," Sven said. He seemed to be their leader, Ingrid noticed. Funny how that was. Freya was still furious, but she was placated by the knowledge that there was a rescue plan forming.

Freddie said he had an announcement to make, and he cleared his throat and looked suddenly happy. "Well, there is a bright side to all this," he said.

"What bright side?" Freya snapped. Had she finally found her one true love only to lose him forever?

"Well, for starters, Gert and I are engaged," he said. Gert smiled shyly.

The family was shocked into silence.

"Congratulations?" Freya said.

"I thought her name was Hilly," said Joanna, looking suspiciously at Gert.

"No, that's Brünnhilde, one of the Valkyries who took Killian away," Norman said. "The one Freddie's been keen on since the Ring of Fire challenge. I always thought she was too much trouble for you," he told his son. He held out his hand and Gert shook it.

"Look, I know you've all been through a lot, but I'm on your side. I've despised Henry Liman since he adopted me and my sister after we were orphaned in Midgard when the bridge fell," Gert said. "He never treated us the same as his precious Brünnhilde."

"Her real name's not Gert. It's Gerðr. I think you might remember her now, yes?" Freddie asked.

Ingrid nodded and hugged her future sister-in-law warmly. "It's nice to see you again, too."

"Well, then!" said Norman, blowing his nose, while Joanna still looked perturbed. She had her son back only to lose him again, she thought. A mother's love was tested in so many ways. But she remembered this Gert and that she had been good for Freddie. She would calm him down, she thought. She had pieced together a little bit of his life here, with the video game addiction and the harem, and Gert was just the antidote he needed.

Freya nodded. "We'll need all the help we can get," she said.

Joanna patted Freya on the back. "I think I need some fresh air," she told Norman, who nodded.

WITHOUT CONSULTING EACH OTHER, they walked out of the house and through the forest toward the place where Anne had been buried.

To Joanna's satisfaction, neither the burial mound nor the blank tombstone appeared underneath the oak tree.

"Good." Joanna nodded. "I hope they had a happy life."

"As happy as one can be with a mortal," Norman ruminated. "A brief happiness. I hope Ingrid knows what she's doing with that detective of hers."

Joanna took her husband's hand and squeezed it. "She'll make it work. I have a confession to make. You know, come to think of it, I never really liked French food."

Norman smiled.

THEY WALKED BACK TO their home to find Ingrid and Freddie standing in shock in the living room.

"What happened?" Joanna asked, alarmed. "Where's Freya?"

"She just . . . disappeared! She was right here . . . Then she was gone," Freddie said, raking a hand through his tousled hair. "But first something appeared on her neck . . ."

"Like a noose," Ingrid said. "I saw it, a red rope burn around her neck—pulling her backward."

Joanna knew immediately what had occurred. "The passage—she's been sucked back into the passage . . ."

"Back to Salem where Loki is waiting to have his revenge," Ingrid said. She held Matt's hand and looked at her family. "This has to stop where it began. We'll all need to return. Follow her back through the passage of time and prevent the witch trials from happening once and for all."

The Nine Worlds of the Known Universe

ᴐᴄ

Asgard—World of the Aesir

Midgard—Middle World, Land of Men

Álfheim—World of the Elves

Helheim—Kingdom of the Dead

Jotunheim—Land of the Giants

Muspellheim—The First World

Nidavellir—Land of the Dwarves

Svartalfheim—Land of the Dark Elven

Vanaheim—Land of the Vanir

The Gods of Midgard

The Beauchamp Family Tree
(The Vanir)

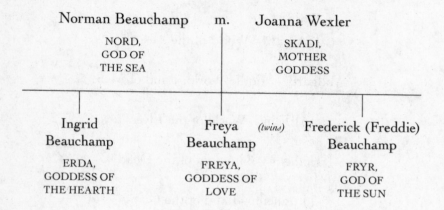

Norman Beauchamp   m.   Joanna Wexler

NORD,   SKADI,
GOD OF   MOTHER
THE SEA   GODDESS

Ingrid   Freya   *(twins)*   Frederick (Freddie)
Beauchamp   Beauchamp   Beauchamp

ERDA,   FREYA,   FRYR,
GODDESS OF   GODDESS OF   GOD OF
THE HEARTH   LOVE   THE SUN

Jean-Baptiste Mésomier (MUNINN, GOD OF MEMORY)

Arthur Beauchamp (SNOTRA, GOD OF THE FOREST) *(Norman's brother)*

Anne Barklay (VERÐANDI, NORN OF THE PRESENT)

The Gardiner Family Tree
(The Aesir)

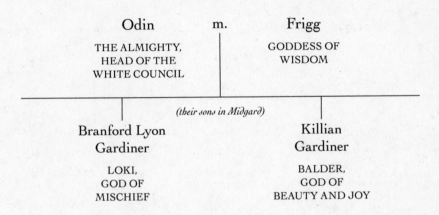

Odin   m.   **Frigg**

THE ALMIGHTY,   GODDESS OF
HEAD OF THE   WISDOM
WHITE COUNCIL

(their sons in Midgard)

Branford Lyon   **Killian**
Gardiner   **Gardiner**

LOKI,   BALDER,
GOD OF   GOD OF
MISCHIEF   BEAUTY AND JOY

The Liman Family Tree

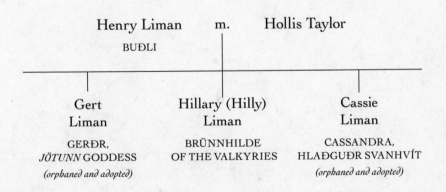

Henry Liman   m.   **Hollis Taylor**

BUÐLI

Gert   **Hillary (Hilly)**   **Cassie**
Liman   **Liman**   **Liman**

GERÐR,   BRÜNNHILDE   CASSANDRA,
JÖTUNN GODDESS   OF THE VALKYRIES   HLAÐGUÐR SVANHVÍT

(orphaned and adopted)   *(orphaned and adopted)*

Acknowledgments

~⚬~

Thank you to everyone at Hyperion for all your enthusiasm and faith in the witches!! Ellen Archer, Kristin Kiser, Elisabeth Dyssegaard, Marie Coolman, Kristina Miller, Bryan Christian, Sarah Rucker, Mindy Stockfield, Maha Khalil, Mike Rotondo, Jon Bernstein, and Sam O'Brien. Big love to my editor, Jill Schwartzman, and my agent, Richard Abate.

Thank you to all my readers who have welcomed the witches into their lives.

To learn more about the world of
Melissa de la Cruz, read:

Wolf Pact

An original e-Book featuring
Arthur Beauchamp and the adventures
of the Wolves of Memory

COMING FALL 2012

THE BLUE BLOODS SERIES

The Gates of Paradise

The seventh and final book in the bestselling epic saga

JANUARY 2013

The story of the Witches of East End continues with

The Winds of Salem

JUNE 2013